# LUCKY 3

## KNOWLEDGE IS THE KEY

**Lesley Ann Eden**

MAPLE
PUBLISHERS

Lucky 3 – Knowledge is the Key

Author: Lesley Ann Eden

Copyright © Lesley Ann Eden (2024)

The right of Lesley Ann Eden to be identified as author of this work has been asserted by the author in accordance with section 77 and 78 of the Copyright, Designs and Patents Act 1988.

First Published in 2024

ISBN 978-1-83538-373-5 (Paperback)
        978-1-83538-374-2 (E-Book)

Cover design adapted from a painting by S.J.Jameson. Witches Stitch.

Book layout by:
        White Magic Studios
        www.whitemagicstudios.co.uk

Published by:
        Maple Publishers
        Fairbourne Drive, Atterbury,
        Milton Keynes,
        MK10 9RG, UK
        www.maplepublishers.com

*"The limits of my language are the limits of my world"*
*– Wittgenstein*

*"The limits of my knowledge limit my understanding"*
*–L.A. Eden*

# CONTENTS

# AUTHOR'S NOTE

Knowledge is the key to all understanding. Wittgenstein stated that 'the limits of my language are the limits of my world'. It is equally true that limited access to knowledge inhibits your perception and the more knowledge you acquire, the more you expand and enrich your multi- dimensional awareness, which is imperative for survival in the Brave New World looming on the horizon. Acquiring information and assimilating knowledge leads to wisdom, insight and aids good judgement, especially when awakening to the 'fixed state' of existence, which can imprison the mind in an illusory dome of synthetic reality.

'There are more things in heaven and on earth than are dreamt of...' and it is said that 'imagination cannot muster anything that doesn't already exist on earth or beyond.' My unbelievable experiences and incredible encounters are real beyond imagining and I know from the photographic evidence that I have taken, as proof of what happened to me, I did not muster up unfathomable injuries incurred during the night whilst asleep.

Previously, in 'Return to the Land of Durga', I documented the 'happenings' in diary form, avoiding emotional reactions, as I was in a traumatic daze not wishing to identify with the horrendous events, but now, time has allowed me to be more detached emotionally, in order to enter the past calmly without panic, enabling me to describe in detail what happened.

The concept of Alien Beings residing, hiding, disguised and lurking in our presence is totally unbelievable to many whose life-experience does not expand beyond the 'norm'. My own encounters are equally unacceptable to those who have severed their antenna towards interdimensional data. A common statement from many people I meet is :" I've never had any kind of unusual experience and I'm sure I never will-I'm just not the kind of person to see strange things as I've been brought up to believe..."- that's where I intervene explaining that everyone has the natural equipment to tune into the Universe and beyond, but it's a person's 'belief system' which controls perception and shapes their concept of reality. A person will never see, hear or know anything other than that which their belief system allows. All it takes is a simple desire to want to see beyond the veil and the door will open new dimensions. Desire is all you need to be free from self-imprisonment and if you have dared to take the first baby steps towards self-enlightenment, opening your mind to impossible possibilities, then the truth of what I have to share will resonate.

By the time you read this, more information will have been leaked about the reality of Alien presence here on earth, as already the American Government have admitted that they are in touch with Aliens who are co-operating with them to create higher advanced technology. Scientists already are claiming there are many more species interacting with humans on multiple different levels to help protect earth. The truth about Hybrids of humans and aliens will be acknowledged becoming a known fact. Furthermore, Scientists have now found hidden galaxies at the edge of time covered by cosmic dust and they are observing shadows of a black hole which they have termed as 'bumblebee gravity'.

Researchers are discovering ways of manipulating other dimensions beyond the dimensions that they have already uncovered and soon it will be common knowledge that 'humans are not alone in the universe' and the question- 'do Aliens really exist?' will no longer be viable. Recently the International Space Station team video recorded a vast fleet of UFO's entering earth's orbit and stated that it was estimated that around one hundred and fifty strange craft were flying towards earth.

In relating my paranormal encounters, I was fortunate to meet a man, who, after reading my experiences wanted to share his own horrendous account of what happened to him as a child living near my cottage where my 'nightmare happenings' began. Not only are his accounts real and terrifying, but the experiences tally with those of the boy next door, who was labelled 'mentally unstable' after suffering agonising traumas from his unbelievable encounters with the strange beings. I now believe that all he claims is true. After enduring similar terrifying alien experiences, his cry for help strikes a deep chord. Additionally, the little five year old girl next door, whom I believe was also taken by the same beings, suffered strange burn marks on her thighs identical to mine and we shared the same mysterious rashes on our legs which appeared from nowhere. Because she was so young, she became extremely ill and had to have cancer treatment for a year, whereas my recovery from the burns was swifter and I didn't have to undergo cancer treatment. I think we were both abducted in our sleep to be guinea-pigs for strange tests perpetrated by unknown beings.

It is for these people and myself that I wish to script our authentic reports, as our stories need to be heard and revealing the truth helps us to come to terms with the injustice of our abduction torment and bear the silent pain we all share.

All character names are fictional but all events and happenings are true.

(If you have any information and knowledge to share which might shed some light on what happened to me and others, I would love to hear about it. Please contact lesleyanneden@yahoo.co.uk)

# BEGINNINGS

Rosie takes the red file from the safe, feeling apprehensive about its contents, as Lucky had warned her that it would expose disturbing information which might prove difficult to process. Just as she is about to place the file on the desk a bundle of photographs fall out on the floor. At first glance the photos are a mixed jumble of patterns but on closer inspection, she deciphers detailed pictures of bruises, burns, indentations, injection marks, scratches and cuts on various parts of a body. They are shocking to examine and it takes Rosie a while to ingest the alarming evidence. On the back of each photo is the date of Lucky's account of the injury she sustained during her extra-terrestrial encounters.

Rosie flops into a chair feeling sick at the sight of the wounds- she had no idea that Lucky had suffered such horrific ordeals and it takes her a while to regain her composure. After a few moments she scoops up the evidence and folds the photos neatly in her desk drawer to inspect at a later date when she has come to terms with the gruesome testimony. She carefully opens the red file and reads the first page:

Hello there Rosie,

Bet you thought your work was finished? Well, you know me, there's always surprises in store! You have probably seen the photographs? They are proof of what happened to me and on request anyone can view them, as they support the truth- as you can see the injuries are not something I could inflict upon myself. I have written a truthful account of all that occurred and I believe that some of the injuries inflicted upon me were not alien orientated as such, but experiments undertaken by a secret American Army Force working undercover, underground in Britain in conjunction with aliens.

There are many aliens here on earth- (I hate the term) because it is so general and there are numerous species from countless planets, all with varying agendas, some have good intentions to help us and some are not so benign. It would be useful to invent specific words to describe all the multi-various aliens, like the Eskimos, who have twenty six separate words to describe 'snow'! We do however, have a few named species such as the Insectoids, the Preying Mantis, the Lizards and the Reptilians together with the Nordics and the Tall Whites, the Greys and the Trantaloids to name but a few, so perhaps we will devise specific terms when humans are openly interacting and living side by side with them when our atmosphere has been adjusted to accommodate all kinds of extra-terrestrials here on earth?

The U.S. Government has been co-operating with Aliens since 1954 and have denied all knowledge of their pact with them. President Eisenhower signed a treaty with Aliens allowing the abduction of humans for testing and experimentation in exchange for advanced technological knowledge. Sooner or later all this will be revealed, together with more evidence which has been kept a dark secret for decades and the many thousands of people who have been abducted and subjected to all manner of invasive tests will have some kind of recompense, knowing their ordeal was real and not fantasized.

In revealing the truth about my experiences, I must stress that throughout all that I endured, I held onto the belief that my spirit could never be destroyed and above all, I was and am still taken care of by the 'I AM' of 'ALL BEING'. There is only love, light, goodness and harmony which helps to guide us through the daily quagmire of living. The world in techno-transit cannot be allowed to suppress the evidence of the 'impossible and unbelievable' any longer and the truth of what is really happening must be told.

After leaving a disastrous relationship and giving up a wonderful job as a Performing Arts Principal for a company, working across four different countries in Europe, I found a wonderful, quaint, unique cottage situated in a row of four, renovated from stables belonging to the manor house at the end of the road, now turned hotel. Mine was the only one with an upstairs, from which I had a panoramic view of everyone's garden and the large factory complex beyond. Somehow I was lured into buying the cottage and was beguiled into owning what I thought would become a lovely home which turned little by little, into a horror house of terrifying ordeals. In hindsight, I wish I had taken more notice of the boy's plight next door and believed his blood-curdling warnings, as what he claimed, I later discovered were real experiences.

This is my account-

# THEY'RE UNDERGROUND!

"They're underground! They're fucking underground! The fucking bastards are underground!" the voice shrieks across the garden shattering the afternoon peace. I am unpacking congeries of boxes and cases, having just moved into a quaint cottage. In the heat of the afternoon, the large patio doors are wide open and the hullabaloo outside is most annoying and disturbing!

"I'm tellin' ya, they're fucking underground!" echoes the high-pitched, agitated voice.

I am curious to know who is shouting and making all the noise and walk into the refreshing breeze, hearing a soothing voice attempting to calm the distraught boy.

"Shh...don't shout dear, it's alright no one is coming to take you away!"

I walk over to the wall and spy two faces peering at me.

"Oh, I'm so sorry we didn't mean to disturb you. I'm Marilla and this is my son Rory. He er...has Turrets, so please don't be offended if you hear him swearing. I'm afraid he can't help it. He doesn't mean any harm. He's home from the hospital for a few days - they allow him out- you know for short spells. He won't be a nuisance, tell the nice lady Rory, you won't be a nuisance?"

The boy smiles awkwardly. I study his care-worn, tormented face. His tall slender physique is boyish but on closer inspection I perceive he is a young man of about thirty years of age. With his head cocked to one side he asks:

"Do you like gardens? Susan likes gardens. She likes this garden, but now she is gone. She was always in the garden she was. What's your name? Do you like gardens?"

I smile and affirm that I love gardens and he seems to approve nodding his head vigorously.

"I do hope you'll be happy here?" sighs Marilla placing her arms around Rory and stroking his hair, "he gets so muddled sometimes. Don't take any notice if you hear him banging on the walls at night, as he suffers from frightmares, don't you dear? You do all that silly kicking and screaming for nothing?"

Rory laughs and waves as he is led back into the house but half-way across the lawn he turns and his charming smile twists into a grimace as he flails the air with his arms calling out:

"The fucking bastards are underground! They're down there alright! They'll come for you: you'll see! They fucking will, they'll come for you! They're fucking underground!"

I am shocked by his outburst and his poor embarrassed Mother tenderly escorts him into the house and silence reigns. Ambling over to my inherited pond where I have acquired thirteen Chinese carp, I resolve to plant a row of tall pines along the wall to ensure privacy from prying eyes and further intrusions. Pausing on the edge of the white stone slabs, I watch the fish dart in and out of their rocky, mysterious underwater world. Flashes of orange, yellow and white ripple through the opaque muddy depths, then suddenly lifting their scaly backs and arching upwards they leap out of the water to snatch insects and dive back down into their secret caves. Swiftly the sun dips behind a passing cloud casting foreboding shadows across the grass and I hurry back inside to tackle more unpacking.

I love new beginnings with the chance to create a fresh living space in the quirky, quaint cottage where every room is different. I need to immerse myself in my new surroundings to forget him. I thought he was the one who would be my everlasting love and I gave up a wonderful career to be with him, but one Sunday morning when he was ostensibly playing golf, my whisperers whispered his deceit. They told me to search in his suit pocket for evidence of his cheating and although he had many suits, they pin-pointed the correct one straight away and I found a hotel receipt for a double room, non-smoking, in his top pocket! My whisperers are always right and I listen to them because they take care of me and now I am alone making a clean start without him. I run up the quirky stairs holding onto the black, decorative iron hand railings and enter my bedroom which has large wide windows, almost the length of the room. I stand and look across the row of gardens and note that all is quiet on Rory's side of the fence, but on the other side I spy a beautiful little girl riding her tricycle up and down the path. She has long brown ringlets tumbling over her tiny shoulders and a lovely sweet smile as she races her little white poodle along the paving stones.

I look out beyond the cottage gardens to the factory complex fenced in with high railings and note how the car park with its parallel lines of small blue lights look like a landing strip for light aircraft, or, the word drops into my mind-'spaceship'. I laugh at the thought and dismiss it. I remember a cup of coffee getting cold and dash back down the stairs glancing through a small window peeping into the kitchen, perched half way down the stairs, which must have been an original feature when the building was a stable for horses. I make a mental note of the new kitchen design I have in mind with a miniature French Bistro in one corner. I love conceiving ambitious projects for my special new home and feel lucky to be able to make all the decisions by myself.

I love the peace in my cottage and on my first evening I lazily hang pictures and have a restful sleep but this evening, my second night, I am strangely restless, finding sleep difficult. Suddenly high-pitched screaming and wolf-like howling tear through the front room walls downstairs and I know it is Rory kicking and banging, fighting his demonic nightmares and I hear his Mother pleading with him to stop. Through the window the lights of an ambulance pull up outside and I watch two uniformed men hurry next door with a stretcher. The howling stops abruptly and a few minutes later I watch a sedated Rory lying lifeless on a stretcher being carried to the ambulance.

After the horrible cacophony, I drown in the silent aftermath and suffocate in the stillness as the tense atmosphere strains the moment. Grey shadows lurk in corners as I wander around checking all the windows and doors and I am too unsettled to climb back into bed, so I make myself a hot drink and sit watching the night sky lit by the factory complex and wait until the first flashes of dawn streak across the new morning.

A few weeks pass and I enjoy creating my new house and getting to know Daisy, the lovely little girl next door. Rory has been in hospital for a while but has been allowed home for a few days which has been unsettling, as I hear him in the garden swearing and ranting and whenever he spies me, he hangs over the wall to warn me of terrible monsters that lie beneath the earth, but luckily his Mother always ushers him away. This morning, Marilla posted an envelope through my door containing a crumpled piece of paper with a song that Rory composed, with a note imploring me to read it and make a comment. The song is a jumbled mass of words full of pain and anguish and in his scrawled hand writing there is a blood-curdling warning;

"MANGLED, MASHING BRAINS TO PULP SUCKING OUT LIVER AND GUTS

WITH BLOOD, INTESTINES DRIPPING ON A BLACK TABLE … PAIN, PAIN IT HURTS SO MUCH

PAIN I HAVE NO BRAIN, THEY TOOK IT ALL AWAY. THEY DON'T WANT ME TO SAY

I CAN'T TALK THEY DRAINED MY WORDS THROUGH A STRAINER. I CAN'T FIND ME!

TORTURE! TORTURE! THEY COME IN THE NIGHT. THEY WAIT BENEATH US UNDER THE GROUND. THEY COME. I AM LOST...

The ramblings of a poor tormented soul scratched out on crumpled pages tear at my senses and I wish I could help him. Some of the words are muddled and parts of the paper are torn where his pen has stabbed into the lyrics. His chorus line is disturbing:

"THEY'RE COMING! THEY'RE FUCKING COMING. THEY'RE UNDERGROUND. THEY'RE COMING."

I write a short note to Rory thanking him for his song, saying I like it very much, encouraging him to compose more and post it through their letter box, just as my consignment of small conifers arrive and I busy myself planting fifteen small trees against the garden wall to ensure more privacy. The day wears on and intermittently I am aware of Rory's ranting in the garden as puffs of cigarette smoke waft my way. I wish I could ease his pain but all I can do is smile and listen to his gruesome raging.

In the evening I begin to measure the bedroom window for curtains and I can't help but keep glancing at the runway, as I call it, with its little blue electric lights twinkling brightly. I shudder remembering my 'electric blue experience' as the little lights have the same intensity as the blueness that invaded my bedroom when I was living in a rented detached house in a farming village. The 'blueness' was a blue that buzzed: blue that pierced: blue that vibrated and smelt and tasted of blueness beyond blue of echoing waves, resounding of blueness and midnight hues of darker blues when they invaded.

It was late one Sunday evening and I felt myself drifting into sleep when I was disturbed by a faint tapping on my window. I thought it was rain beating against the glass but as it grew louder the whole room lit up in a fluorescent disco blue which pounded and throbbed, vibrating into my body and I blacked out. When I came round, I was aware of beings standing at the end of my bed as though they were completing some kind of operation. I tried to sit up but they told me to think of something happy as I hypnotically floated back, swimming into a deep sleep. In the morning I was alarmed to remember the incident, and tried to forget it, but when I was taking a bath, I saw implanted in a vein on my right ankle a dried blood clot. I washed it and found what I thought was a small cyst and I tried to burst it but it was unlike anything that I had ever encountered.

Something was stuck inside my ankle! I researched the implant and the 'blue experience' and was amazed to find that hundreds of people, women, men and children had experienced the 'blue' ordeal and like me became afraid of the colour after the encounter. I also found that in America, Dr. Roger Leir was removing the same kind of implants thought to be placed in peoples' bodies by aliens. Dr. Leir in his ground-breaking operations had removed countless- what he labelled as, 'tracking devices' from various parts of humans made from unearthly material. The tracking device remains in my ankle and I know I have others. When I go to airports I am always stopped, as I set off alarms and the x-rays reveal strange pieces of metal in odd areas of my body. On the last count I had seven different metal objects planted under my skin in various places, especially on the left side of my body.

Now in the darkness of night, I watch the little blue lights and wonder why I thought it was the factory's car park as no cars, lorries or bikes clutter the tarmac. It's strange to see the space so vacant for such a large work place. The factory is a well-known fruit canning complex, hiring coach- loads of foreign students bussed in overnight who disappear in the early hours of the morning, but there is never any sign of them in the factory grounds. I keep staring at the lights, hypnotised by their electric intensity and out of the corner of my eye I detect some movement and turn my gaze to the large warehouse on the right. Two people in white suits with white space-like helmets appear to chat for a few seconds then vanish into the night. I argue with myself that working in a food factory there must be some protective clothing worn by the workers, but I can't help thinking that the uniform closely resembles astronaut's space suits. I dismiss my suspicious imaginings and jog downstairs to look at curtain designs to jolly myself into happy thoughts but harrowing screams, screech through the walls as Rory begins his kicking, pounding and howling. All I can do is turn up my music to drown out his suffering until the ambulance arrives to take him away.

Once peace is restored In the quiet of the night, I sleep well and in the morning between waking and sleeping a strange voice tells me: "You are not alone!" It isn't my whisperers but a different intonation accompanied by a low reverberation. In the lower half of my right leg there is a peculiar electric buzzing directly over the implant. It feels like it is being deactivated. The whizzing vibration moves up my leg in a circular motion and hurts in a weird kind of way, but it's bearable. I am not fully conscious and fight through a haze to wake, but I am in a trance and hear noises in the bedroom, but I can't surface to see what is happening. Thankfully the odd ordeal doesn't last long and the electric buzzing ceases, but my leg cramps and I fully wake to the intense pain of a muscle spasm. I jump up and down and thump my foot on the floor until the calf muscle relaxes. Somehow I know the energy has drained out of the little implant and the hard knot on my ankle is now a soft shell. I am not sure whether I am grateful it has gone or whether I miss it? But I suspect it will be replaced and I know they will come again. Do I feel lucky? I am not sure! But I push away negative thoughts and know that I will be lucky, for I AM Lucky.

# WHEN THEY CAME

I was not wrong when I predicted that the defunct implant would be replaced by another device in a different part of my body and this morning, when I was cleaning my ears, a strange black object fell out of my right ear drum. I thought at first some wax had become dislodged, but to my surprise it was a tiny black wheel with serrated edges. The material of the object resembled black patterned iron. In the centre of the wheel was an intricate design like a miniature mechanical wheel inside a pocket watch. It was covered in dried blood and after cleaning it, I placed it inside my dressing table drawer for safe-keeping but now I can't find it. It seems to have completely disappeared. I presume if it has fallen out of my ear, they will attempt to replace it with something else, somewhere else! The idea is unnerving as I have no notion of who 'they' are and what 'they' want. I hurry to prepare for school, as having left my wonderful job, I have taken a post in a local secondary school where my children were educated.

Time is, as time does, as time lingers or races and now it is half term and I am exhausted. I feel run-down and in need of a rest. Yesterday I felt an awful pain in my groin and thought a boil was festering, but on closer inspection and probing, I extracted from under my skin a white object resembling a grain of rice. I was astounded to think it was embedded in my groin. It was plumper than a grain of rice but with the same kind of smooth, glazed, cream finish. Strangely at the end of each tip were microscopic serrated edges like the black wheel that dropped out of my ear. It was incredibly hard and I tried to crush it to see what was inside, but it was indestructible. I left it on the bedroom windowsill where I could see it, but now it has disappeared; like the wheel it is nowhere to be found. Research has shown that Alien implants are sometimes embedded in the genitalia area because they are difficult and painful to extract.

Finding a second object is alarming, especially as it is now defunct and I know for sure they will try again to insert another device. They will come and I am helpless to stop them. I can't tell anyone as people will think I am crazy and I don't have any proof of the implants as they have vanished and the shell over the vein on my right leg, now looks like a cyst. I stare out of the bedroom window reminding myself that I still haven't made curtains, but no one can see inside the bedroom, unless of course they have the device that infiltrates buildings. I know the device exists because my ex-husband, who worked for the government as an informer in Ireland, told me about all kinds of 'snooping' gadgets that they used to obtain secret information.

The last of the summer rays sparkle across my pond and the fifteen ducklings that hatched in my garden and destroyed all my plants and vegetables during the summer, have finally fled. I gave them all names beginning with the letter 'D' and Daffy, who was the runt of the batch with a deformed beak was the last to go. It seemed she didn't want to leave. She formed an attachment to my youngest daughter and it appeared that she was waiting for her to visit to say good bye. It was a Saturday morning when she called and Daffy was paddling in the pool when she spied my daughter and waddled over to greet her. At that moment a male duck flew down and Daffy reluctantly spread her wings and flew away. She never appeared again after her farewell quack and now the garden has a chance to recover from the duckling invasion and I decide to have my morning coffee on the patio to soak up the sunshine before the onset of the grey winter days.

With my coffee in one hand, I slide open the patio door and am immediately overwhelmed by a fresh minty scent in the air mingling with a clean soap- smell which is invasive and overwhelmingly unpleasant as it stings my nostrils. I look up into the sky to see if any craft is responsible for crop spraying, but there is nothing. I wonder if the factory is emitting a chemical from one of its chimneys, so I screw up my eyes tightly, in a screeing mode (which is an ancient psionic device to see other-worldly things- like looking into a crystal ball or a bowl of clear water) and I see silver microscopic particles teeming in the atmosphere. I am wary of chemical substances sprayed in the sky, as chemtrails have become part of our daily grey lid sealing of the ionosphere in an opaque dome to block out the sun and Alien craft, which the government wish to keep secret. Chemical substances are sprayed in our skies such as barium, strontium, aluminium and sometimes traces of blood have been found in the chemical residue. The government's excuse for such barbaric pollution is to prevent global warming, but my whisperers say differently- they claim that it is to change the earth's atmosphere in preparation for aliens to breathe on earth unaided, because at some point in the future there will be many species of alien living freely on earth.

The use of chemtrails, however, is as old as air flight itself and its invention can be traced back as far as Leonardo Da Vinci, who mentions the use of sulphide of arsenic as a means of killing an enemy with bombs filled with the toxic substance. Our government have admitted to spraying various viruses in certain parts of the country in order to test the public's reaction and vulnerability to specific microorganisms and to test recovery rates. The new appearance of 'Morgellans Disease' has alarmed Doctors, as they are perplexed by the appearance of tiny threads of living organisms wriggling underneath a patient's skin. Some scientists are blaming the components mixed in the chemtrail chemicals to be the source of the new disease.

All these facts run through my mind as I step outside into the pungent air and am shocked to see a blackbird standing perfectly still by my outdoor table. Normally the birds scatter at the slightest hint of noise or intrusion. I am a little afraid of birds and the sight of the unnatural statuesque position of the black bird worries me. I scrape my chair on the patio slabs in the hope of scaring off the bird but it doesn't budge. The thought crosses my mind that someone has placed a stuffed bird on the patio as a joke but as I creep closer, I see its little chest feathers ruffling in the wind and its eyes are glistening. I sneak nearer and nearer and it still doesn't move. I dare myself to touch its head and with a trembling finger I brush its feathery skull, but it remains motionless. It is a living statue. I have never seen anything like it before and search around to see if any other birds have been affected, but the little Blackbird is the only one stunned and frozen to the spot. I recall Alfred Hitchcock's scary film 'The Birds' and flinch at the thought of being attacked suddenly if the bird wakes, but despite jumping up and down in front of it and waving my arms madly at the poor thing, it remains in a trance.

As I investigate the garden, I notice hanging from bushes and trees and trailing through the grass, a thin film of white sticky cobweb-like slime glistening in the sunshine. I have read about such substances formulated from the fall-out chemicals from chemtrails and am careful not to touch it, as the general consensus suggests that it might be radioactive. I had also heard on the news that certain schools in Leeds had been scourged with the slimy stuff coating playground equipment and playing fields and the children had called it 'fairy foam' and were not allowed to touch it or play with it. I decide to have my coffee indoors to be on the safe side, wondering if the fate of the bird was an indication that whatever was sprayed in the atmosphere could have a sedating effect on the populace?

After coffee I go upstairs to re-measure the windows for my curtains and my attention is drawn to the factory. I blink and rub my eyes as the buildings seem to be coated in a shimmering haze, like a mirage on a hot day. As I gaze at the sheds, they appear to be immersed in a gigantic bubble and like the bird outside, I am glued to the spot, mesmerized by the strange apparition. My mind grapples with what I think I am witnessing – is there really a massive soap-bubble encompassing the warehouse? I begin to suspect that the smell in the atmosphere is leaking from the factory. Perhaps one of the cleaning machines has broken, producing a mass of suds, like too much detergent overflowing in a washing machine? There is no sign of anyone in the factory and no vehicles in the car park and no sound of working machinery. I am glued to the scene until the bubble disintegrates leaving me doubting the reality of the strange illusion. Back downstairs on the patio, the bird has disappeared and the 'fairy foam' has melted in the sunshine. Puffs of smoke waft across the lawn and I hear Rory in the distance chanting obscenities and I resolve to try to enjoy a restful half term.

Strains of old tunes sift through lost songs of yesterday, blending in with today's melodies as I sit at the piano inventing new chords for tomorrow. The cottage likes my music and apparently so does the little girl next door, who sits on her Mother's bed with her ears pressed against the wall when I play. Her Mother says Daisy would love to learn to play the piano and I agree to take her for lessons after Christmas. Losing myself in the music, I am taken out beyond the moment and drift with the orange glow of the dying sun to a golden desert, where the dunes endlessly rise and fall. I float over the ribbed gullies to a high sand mountain and sit on the top looking out across a rippling sea of tangerine earth enveloped in the glow of dusk. Ancient voices whisper, like the hush of sifting sand through an hour glass:-
*"Orange is the colour for change; a transition is on the horizon!"*

I listen to the voices discordantly in unison, while immersing my bare feet in the soothing warm sand growing damper as the sun sinks. The voices whine on the wind:

*"Earth colours nurture the soul. Seek solace in nature, for Mother Gaia watches and waits for you to join her life cycle. Birth, life, death is your planet's pattern. Orange is the magnificent flame of the closing sun, like the autumn majesty of dying trees when they become their most brilliant before the bleak, black winter and the orange flare of the falling sun before nightfall blends passionate red and sunny yellow, to animate a power beyond imagining. Use the colour wisely, for orange has one of*

*the strongest physical effects on humans. The colour orange can help to bring a transformation into your life. It is the colour that represents enthusiasm, adventure, creativity and courage."*

I am not sure why I have wandered into the desert, allowing myself to drift off whilst playing the piano. Sometimes it is easy to let my mind wander while I play. It is a moving meditation technique where I find myself closest to truth and as I stand before the Ancient Wise Ones they ask why I have ventured into their domain but it is hard to answer their question and they encourage me to write a question in the sand with my finger.

"Why are the young taken before they have time to live?" I write the question without thinking, realising that subconsciously I am mourning the death of a young student. She was brilliant, beautiful and talented beyond measure. She was only sixteen and killed outright by a lorry. I mourn the world's loss of her presence. I mourn for her parents, friends and teachers who loved her. Yet I know she came back to class amidst a terrible thunder storm and as the lightning struck through the classroom windows, a beautiful red butterfly, Ruby- red, just like her name, settled on my desk. The whole class watched silently as she fluttered near my fingers and we all experienced in silence, the magic of the moment. She stayed for a brief spell, then flew up and up until she disappeared into the ether.

Now a rising wind unsettles the sand blowing away my question. The grains sift through invisible fingers as the Ancients gather to answer my question and surround me in a circle, cloaked in grey primal gowns with their creased, leather-worn faces peering down and their marble-glazed eyes boring into my thoughts. Like an ancient, antediluvian choir the strained voices chant a sing/song melody:

*"Don't try to snatch the wind or contain it in your hand,*

*Creation is too vast to count the grains of sand,*

*Melting miracles of snowflakes and bubbles flying high*

*Perfection in the moment, but their nature is to die,*

*You cannot trap a sunbeam or clutch a lightning spark,*

*You'll never find the answers, when you're searching in the dark."*

The song lingers or is it me from afar playing a remembered tune? Their answer is misted in riddles and although I am not ungrateful for the message, I am left unsatisfied. I want answers for her untimely death. They hear my thoughts and a single voice rides close on a sharper, colder wind shifting the sand below like a quivering sea- adding:

*"understand as of now your mind is too small; your brain too condensed to understand the bigger picture. You are blind to see beyond the plan of now, but one day you will understand all. Your student has not gone, but only walked through another door to her destiny."*

I nod, acknowledging their wisdom and before I can digest the message another voice breezes in droning on a lower note:

*"The planet earth is a seat of learning where every seed can grow in the light, but it is a matter of choice for everyone. Know that beyond and beyond and beyond is a reason for every footstep; for each decision made; for every lost second and every found gift. All living has a purpose; all exits are deliberate. Don't question the length of a lesson, for it has its own dynamics, but understand this- a moonbeam contains millions and trillions of microscopic particles- singly they are invisible, yet together they shine as one."*

I understand the lesson and know that my student shone like no other and among the stars she still shines. Another voice, higher than the others sings sweetly, as the orange ball of fire in the sky sinks low over the unsettled dunes: *"Everyone's story is perpetual. It is always on the move, always shaping, always developing, like the little seedling in the dark underground making its journey to the surface where it blooms and flourishes in the unceasing elements and once its cycle has run its course, it returns to the earth where it begins again a different life cycle- to be born, to develop then depart, but it is always journeying, always moving, always in transit and no one knows how long the journey will take, no one knows the full purpose- only that it continues-therefore there is no death.*

*Lose your fear of death, it is illusory. This is your answer."*

The voice dies. The ancients fade and I am back inside my fingers gliding up and down the keys. I have been away for a while and now the chords play in the front of my head and I am conscious in the moment. I ponder the message and understand the meaning of life's passage and its purpose a little better and I accept the mystery of physical death with a deeper appreciation of the greater picture. My darling girl, my wonderful student, you live somewhere else in a different sphere and will shine your goodness and beauty for others in another dimension.

I stop playing and walk to the window admiring the last golden/ orange rays of the dying sun, recalling the ancient spirit's words about orange- the colour to help bring about change and I am uncertain of what that might mean or create in my life. So much has changed already and I am grateful to be where I am in the now of the present. I go to bed and prepare to sleep placing myself into the hands of the Universe, the Great Architect of All Being, who knows eternity and beyond.

It is just before dawn as I stir in between a state of sleeping and waking. A draught of cool air wafts across my left hand and over my face as if someone or something is deliberately blowing cold air in my direction. I attempt to open my eyes but I can't. The cold air coils around me like slow smoke enveloping its victim. I suspect I am floating outside in the atmosphere – but how can this be? I am paralysed and not able to open my eyes or move my body. Trance-like I float in nothingness. I am totally helpless but conscious and I remember the little blackbird outside, stunned in a trance, unable to move. My mind is alert and alive, yet in the front of my brain a block prevents me from feeling afraid. I am not afraid. I am not anything. I am just drifting and floating in a helpless zone. I am in my body, yet not of it! Did I die?

Now I am lying on my left side. Am I in bed? No! I am lying on a dark flat table. Rory's song describing lying on a table echoes in my mind. I can't see through my eyes, yet I see. There is someone or something sitting next to me. Its head is a little higher than mine but I am confused because if I was in my own bed then someone would not be able to sit next to me as there is a heavy set of drawers next to my bed. Now my left arm is raised above my head and my hand is being held by a hooded creature. It has dark grey/blue skin with bony hands and long skeletal fingers. Its hands are not like mine. The index finger is long and scrawny and maybe it only has three fingers? I don't know, I can't say. I don't understand what I am seeing or hearing or feeling, not through my normal senses but beyond. It takes my left hand and telepathically asks my permission for a substance to be injected into my vein. I comply. I don't know why and almost instantaneously it injects a sharp needle into a vein in my left hand. It says it is to heal my arthritis as later I will be called upon to do a job for them in the future. It hurts. It's not a dream. I know the difference between real pain and dream pain. This is real! A cold substance enters a vein in my hand and begins to ride up my arm but near my elbow on the intersection where the veins meet, there is a blockage. There is something wrong. It hurts!

Invisible hands work on the obstruction and massage it until the cold fluid is free and flows up through my arm directly across my shoulders in a straight line across my collar bone, down my right arm, over my pelvic girdle and into my thighs. The sensation is peculiar in this area of my body. It is like a warm tickling, yet the opposite- like someone is tracing an ice-cube over my skin on a hot day.

The substance does not go near my head. Voices explain that it will not go into my brain. I know what the liquid looks like without seeing it. It is a white opalescent creamy thick solution with a tinge of glowing purple, iridescently shining through the opaque substance. The thing clarifies that the injection will make me better and stronger in order to meet the changing vibrations of a different world to come and that my special psionic gifts will be needed in the future to communicate with others not of this planet. They reveal, as though watching a film, many different types of alien from the future – some are helpful and benign, while others are brutal without empathy or sympathy for humans. They continue to explain that there are many different types of alien species already living on the planet side by side with humans who are mostly unaware of their presence. The picture of the future is frightening because it is unrecognisable from the earth of today. A clever, deceitful de-population programme is activated which poisons both mind and body of humans across the planet.

Mass fear enables a smooth transition from easy compliance to full-blown slavery where humans are stealthily metamorphosed into semi-robots. A New Global Elite rule the world which is sealed under a chemical dome and the weather controlled and regulated from a central station in space. Food is made from synthetic, chemical ingredients and some human body parts are distributed to the masses on a daily basis. No one prepares or cooks food as everything is despatched to the masses according to their position in society and the level of the hierarchy depicts the scope of choice available. The lesser beings have no options and the highest social strata have the greatest advantages in all scopes of living possibilities and as I see the great divide amongst the people, I realise that not much has changed from today, as hidden in the techno-advanced, futuristic paradise is the same lamentable plea of the poor.

They show me tribes living on the outskirts of the great Cityscapes and their struggle to survive eking out an existence from the radio-active earth. Then I zoom into strange biological labs where bodies are fermenting in glass cases, where hybrids of humans and aliens are constructed. They show me a set of hybrid children playing in a glass nursery and ask me to cuddle them, but I cannot. I am distraught. Tears drip down my cheeks but I am not crying. I cannot cry I am immobilised. They tell me that when I wake I must not eat heavy food for a few days and to avoid alcohol. They show me a picture of something white and lumpy like rice pudding explaining it is a good remedy for de-toxifying the body. It is Tibetan mushroom kafir which has wonderful healing properties.

I wake in my bed, slowly becoming aware of my normal reality, trying to analyse the process I experienced. It was not a dream. I look at my left hand and find the injection mark above a vein. It is sore. It is real. I did not imagine the ordeal. I get up feeling dizzy remembering their caution about food. I feel sick like the aftermath of the effects of a general anaesthetic after an operation. I crawl into the day and prepare to teach after a relaxing half term, traumatised by the horrific violation. I want to scream to the world what happened, but instead I wear my teacher's all-in-control face and pound through another day of challenging teenagers. After school I pick up my youngest daughter to drive to a school to teach dance together and I am brave enough to show her the injection mark. I cautiously attempt to explain what happened, hearing myself describe the impossible and she smiles sweetly. I know she thinks I have imagined the whole dramatic episode. I can't blame her for it is too fantastical to comprehend and I drop the subject. It hurts that I can't share my experience with anyone.

The evening wears on and I become tense. Perhaps if I am honest, I should admit I am afraid to go to bed. They told me not to drink but I need a glass of wine to stop the fear. I keep telling myself I must have imagined it, but I know I didn't. I know they will come again but it's not knowing that scares me. I go to bed looking suspiciously around, searching under the bed, behind cupboards like a frightened child making certain the big, bad monster isn't lurking and I delay turning off the light until I dare myself to be in the dark and hide under the bed clothes with pounding heart and dry mouth, waiting, listening for the unknown.

Somehow I fall asleep and am grateful to wake in the morning to greet an ordinary day not contaminated by the fear of a paranormal abduction. I want to do ordinary things; I want to be ordinary but loitering in the back of my mind is another reality waiting to pounce. I go to the hairdressers to enjoy being pampered by my little happy hairdresser who is always smiling, but today she is heavy with a deep sadness and when I ask her what is wrong, she is reluctant to share her grief, but eventually she talks. She explains that her Dad who was always happy and optimistic about everything had suddenly changed and had become depressed and non-communicative, hiding away in his little flat and not wanting to go out. She said that things got worse and he had been transferred to a psychiatric hospital. "Please don't say anything," she continues as she blow-dries my hair," but he said that beings came out of his television screen and gave him an injection, saying that it would heal his asthma and that he was needed to do a job for them in the future and they told him to just eat soup for a while and now he won't eat anything else!"

Shocked- I try to disguise my inner alarm bells and cough dramatically. She stops and asks me if I want a glass of water, but I regain my composure and sympathise with her situation. I cannot share my experience with her, but can only offer her my commiseration and try to reassure her that all will be well.


Driving back home, I wonder how many other people these beings visit and I begin to query Rory's claim that 'they're underground!' and question the fact that he might be telling the truth?

In the afternoon I board a train to Leeds and manage to get a seat just before a strange little man with black, unkempt hair takes the seat directly opposite me. He is wearing a fashionable fawn mackintosh with smart gear underneath. He appears drunk or high on drugs and immediately begins a conversation in which I am reticent to participate. He drunkenly asks me to marry him and the two gentlemen in the seats opposite are highly entertained by his blatant approach, but they also show concern for me and try to steer the conversation away from me by asking him his occupation. He tells us that he is in sales and visited York for business staying one night in a small hotel. He continues at great speed hardly taking a breath: "and do you know, you just wouldn't believe this, imagine this, I'm sitting watching the TV mate and what do you think comes out of the bloody thing, mate?"

The two gentlemen and I don't reply, although we are intrigued to know what comes out of his TV.

"Well, it's a bloody, fucking swarm of bees mate! Well they look like bees, hundreds of 'em, all buzzing out of the bloody screen."

"You were definitely drunk, or high!" adds one of the men.

"Don't think so mate! I know what I saw alright! They all come out of the TV and then turn into creatures mate. One holds me down while another injects me with stuff and I black out! When I wake they've gone! What do you think to that then mate?"

Inwardly, I freak! I feel weak and sick and stop listening while the men point-blank refuse to believe the story, claiming the man was drunk, but he continues to insist his experience was real. On nearing the station, I rise and say goodbye, rushing to reach the door for air, fighting my rising unease. I don't know what to think and yet I know what happened to me and I can't deny the reality of it. Two outside accounts of similar happenings are alarming and I am more fearful than ever for the next encounter, for I know it will happen. I know they will come. The black, bleak, industrial factories surrounding the city echo my inward darkness as I step off the train and I try to lose myself in the busy hub of the noisy passengers rushing to their destinations. I cajole myself into a fake sense of fun as I shop for new clothes in the modern precinct, allowing the imposing pop music to flood my mind free of speculative scenarios with alien creatures.

Now, back in my new home with the welcoming warmth of a glass of whiskey, I feel fine and tell myself that last night I was lucky and 'they' didn't come, so perhaps tonight I will be lucky for I am Lucky.

# HAPPINESS IS A CHEMICAL REACTION

Sitting in my little conservatory, watching the evening sun settle behind my garden wall, I rejoice that all is peaceful. Only the wind humming through the trees echoes a doleful melody. It sings a gloomy tune from the past when false love left me empty, entrapped in a web of lies and deceit and my spiritual guide, Grandfather- a great Chinese sage, entered my life. He helped me so much during the bleak, depressed times and now facing new fears he appears in my mind saying;

*"Create within you the right kind of chemistry for happiness to overflow."* He is concerned that fear of another visit from Aliens is disturbing my concentration and debilitating sensible thought. I listen to his wise words:

*"fear is an emotion which produces a strong chemical reaction affecting the mind and body, causing dis/ease mentally and physically, for emotions are chemical reactions to situations, places and things and can become addictive. Certain emotions are toxic by nature and negative emotions alter your mental state, which in turn triggers physical sickness. That is why 'fear' is such an effective weapon, my dear and openly exploited especially by the media and also surreptitiously by those in powerful positions."*

I try to take Grandfather's advice to dispel my rising fears of another Alien visit and his gentle voice continues: *"emotions have the power to create unreal and fake attachment to illusions causing disillusion. For example- falling in love, is one of the oldest ersatz feelings that humans can experience and most prone to false delusions, as many people abuse this kind of love in an egotistical adventure to enhance their self-esteem and unless their attachment is honest and selfless it will fail and fade. Fake love must not be mistaken for genuine 'love' which humans share for their fellow humankind, for truthful love is the essence of everything."*

I understand Grandfather's teaching, realising I must not live in fear, but it is difficult when I know for sure the Aliens will come again. I walk into the garden in the beautiful twilight evening with pink and purple flashes streaking an orange dying sun and in the dimming light I can just make out golden- yellow Chinese carp darting in and out of their hidden caves, where they are totally unaware of the world beyond their watery kingdom. I wonder if my world is as limited as theirs?

*"Yes, my child,"* Grandfather whispers," *the fish live in their own contained domain, completely unaware that they are part of another world much bigger than their own. It is like here on earth where your world lies within further worlds set apart from others which are hidden within universes and multi-verses and cosmic realms within celestial galaxies, that expand and contract as multi-dimensional forces organically change the game. You are part of a ginormous whole, yet infinitesimally small in the hierarchy of greater beings. The fish have no knowledge or concept that they are being watched from above, like you have no concept of who or what is observing you."*

"That is what I am afraid of Grandfather!" I exclaim.

He quietly chuckles stating, *"well, if that's all you're afraid of my child? You are lucky!"*

At that moment Grandfather disappears as my meditation is broken by Rory screeching across the lawn, "they're coming, you know they're coming, I told you, they're underground, they're fucking underground!" Calm descends as his Mother leads him quietly away and stillness hangs heavily in the air after the raging outburst. A gentle breeze rises through the bushes whispering;

*"Apprenticeship to warriorship means taking the Gladiator training...be brave. Go assertively into the dark night!"*

I am not sure what that means. The fish are now nowhere in sight, only the dark top water flickers.

Tinkling, peals of laughter echo over the wall, as I hear Daisy teasing her pet dog Snowball before she goes to bed and I envy the cosiness of Mother and child snuggling together through the dense, dark night. It is late and I have stayed up, putting off going to bed, dreading another Alien visit and now lying in bed, like a frightened child, I listen intently to the stifling stillness, hearing my heart pounding through my chest. I tell myself not to be stupid; but I can't stop the rising fear from tormenting my sanity. I manage to slip into a semi-slumber but the sound of dull footsteps climbing the stairs renders me alert. A slow 'thud' 'thud' along the carpeted corridor stops my heart. The door handle rattles and I shoot bolt upright in bed. I scream silently. My mouth is open but there is no sound. An unknown force pushes me back on the bed and the covers lift off my body. Something is holding my feet tightly together and I am raised up onto something hard like a stretcher. I fight internally with all my might conjuring up an inward force shouting, "stop it! I want it to stop!" I imagine a powerful energy pushing them away and to my surprise everything ceases. I am back lying in my bed in the strained silence. I marvel at my victory and remember the message about 'Gladiator training' and the 'apprenticeship to warriorship'- it seems it has begun and I intend to battle my way through whatever is waiting.

Time turns the handle of the clock, as I daily fight classroom battles, crusading my way through hordes of unruly teenagers who definitely don't want to learn how to write or speak their native language. I stride towards the noisy classroom, dreading the usual fracas from the worst class in the school as two boys rush past, shoulder bashing me into a corner and I shout demanding them to stop, calling them 'impertinent boys'. One turns around and punches the other shouting,"er...Miss called us 'impotent' what does that mean Miss?" As I regain my balance they run off giggling. It has been a month since the last Alien encounter and I have become almost complacent about another attack. Perhaps the daily trials of school have overtaken my nightmare anxiety and I have fallen asleep most nights exhausted from the stress of teaching lunatic juveniles.

Now in the early hours of a Wednesday morning, just before dawn, I am aware from a sleepy distance, footsteps plodding outside my bedroom door. Immediately I know they are here. The air around me changes as though I am transported elsewhere. I am semi-awake and not able to pull myself through the sleep barrier into conscious reality and the physical paralysis, like before, prevents me from moving. A grey/blue being sits beside me and telepathically communicates explaining that I need another injection to help transform my energy vibration to a level where I can receive information from extra- terrestrial entities. Before I can refuse their request, they place a sharp needle into the same vein in my left hand like before, and a white substance, this time with a lime green tinge, is injected into my arm. It has an iridescent glow like fairground candyfloss. Again the cold substance hits an obstacle in the crease of my arm and they withdraw the needle. This time they puncture another vein and the liquid travels along the same path as before, avoiding entering my head, but on this occasion the sensation is unpleasant and I feel sick. The nausea increases as the liquid travels through my stomach. It is unbearable and I cry out writhing in agony. I hear a distant voice commanding someone to turn me on my side to alleviate my pain. Invisible hands roll me on my left side. Momentarily, the pain lifts but the liquid leaks into my head. Every nerve, every vein, every sinew lights up like Blackpool Illuminations. An incredible light show flickers and flares like the greatest firework display on New Year's Eve. Like a pin-ball machine, parts of my brain ping into play as the liquid bounces off each cog blazing a bonfire beacon in my head exploding like Mount Vesuvius until I black out!

It is morning and I am fully awake. It must have been just a few hours ago that all hell was let loose in my head? Now I am fine. The sickness has passed and I don't even have a headache after the wildest party in my head. I remember they told me not to eat heavy food or drink alcohol and just eat mild, sloppy, milky food but I have no intention of following their demands. I will not become a slave to their commands. At school the rocky terrain of bullyboys, misfits and kids who've been in goal for the night, pull my full attention and I don't have chance to think about the impossible happening that occurred in the early hours of this morning. I attempt to analyse my feelings. On the one hand I am terrified of their presence and yet they make me feel important. The experiences are way, way beyond imagining and I could never envisage encounters of the third kind happening to me in the way that they are unfolding. Wine is a comfort after a hard day at school and helps to calm my nerves waiting for another alien attack. It's not so much the invasion itself, but more the anticipation of the initial scary contact.

Alone as I drift into a cosy haze of acceptance, my peace crashes as Rory screams and wails on the other side of the wall. I am beginning to understand his nightmares if he is going through the same torture as me, or worse. I know he is trying to warn me as he bellows, "they're coming for you, they're fucking coming for you. They're underground! They're coming for you!"

Tears stream as I hear his Mother attempting to calm him and in the silence that follows, I know he has been sedated. I quell my fears with wine, telling myself that just another glass won't hurt, but I know I have to be careful not to fall into the trap of alcoholic reliance. Bed is a relief and I drift into oblivion.

Twenty six days and nights have passed without a peep from them and I don't know whether I am relieved or feel abandoned? There is something horrifically addictive about their visits and yet I dread their coming. Somehow just before they appear, my body knows they are coming, as I become unnaturally hot and my heart-rate increases – or is it that they prepare me in advance? This time my body heat rises rapidly and I am prepared, but as always I am unable to move. Mentally I am aware of what is happening and as they hover over me I demand to be given a name. This request surprises them and they take time to show me a long line of written letters and symbols which I cannot comprehend and although they try to teach me the sounds of the signs, it is impossible to reproduce them as there are no similar resonances in our language. I ask them about what happened inside my head on their last visit and demand to know why. They quickly reply almost before I ask the question: "better for communication!"

I ask them about other people who are abducted and again the response is prompt:

"more people than you can count are being prepared for future development on planet earth but they are afraid to speak out for fear of being placed in a mental institution, but eventually all will be revealed for a purpose. Many millions, for it is a global phenomenon, are experiencing the same tests for a reason, which we cannot at present divulge. Just know you have been chosen!"

The visitors fade without further interference and I am left wondering why they came just to give me information and I fall into a relieved sleep.


A few weeks pass without any contact and during this time colours have become more vibrational and distinct, especially at twilight when hues of all the plants, flowers and trees zing with energy. I think it is because they have done something to my brain which now has the increased ability to be in tune with colour vibration. It seems I am more sensitive to colour-positive power as each colour speaks uniquely as it transforms into pulsing energy. When I step into the garden at twilight, I am mesmerized by the powerful, joyous cacophony of vitality, like an orchestrated symphony of colour and vigour from all the living plants, flowers and trees. Grandfather said that happiness is a chemical pacing through the body and we should allow it to flood our being and I understand now, how vibrational energy is a complete formula unto itself and human beings should seek to dwell in the flow of happiness. I ponder this new gift as I stand at my kitchen sink. I am thrilled at my transformation of the old kitchen, having hired a special designer to create a Bollywood spectacular film set with red shiny marble work tops, black and grey cupboards with a French Bistro corner set with black ornate table and chairs and my wonderful, innovative black, shiny porcelain sink- so unusual! My Grandchildren laugh at my eccentricity saying it is 'glitzy' like me and in creating my wonderful new colour-raged space, I am somehow freed from my secret terror of the alien visits – some might say that my internal anxiety has pushed me over the edge of normality, but for me my showbiz kitchen is a welcome escape.

I clean my new black sink, polishing it until it gleams, whilst listening to my whisperers enhancing my thoughts on my recent colour revelations;

*"Colour is a powerful gift to be used for healing and general well-being. It enriches surroundings and affects emotions but is generally taken for granted. You cannot imagine a world without colour.*

*White and black are not non-colours but poles of integrated, myriads of colours which have their own power-driven components. Turn on your cold water tap!"*

At first I am surprised and a little bemused by their request but I follow their instruction.

*"Now focus your attention on the running water. Watch it flow. Allow your gaze to go deep into the stream. Go further and further into the rippling, rolling, pulsing energy. Now see the myriad of multi colours like a rainbow river gently cascading down a small waterfall. Slowly move towards the tumbling surge, noting the constant bubbling of the flow and move inside the swell. Merge into the waterfall and step out the other side into a white Gardenia garden. The water is pure energy and you will not get wet."* I follow instructions and walk into the waterfall and out the other side into a white garden amassed with delicate star-petal Gardenias frosting the ground like the first snowfall in winter. White Gardenias blanket the gentle rise of hills beyond, cloaking the forest in an endless white lace coverlet. The sweet, divine, exotic perfume lingers in the air, riding the gentle breeze with intoxicating dreams of innocence and promises of purity of heart. A soothing soprano voice explains:

*"White represents a new beginning. It cleanses the soul and brings peace and calm to the troubled mind. Breathe in the essence of whiteness and it will cleanse the sterile, static minefield from stress, anxiety and fear. By bathing in the freshness of white particles floating in the atmosphere your mind and body will be refreshed anew. Allow your body to soak up the essence of the snowy veil enveloping you, for you are pure, untainted and whole as you are meant to be. Take time to linger in the unworldly, gentle paradise, for here you can reclaim your soul energy. When you are ready, walk back through the welcoming waterfall and find yourself in your kitchen and turn off the tap.*

*Whenever you feel the need to enter the white world of healing, you will know how to reach the white Gardenia garden."*

I wake from the 'moving meditation' and am totally calmed by the white experience. My guide whisperers have given me a precious gift, inspiring me to seek more knowledge of colour energy to teach and share with others. As the evening wears on I feel as though the 'visitors' will come, although I am not sure whether I am missing them and wanting them to appear. I seem to be losing my horrific fear of them and instead a strange emptiness invades my mind when they don't appear. I don't understand this secret yearning. Have they made me feel this way? Perhaps to co-operate with them it is necessary for me not to be fearful? I do not know the answer but wait with a peculiar sense of expectation.

I fall asleep but just after midnight I feel my arms hoisted up as though someone is trying to pull me up off of the bed and as I am placed back down something sharp cuts open a flap in the muscle at the top of my right arm. It hurts. Something is placed under the skin. The flap is quickly sealed as the skin miraculously folds back. The operation is swift, performed in a split second and now I am in agony. They seem to have sliced into my muscle and the pain is intense. Something has been planted in my arm. I feel them roll me over on my left side to alleviate the pain, then they show me a small tablet with orange, pink and purple fluorescent symbols inscribed in thin stick-like pencil signs which I don't understand. I am frustrated at not being able to comprehend the codes as they are totally unlike anything I have ever seen, although bar codes for items in shops are similar to some of the icons and they tell me:

"Tracking gadgets will be used in all humans in the future. Implants under the skin will be enforced for everyone. Tiny micro-chips will be injected into all humans under the guise of health-care benefits. Everyone will be controlled from the central government base. Many humans will die in the process as the first batch of micro-chips will be experimental and will have fatal consequences.

When a lethal virus strikes globally, everyone will be forced to be vaccinated. The micro-chips hidden in vaccines will alter human DNA and the immune system will be weakened. Billions of humans will suffer strange illnesses and die from heart attacks, especially in fit athletes and young professional football players. Thousands will be exterminated by radiation contamination installed from electromagnetic, high force 5G power points. These will be established around the world to work in conjunction with the implants and micro-chips to eliminate the population. The techno resource implants will act as mind-control devices. "

I am shocked by the information and ask if this is in preparation for an Alien invasion. There is silence and then a voice mechanically speaks:

"Alien invasion has already begun and will continue. Control of humans has been surreptitiously enforced for many years. Step by step changes in the human world for Alien benefit has been enforced without humans noticing. Your air, your food, your bodies your minds have been captured and altered and will be further metamorphosed until planet earth is unrecognisable. Humans are so stupid and gullible. Like the fish in your pond, humans see only what they wish to see."

I wait in the stillness for more, but they fade. How do they know my thoughts? They mentioned the fish in my pond where my thoughts had meandered earlier- how could they know my thoughts?

Now I am left with a terrible nagging pain in my arm like a constant tooth ache and I cannot find a comfortable position in which to fall asleep.


In the morning after a fretful night, my arm is stiff and I can't lift it. I force my arm to work, refusing to accept the pain and continue teaching dance to the best of my ability, not giving in to the excruciating stabbing twinges. Whatever they have planted inside my muscle, is causing me great concern and they know I cannot go to the Doctor for help as it would lead to all kinds of other questions and my life is difficult enough without added stress. I battle on quietly adapting to living in two separate worlds- one, my immediate reality of surviving the diurnal round of eat, work, sleep and the second- an off-earth unworldly world of aliens and secret horror-show visits of scary creatures who come out at night, like Rory predicted.


The pain at times of the implant is almost unbearable, especially at night when trying to sleep because no position offers respite from the niggling ache and tonight I feel instinctively that they are coming. I hear them approach and my body heats up. I am semi-conscious and know when the paralysis sets in they are around me. They place something in the right side of my brain which eases all pain, stress and tension. I float like a gentle sail in the breeze on a calm ocean and I am detached from reality and feel no pain. I drift into peaceful oblivion for the first time in a while since they sliced my arm open. This feeling however, is not the flooding of happiness, like the chemical reaction Grandfather spoke of, it is rather a numbness of nothingness. Perhaps they made a mistake when they sliced open my arm and they want to make amends and take away the pain? I sleep in peace drifting away from the torment.

In the morning the pain has dulled and I can lift my arm higher than before, but I am still aware that there is a foreign implant in my arm. The weather has grown colder and the autumn nights close in. I still haven't made bedroom curtains and the lights from the factory at night begin to annoy me. The little blue runway lights twinkle and are seemingly purposeless and the mystery of their existence irritates me more and more. There is something about the factory that is unfathomable, something that fires unreasonable anger within me and I don't know why I have mounting resentment for the strange buildings at the bottom of my garden. At first the factory never bothered me but now I hate the look of the sheds and the secrecy surrounding the place.

Recently a black helicopter has been hovering over my house. A friend said jokingly that I must be under surveillance by the secret police, but I didn't find the joke funny. The other evening a young girl came to receive psychic counselling and we were sitting in my office, when overhead we heard a loud drumming, invasive pounding, so we both simultaneously shot outside to investigate. It was a black helicopter hovering over my roof disturbing all the plants and flowers in my garden.

When we went back inside it was seven o'clock as I noted the time in order to keep to our hourly slot and after what seemed like only five minutes, the time was nine o'clock. We were only supposed to have an hour's session but two hours had disappeared and we were both shocked and couldn't remember what we had discussed during the two hour lapse. It was very strange and something we both couldn't fathom.

I think I must be developing a distrust of everything around me. I am becoming paranoid about ordinary things like white vans parked in the layby outside my house. White vans come and go at very odd times out of normal working hours and men in jump suits pretend to mend telegraph poles or fix council street lights. White vans without trade identification, park for hours without visible signs of any kind of work being undertaken and sometimes when I come home from school and a white van is parked next to my space, I get the feeling I am being watched. Sometimes when I enter my house I get a strange sensation that someone has been snooping around. It's just little things like a cup might be slightly out of place or the sliding glass door into the conservatory might not be closed properly or the tv control is not exactly as I left it. It is unnerving and I tell myself that I am imagining everything but I can't shake off the impression that eyes are watching my every move!

A friend arrives today for a few days and is staying in the grandchildren's bunk room where I hope he manages to sleep well. He is autistic and can only tell the truth of what he sees and hears, so if anything strange happens he will tell me. I don't speak of the visitors in case it scares him as I watch him contentedly display his helicopter collection on the empty shelf and his porcelain statue of Fiona, Shrek's wife. He is very attached to his few possessions and takes them with him wherever he goes. He is an amazing artist and has a brilliant mind for inventing computer animation. His world, like the fish in my pond, is very enclosed and he does not understand human emotions and has never experienced unworldly beings or psychic phenomena of any kind, so I am concerned that he is not disturbed by unusual activity in the night.

I have almost come to accept the strangeness of altered reality in which I live, as being normal and having him in the house is a comfort and a worry. The first night all is well and I am relieved he was not disturbed by strange visitors, although the sound of the central heating pipes apparently kept him awake as he has ultra-sensitive hearing. I am in the kitchen waiting for him to appear for his breakfast after his second night and he sheepishly creeps into the kitchen looking pale and upset. I ask him what's wrong and he shakily replies:

"There is something bad about this house!"

I look into his eyes and he turns away as he is not good at holding or returning a stare and I gently enquire what's wrong. He takes his time to reply and answers:

"Well, I was almost asleep when all the lights of my helicopters switched on all by themselves and they weren't even plugged in! The blades whirred into action moving around without electricity and they knocked poor Fiona off the shelf, but luckily she landed on the carpet. She wasn't broken, but all the helicopter lights flickered and jumped around. They did it all by themselves. I didn't know what to do and when I got up it all stopped. I sat on the bed and wondered why it happened. I knocked on your door but you didn't answer. I opened the door and you were asleep but there was a thing sitting by your bed. A little creature thing with big eyes sitting by your side. I was shocked and went back to my room but I couldn't sleep and now I'm going home!"

I am horrified and stunned to the core, firstly because of his helicopters shooting into action without electricity and secondly he actually saw an Alien sitting by my side. I feel dizzy and want to vomit. It's one thing knowing my strange experiences are real, but to have someone actually witness an Alien sitting next to my bed is horrendous. It makes everything more real and terrifying for me to handle.

The surge of electric energy when the visitors are present must have shot the helicopters into action and he must have been terrified, but I do not recall a visit last night! I understand why he has to leave and I am sad as he waves goodbye carrying his little suitcase.


Life goes on and I know I have to come to terms with what is happening to me or go mad! I am not going to be pushed out of my quaint cottage by strange beings and I resolve to battle on. It is early evening and the house is still and a pang of anxiety shakes my confidence as I watch the night sky bleed into the last rays of daylight. Fear creeps in when I least expect it and I struggle to push away the rising unease of what they are going to do to me. In the stillness, the phone rings and I jump in surprise and rush to answer it. In the midst of fear and panic, something wonderful takes me out of the quagmire of despair and lifts me up into the bright light of hope.

I am being offered the job of choreographing a highly prestigious event which will be televised world-wide and the idea fills me with great happiness beyond belief. It is wonderful recognition for my life's work and the thrill of the responsibility is overwhelming. I sit at my desk after the phone call and feel fortunate to be chosen, for the opportunity will open up new doors and no matter what is happening to me on another level, I feel I can handle it, because the powers that be have given me the chance to express my creative flair at a very high level. Grandfather is right - if you allow 'happiness' to flood your being then the whole world changes and everything seems brighter and clearer as the chemical change within your mind and body heals fear, bringing new confidence and energy. I am blessed and lucky to have something so inspiring to take my mind off the alien intrusion in my life, yes I am indeed Lucky!

# UPGRADED BIOLOGICAL CONTAINER

Rosie sighs and sits back assessing the information from the first half of the file. She is shocked and upset to think that Lucky endured so much in silence, realising that the actual truth of the facts are more horrific to digest with the photographic evidence. She turns over the next page and finds a letter addressed to her from Lucky which reads:

'My Dear Rosie,

I guess by now you will have read the first section of my experiences and I want you to know that everything happened as I related it, nothing is embellished, in fact quite the contrary as I have tended to play down the impact of some of the encounters. You may wonder why I didn't speak about my experiences earlier, but to be truthful, I was afraid of ridicule, afraid of the adverse publicity for my school and fearful that I might be considered insane.

As you read this you will know that the climate of 'acceptance' for believing in Aliens has changed and is very different, as public awareness of Alien presence on earth has increased and become credible. The news is flooded with the release of secret documents revealing the truth about crashed UFO's, Alien visits, the discovery of Alien corpses and videos of alien investigative operations, together with whistle-blowers revelations about U.S.A.'s interaction with visiting alien species. There is too much evidence and documentation to refute the idea that aliens exist. The U.S. Government have confirmed that there are five million Aliens alive on earth, which is a conservative estimate, as there are probably colonies living below earth that have not been counted. Scientists are back-tracking on previous statements about life not existing in other universes and are now speculating that it is very likely that there is life in other realms of the cosmos. These are not predictions Rosie, but facts which have been leaked. I know you are with me and believe in me, but what I am about to reveal next, takes a great leap of faith, as even I find it difficult to believe. Please stay with me to help get the message out to people because now is the time to act and reveal all.'

Rosie wipes away a few stray tears as Estrella enters with a welcome tea tray.

"How's it all going Rosie?" enquires Estrella, placing the tray on the desk awash with papers.

"Er, well, it's taking shape," replies Rosie, recovering her composure.

"You know Rosie, Mum told me once that one day she would tell the truth about everything and that when it was time, it would be the right thing to do. I suppose that time is now, so don't hold back on anything, as it's what she wanted, so tell it as it is!"

Rosie smiles and nods as Estrella leaves her in peace to continue reading from where she left Lucky receiving a phone call to ask her to undertake a new choreographic project.

The new venture lifts me out of a grey depression and a draining, stressful teaching post. The choreographic assignment is exhilarating and helps me tolerate the daily onslaught of unruly teenagers and prevents me from worrying about alien visits. But one of the two directors hates me and has given me the title,' Dance Director' of the project, instead of ' Choreographer'. It seems it is the boss-man's way of trying to control my work when his green-eyed monster appears and we clash over conceptual ideas. The other director is wonderful and truly appreciates my creative input.

The hateful director never allows me rehearsal space or time and I continually have to fight to gain access to these basic requirements for the job. He loathes the fact that I can handle large numbers of people and teach them to dance, even if they can't put one foot in front of the other and he keeps sending new recruits, hoping that I won't be able to cope and will quit the job. But of course the challenge spurs me on!

Where is the now? It is evening and grey shadows lurk in the hallway as I rush through from the sitting room to the kitchen, avoiding eye contact with what might be lurking on the stairs! There is no one there, but the eerie presence of what is to come lurks forebodingly. I promise myself a hot toddy with ample whiskey to scare away the night tremors and of course is medicinal to ward off a pending cold. The black night outside highlights my reflection in my bright- red Bollywood kitchen and the silver flecks in my red marble work tops glisten under the lights. I know I am lucky to have all of this, but underneath my brave veneer I am battling fear again. I am dreading going to bed because I know something is going to happen; I can feel it. Something is waiting and watching and I can't escape. I want to run outside and scream to the stars that I am a victim of something, but I don't know of what? Poor Rory springs to mind and I appreciate more and more his private torment. He has been in hospital for a while and I haven't heard his tormented screams, but the horror of his words stick in my mind as my own panic thickens, stirring up terrifying images.

After another whiskey, I force myself to go to bed, being self-conscious of going to the bathroom and getting undressed, as I feel every move is monitored. In bed I make myself turn out the light and lie clutching the covers up to my chin in abject terror of what is to come. I close my eyes but my mind is too active to sleep. My heart paces faster and throbs as though it will break out of my chest in anticipation of the first thuds on the stairs. I hear it! Thud! Thud! I stop breathing in the hope they won't find me, but several thuds later and a rattling of the door handle they arrive. I know they don't have to do all that drama but I think it is their way of leading me into an hypnotic trance, preparing me for their entrance, because by the time they are hovering over me I am immobilized and feel the air changing around me as I am taken without a physical struggle; yet I am conscious of something happening.

I can't see where I am, but I have the strange sensation that I have been moved underground in the factory premises into a dark laboratory where they place me on a table. Rory's words echo in my head…"They're underground….they put you on a table…!" I black out and when I gain consciousness I am lying on my stomach with my head facing out into the dark. I am aware of beings walking around taking care of other humans lying outstretched on black tables. When I regain my senses, I am sickened at what they have done to me! My chin is resting on the table and my mouth is opening and closing like a fish out of water gasping for air. My jaw is moving up and down and I can't breathe. Someone calls for help as I panic and try to struggle. I can't believe they have cut my bottom jaw open and taken it out, but in putting it back together again it doesn't fit properly and I am wrestling with my mouth open, struggling to speak. Excruciating pain is all I know! A man in a white coat draws near with a being by his side and tells me to breathe deeply. I try but my breath isn't coming from inside me; it is entering my body from far away. Far away, far away, I am separated from my body until eventually I feel my breath rising and falling inside me. I am back in my own bed and I black out.

In the morning when I wake I remember the nightmare assault. I touch my jaw and it feels fine. How could they do that? Why would they take out my jaw and replace it? I get up and look in the mirror.

There is a strange line under my chin as though the skin has been glued together. The line isn't straight and it looks like the skin has been heat-sealed leaving a small scar running the length of my under jaw. It doesn't hurt and no one can see it unless they look closely but the evidence of some kind of operation is there and can't be refuted, but why, why? It doesn't make any sense? I hurry to get ready for school going into automatic drive in an attempt to bury the horror of the night, pretending in some stupid way to convince myself it was a nightmare dream, but I know it was real!

Throughout the day I am aware that subconsciously I keep touching the scar under my chin to see if it has disappeared, but it's still there. In the evening my eldest daughter visits and I want to know what she thinks of the mark underneath my chin, as she is a midwife and has great knowledge of repairing skin tares. She examines the scar and is puzzled by it, saying that it looks like a new method of sutures, a technique of stitching the skin together with a glue-like substance. She asks how I got it and I try to explain that I fell as a small child, which is the truth, and cut my chin open but I wasn't taken to hospital and my Grandmother bound the skin together. The other alternative is to explain the abduction but I don't think she or I am ready for that! So we spend a pleasant evening catching up on old times and when she leaves I am left alone tidying the kitchen to avoid going to bed.

Questions go round and round in my head...why do they come at night? Why are they doing this to me? Will it stop? How can I escape? Why my jaw? But I have no answers. I don't seem to have any discomfort from the invasive operation but at the back of my throat is an irritation like a tiny hair which is stuck and I keep trying to swallow it, but it remains.

In my research I find that fine hair-like strands attached to alien implants have been removed from some abductees and I wonder if that is the case with me? Lately I have found that on the verge of sleep I am suddenly woken by a loud metallic, cracking sound in my nose, ears and head. It is most peculiar and like the ringing sound of a Tibetan bowl, the reverberation continues until it ceases. I have read the noise is a reverberation from metallic implants and has been recorded by many people experiencing the same phenomenon.

Now I am lying on my stomach in bed and I am angry. Fear has turned to rage and I am seething with fury at being used for some secret alien agenda without my consent and paralysed in order for them to impose horrific operations. I decide to use my psychic ability to 'remote view' the factory – it's a skill I have always had as a tiny child and when I was bored at night I would travel out of my body to explore places. I never knew anyone else did it or that it had a name, all that I knew was that it entertained me. My chin operation was grotesque and I suspect that I was taken to an underground facility nearby-which has to be the factory? I close my eyes and allow my mind to freely wander outside my body coaxing myself towards the factory where I see a night watchman strolling around near a small guard box like a telephone booth. It is chilly and his large frame is ungainly as he tries to keep warm, clapping his hands together. I sail past him like a smooth breeze and dip into a large warehouse where two men in black uniforms are sitting at a desk at the entrance watching two camera monitors. They seem bored and are making jokes about futile things.

I hover past them and enter a massive store room, where, to my amazement, hanging on large racks are Grey alien suits hanging in rows. I glide closer to inspect the uniforms and see that the fabric has fine veins woven through the material like a very thin spider's web texture which probably, when worn, is a form of communication system attached to the brain and hooked into a main computer system. The Grey Alien being known for its large almond shaped black eyes, I see from the costume, are not eyes at all, but a form of eye protection like sunglasses shielding their eyes from earth's harsh solar beams. I suddenly realise that the Alien beings who have been visiting me are non-bio robots who don the costume and obey orders from a central computer.

An invisible voice interrupts my thoughts stating that not all the Greys are robots and some are genuine beings who have to wear the outfit to protect their natural essence from the earth's electromagnetic rays and that the stereotype costume is not their actual appearance. The voice ushers me out of the warehouse and I am back in my body. The being chides me, instructing- "It is not

for you to decide the order of things. You will be told all when it is
time. Do not enter forbidden territory when you have no authority
or understanding of things beyond your comprehension. Everything
that is happening in secret on your earth is for your own good. The
human species is being upgraded and the old model Homo Sapien
is being revised. Your biological container, which is your body, is
being modified and improved to adjust to the world, which is being
gradually transformed. Humans with the capacity to use 'thought
energy' will be saved for the new Tachionic Thought Particle energy,
where thought power is the most prominent form of communication.
Temporal technology and the ability to time travel will be commonplace and the new upgraded human container will be a better
model designed to travel speedily through space and time. So do not
interfere with what is coming; you cannot prevent the evolution of
your species by those who designed you in the first place!"

The voice fades and I regain my full consciousness. Intuitively I
knew that something was not quite 'normal' at the factory base and
now having seen the Grey's costumes hanging up in rows on coat
hangers, I know for sure that the fruit canning operation is a front for
something sinister. I wonder if there are similar underground labs all
over the country where Aliens are abducting people and performing
all kinds of tests on them? I search the web and find reports from
people who claim to have information to verify that my suspicions are
valid, as whistle-blowers are speaking out about secret underground
bases where Aliens live and are creating hybrids of humans and other
alien species. Already renown physicist, Michu Kaku has stated that
the next hundred years will determine whether the human species
survives and I guess that higher intelligences are devising ways
of making sure the Homo Sapien species not only survives, but is
upgraded into a more advanced container, suited to cope with the
new world frequencies.

Back at school the smell of damp wool permeates the air with
sodden coats hanging on pegs in the corridors and wet slippery floors

like ice rinks lead the way to cold form rooms and I feel trapped in a classroom of mini volcanoes about to erupt at the slightest provocation. Why am I always given the difficult ones? It's like attempting to tame a cage of wild animals. It is too dangerous to turn my back on them for a second to write on the board as something terrible would happen, so I devise ways of teaching making sure I always face them and the constant strain of keeping discipline is taking its toll. I want to escape. I need to escape. I need to be far, far away from the alien torment and the school dramas. I have a free lesson and instead of marking delinquent's books, I sit at my computer in the staff room amidst a few teachers coughing and blowing noses, while the dinner lady tidies up the coffee cups and the left-over dry biscuits and I fall into a dream of distant places where the sun is shining and the pace of life slow and dignified. I descend into an ambedo trance noting the antics of a small blackbird searching for food. His little beady eyes peer at me through the window as though he sees me and then scuttles through the dark skeletal bush to the brittle winter ground to find food. I feel like the little bird searching for sustenance in a barren land. Trance-like, I allow my fingers to wade through beautiful photos of exotic paradises and with my limited computer skills I follow one site after another until the words 'CREATIVE WRITING IN GUATEMALA' flashes across the screen and I know that is exactly what I want to do. The thought thrills me and although I have never booked anything on line before, I follow the commands diligently until I have booked and paid for- not creative writing in Guatemala but a six week expedition across Central America, Mexico, Guatemala, Belize, Antigua, Caye Caulker, trekking through the Rain Forest and exploring Mayan Temples in the jungle, staying in primitive accommodation.

When the transaction is complete I am utterly shocked! I must have been in such a deep meditative state that I was lead to book such a terrifying expedition. I am petrified of insects and small creatures and spiders, so I can't understand why I have placed myself in such a precarious position, travelling alone in what could be a very dangerous situation, as many people have been kidnapped and held for ransom on the Guatemalan border. I understand the guide will be experienced and lead his small party with great care, but nonetheless I am suddenly in a state of panic. The bell goes and I wake out of my stupor and rush to my next lesson, still in a daze, but a voice in my head pacifies me stating:

*"You will always be where you are supposed to be. The Universe designs it this way. You are meant to take this trip. Do not fear, but rejoice in a new exciting adventure!"*

I push open the classroom door to find a pile of boys on top of each other fighting and screaming and I drop my books to separate them as one accidentally kicks my shin. A senior teacher nearby comes to my aid and bellows at the boys like a fog-horn in a mist and they pull away from each other instantaneously - such is his vocal skill and years of experience in dealing with obnoxious boys.

I envy his talent and am relieved when he shunts the reluctant perpetrators to his office and I am left to deal with the less unruly until I am released by the afternoon bell.

Back at home after a late evening of more teaching, I flop into a chair with a glass of wine and mull over my astounding adventure that I inadvertently booked, maybe I was guided to take it in my desperate need to escape everything, but to take myself out on such a daring expedition is ludicrous as I am such a scaredy-cat and I have no idea how I am going to cope with the intense demands of the journey. Physically I need to be fitter but my knee is worn out after years of dance and my hip is not good. I ponder all the necessary vaccines that I will need to travel across so many countries, trekking in far out places, so I will need a rabies injection. There is so much to organise and research that I am hardly fearful of going to bed, although the dread of 'them' is still there. I climb into bed with a mind full of 'what ifs?' I try to lie on my right side but the muscle which they sliced open still hurts and I have to hold it tightly to try to alleviate the pain. The air changes suddenly and I am immobilised. They are here and they roll me on my back.

There is no time for fear. Everything happens so quickly. Something icy cold is being poured down my right arm where they cut it open and it is trickling into my chest. It is so heavy like a great weight placed over my ribs and I can't breathe. My lungs are collapsing and I'm suffocating. Hurriedly they roll me over on my left side. The weight of the cold substance is overbearing. I feel them panic in an attempt to stop my lungs from giving way and I drift in and out of consciousness as they correct the problem. The heaviness begins to dissipate and my breathing returns to normal as they disappear and I am left completely at a loss as to the reason why they came to perform another injection, unless it was to help the pain in my arm, but my mind tells me that it is for another purpose. I think it is all part of the plan to upgrade the human container to prepare humankind for a different world and I am certainly going to be travelling in a strange new domain in months to come so perhaps they are preparing me for this venture. I am not sure whether I feel lucky to have this treatment, but I know that whatever happens to me is for a reason and I suppose in this way, yes, I am Lucky.

⊹⊱⋅⟨◇⟩⋅⊰⊹

# VENI VIDI AMAVI – WE CAME, WE SAW, WE LOVED

Standing in the middle of the massive arena being built for the outdoor performances of the prestigious project I have been asked to choreograph, I marvel at the magnitude of the production.

With a cast of hundreds and star appearances by major actors, the dramatic impact on audiences will be overwhelming. The 'theatre' has and always will be my Church, as there is nothing quite like the great surge of energy generated on mass, during a performance, which is magnificent beyond understanding and greater than any religious ceremony.

The dual interaction between performer and audience is the highest form of communal telepathy humans can ever encounter on earth and during a show, performers and audience subconsciously agree to engage in a fantasy world, imbued with a heightened reality more real than reality itself. Perhaps that is why I love the theatre so much and have made it part of my life's work. Here on the stage is a greater sense of life and 'oneness' than outside in the everyday world and the thrilling communion between everyone in the arena is intoxicating, especially just before a performance begins, where expectation rises and ascends to a crescendo. The opening bars of the overture commands silence and everyone enters the enchanted kingdom of make- believe; fully accepting to suspend our disbelief for a short time whilst enveloped in the magic.

I walk across the vast stage pacing out steps where the performers will dance and as the clouds disperse, a shaft of golden sunlight beams through the steel canopy encasing me in a bright spotlight and a warm surge of energy wraps around my head as my whisperers speak:

*"Entering life on earth is very much like accepting the same terms of agreement as when you enter the theatre, either as a performer or audience- remember; "All the world's a stage, and all the men and women merely players; they have their exits and their entrances..."Like on earth there is birth and death. Entering earth's illusory zone and participating in the illusion is a personal choice and the power of each performance depends on individual, unique private application to the role."*

I understand the meaning and find the analogy between the theatre and life on earth very illuminating. Amidst the banging and clattering of carpenters hammering the set, the noise echoes into the town, alerting people that something great is being prepared for their entertainment and my whisperers continue:

*"Planet earth is a school for spiritual enlightenment where difficult lessons must be repeated if not learnt the first time around. Transcendent advancement is part of the spiritual training on earth and 'Karmic Law' ensures 'self- payback' for damage caused to another human, whether physical or mental. Karmic Law is not an external police force, as many people believe, but rather an internal, self- judgemental device, administering appropriate self- punishment when necessary."*

I watch a clutch of workmen creating and making invisible trap doors in various places on the stage and I note another analogy of life- which is, that we spend too much time avoiding life's hidden trap doors and being continually fearful that we might fall into an abyss at any time; but my whisperers remind me that:

*"it is not the falling which is important, but how you get up. Like in African dance, performers are taught that the fall is inevitable but the getting up is Art. So it is in life, downward spirals of self- doubt and fear can keep you trapped in your own darkness, but the light is always there*

*if you allow it to shine and you will rise up eventually in enlightened brightness."*

I recall my time in China, when I was learning to be a Panda keeper and being woken in the dead of night to receive some terrible family news. I was distraught, feeling alone and unable to rush home. Emotionally, I was at the bottom of a deep dark well, unable to climb out, drowning in the depths of despair and when I was at my lowest, calling out to the Universe in sheer desperation, a bright light came from nowhere blazing on the edge of my darkness and I looked up and followed it. Rising high, high into the starlit sky where the dazzling glow filled my empty being, I was told that all would be well and that my energy would be received if I believed in the true healing power of love. 'I believe in love'. 'I believe in love'- I cried in the darkness and 'love' filled my heart with eternal sovereignty, gathering force from all around, entering my Sacral chakra up through my body and out from the top of my head, spiralling beyond the cosmos to my loved one and the healing worked!

Now as I gaze up into the auditorium where the first high-rise set of seats are being erected, I am awed by the fantastic engineering feat of the builders as the massive stadium takes shape. A cold gust of wind sets the protective plastic sheeting over the seats, flapping in a spontaneous round of applause resounding around the stage as I exit through a side wing into a gigantic collection of props and congeries of boxes containing large umbrellas ready for rainy performances in the open-air arena. Gigantic topiary animals on wheels wait eerily for the Noah's Ark scene and bits of the Ark lie forlorn in a corner ready to be assembled. As I look at the Ark, a flashback from the Alien contact connects in my mind and I begin to piece together bits of information they shared. They said that throughout the planet, deep underground, giant space ship Arks are waiting to fly millions of people to other galaxies for a mass earth exodus when the time arises. Underground railway tunnels connect passageways to the Ark complexes and a massive underground railway line travels from

Buckingham Palace, through London, linking important points like the Houses of Parliament and government buildings together with Scotland Yard and other high ranking places, out to Scotland where a deep underground air station is secretly situated. They showed me a forest, which is completely fake, camouflaging a massive circular entrance which folds into the earth when the seal lifts for the space Ark to take off into orbit. They also showed me an ancient underground series of tunnels which link Scotland to other countries all the way to Turkey. They said that particular complex was discarded a long time ago and that new fast track rail systems had been built all over the world, so that if a Nuclear explosion threatened earth, then a mass exodus across the world under the earth would be possible.

The flashback fades as I stand staring at a clump of angel's wings dumped by the arena and rails, upon rails of costumes with name tags fluttering in the breeze wait to be collected by hundreds of local performers. In a daze, I am still zinging with the communication energy from my whisperers who assure me that all is well and that I must consider myself privileged to be shown such secret knowledge.

My mind meanders to the question of 'Karmic Law', as I nearly stumble over treasure chests of swords and Roman helmets and ask my whisperers if evil people really enforce their own karmic punishment. A single voice vibrates through the air saying:

*"all humans no matter how great or small the evil perpetrated to others, will receive their own Karmic punishment instigated by themselves. No one on earth escapes this as it is the nature of Karmic Law, but it is not so beyond earth's gravity, as other species in other dimensions are subject to their own laws."*

When the costume ladies arrive I make myself scarce and wander into the parkland where massive tents are being erected amidst the ruins of fallen masonry from an historic ancient abbey. The place is beginning to look like a gigantic refugee camp complete with outdoor braziers for night fires and I can almost hear the faint folk guitars strumming a communal lullaby. As I wander through one of the tents prepared for my dancers, I can't help asking my voices what happens to horrendously evil people and the reply is prompt: *"You have asked this question before. Do you remember the two visions you received?"*

I nod remembering exactly what they showed me and I bring the scenes to mind. I recall asking about Hitler and what happened to his soul and I was shown a large nursery of cribs with grotesque beings lying abjectly still, bound in their own monstrous incarcerated gore and being told that it would take many eons of lifetimes before the monsters transformed into humans again. I was shown Hitler's cot and was nauseated to watch a black, gelatinous slug-like creature lying in an eternity of black plasma.

I was then taken to a repulsive zone and shown an unforgettable scene of a monstrous man who had committed unspeakable crimes to children, sick patients, the elderly and dead people. I recognised him immediately as he sat terrified unable to move a muscle in an atmosphere heavily clogged with a sulphurous, dark red gas. All around him was decay and destruction with rubble and stones lying in a layer of dust like in a nuclear fall-out explosion. He was wearing a turquoise shell suit and pink-tinged glasses through which I spied his left eye bulging with a disease that was eating him from the inside. He was petrified as eyes from all directions focussed on him. He was surrounded by distorted, small, hideous creatures representing the injured souls he had abused who were poised ready to pounce to avenge the heinous crimes. Jimmy Saville was finally being punished and tortured. The visions were shown to me, but I can't vouch for their validity, as all I know is the truth of what I witnessed.

Having inspected the performance arena, I show my pass to the security guard and he salutes as I slowly drive past. Once our rehearsals are underway, the traffic into the main town will be overbearing and I shudder to think where all the performers will park and I feel lucky not to have to worry about that problem, but the anxiety of returning home begins to rise. Fear of the unknown and what might happen during the night weighs on my mind. My beautiful, quaint cottage doesn't feel like my home anymore and as I enter the hallway, a heavy emptiness descends. I pretend all is fine, but I am conscious of eyes watching from afar. I argue with myself that I have become paranoid about everything, but on the other hand, after what I have endured, it's hardly surprising that I feel scared. I am afraid to tell anyone or share the details of the nightmare visits from alien creatures.

The unbelievable phenomenon of scratches appearing on my arms and back have begun again. It first happened about ten years ago when my youngest daughter was little and she noticed scabs of deep scratches on my arm thinking that our cat had carelessly caught me with her sharp claws and I agreed with her explanation, not wishing to frighten her with the truth. But the fact was that scratches appeared from nowhere perpetrated by no visible person one Saturday afternoon when I was at the sink washing up. My hands were deep in hot soapy water and my arms began to tingle and hurt as an invisible line was carved into my left arm. Then scratches began to appear and bleed which scabbed over and remained sore. At the time I had a boyfriend who was a male nurse and when he inspected the scars he became alarmed, especially when I explained the truth of how they appeared and strangely I never saw him again. After that scratches would appear randomly and remain for a while and inwardly I would fight the force until they disappeared without a trace.

Sometimes I would be swimming in a pool with a friend and my back would become sore and my friend would witness large scratches appearing across my back as though I had been whipped.

He was shocked to witness such a mysterious, vicious attack, but like as always they disappeared after a short time.

On other occasions I would be having coffee with a friend and the warning soreness would strike, as scratches would appear in a long line down my left arm as though a creature with sharp talons was clawing at me. There were many times when I was attacked by an invisible force but I wasn't afraid because I could fight off the energy with my own inner strength. For a long time the scratches never appeared, but just recently the attacks have begun again. I am not upset by this, it's more the thought of alien visitors which terrifies me. I do not know why an invisible force claws my body or from where they are initiated and by whom, but the phenomena is not as terrifying as the alien invasive operations. Perhaps one day all will be revealed.

I am ashamed to say, I find solace in drink. It's only when the night draws in and terror of the unknown begins to taunt me that wine helps to take the edge off the hollow dread, but I don't like the feeling of not being in control and so I only drink enough to calm my nerves and I know even that is not good. I climb the stairs feeling sick with nervous apprehension. I know they will come. It's like climbing the stairway to the gallows-you know you cannot escape what awaits you. I manage to fall asleep, but in the early hours of the morning they are here. I cannot move but I sense their presence. I don't know if I have been moved or if I am still in my own bed, but they take my left hand and inject me again. The serum is red and thin like blood. Is it blood? They tell me it's to rejuvenate my cells. The sharp needle enters the vein in my left hand and I feel the liquid rise up my arm but again it hits a blockage and they push and push until the blood-red substance flows through my body. Spasms of pain attack momentarily then subside. I am riding a roller coaster of stomach cramps. I feel sick. They roll me on my left side to alleviate the pain. It is too much. I black out.

In the morning I wake and feel fine. Why do they always inject me in my left arm? Why does it always hit a blockage? Why do they roll me over on my left side? So many questions and there is no one to answer them. I look at my hand and see the tiny red dot where the needle has punctured the skin, but I marvel at the youthfulness of my hand. It looks younger. I get up and stare in the mirror.

Yes, somehow I look younger! They said the injection was for cell regeneration- I guess it must have worked and I smile- at last something beneficial, but outwardly the effect doesn't last long. As I ponder the idea of cell regeneration, images they showed me return. I see a vision of the future where 'rejuvenation' is common place and 'old age' unheard of as a primitive process from the past and disease of any kind has been eradicated and Homo-Sapien has been upgraded into a super- human prototype. They show me that now is the era when humans are slowly metamorphosing into transhuman beings with super human powers, both mentally and physically. The vision fades and I remind myself that I have an appointment at the travel clinic where they will advise me on all the precautionary injections I will need for my forthcoming expedition across Central America. I am still in shock over actually booking the trip and I don't know how I did it, but the Universe has planned it and so I will plunge myself wholeheartedly into the project.


The nurse at the clinic is very helpful and I receive all the necessary injections to travel across jungle scrubland and rainforest territory, including a rabies injection, as I will be trekking in mountainous areas where hospitals are days away. She also gives me a self-survival kit with two injections to administer to myself in the case of severe diarrhoea, but as she cautions, I will have to choose carefully which bout I deem as an emergency, as there could be a few during the time I will be journeying. My arm aches after the injections and ironically I smile to myself thinking that my body is like a pin-cushion after all the invasive injections from the aliens and now these! The nurse would think I was absolutely crazy if I confided in her about them, but I am sensible and thank her leaving with my little red cross bag supplies for emergencies.

Back home I look at the map of my intended expedition and I am shocked at the territory we will cover and the amount of countries we will encounter. I hope that I am going to be able to withstand the rigours and trials ahead? There must be a reason that I am guided to do the trip and I research information about the Mayans, their culture, amazing astrological knowledge and their temples. Perhaps there is a connection between their myths, legends of outer space visitors and alien gods as their statues, pottery artefacts, and art work is amassed with signs and symbols of outer space visitors? During the night I have a painful reaction to the Hepatitis B injection. The stomach cramps are intense, like giving birth and I roll around in agony almost wishing to suffer a visit from the aliens, rather than endure the gut spasms. I call out to the Universe for help and little purple-pink orbs appear with buzzing healing vibration and I collapse into their loving care. The purple orbs appear when I am desperate for help and their loving energy encompasses me in total restorative healing.

In the morning all is well and I am so grateful to the purple healing energies for taking away the pain and I feel fit to face the terrible teenagers. The thought of escaping gives me greater inner strength to tackle the day's challenges, plus little Daisy from next door is coming in the late afternoon for her first piano lesson and I am looking forward to seeing her. She is such a sweet little five year old with beautiful big blue eyes and long curly ringlets. I hope we will be good friends. As I drive to school waiting in traffic queues, I catch a news article on the radio about solar flares and a memory from somewhere springs to mind. I see in a vision the sun radiating orange/red vibrations out to earth and an object, like an alien spaceship flies into the middle of the red-hot plasma. I am shocked to observe this as I thought the heat of the sun would burn anything that came within shooting distance, but a voice reminds me that I have been shown this event during one of my Alien encounters where they relay future events and strange happenings. Bit by bit I begin to recall the information they shared with me:

*"Alien spaceships, as you call them, are made of a kind of metal which you cannot understand, as there is no earthly equivalent. This material can withstand the sun's heat and the Arctic cold and a certain species of Alien have bases inside the sun where they control the earth's electromagnetic field. The planet Saturn was the earth's first sun, but it was replaced with today's sun and Saturn was imprisoned in a ring of energy which keeps its inhabitants captive. There will be solar radiation explosions which will shift the earth's magnetic poles and this will begin significant changes on planet earth. The frequency of earth's magnetic field, known as the 'Schumann Resonance' will change to a higher resonance and humans will experience a shift in the magnetic poles, feeling the speeding up of time, albeit slight this time."*

The voice fades and I move forwards as the traffic thins. It's strange that I keep getting memory flashbacks from my alien encounters. I know that during the visits they put a memory block in my brain, although I am able to recall some things but not everything and at times I remember bits in bursts of recall. I suspect there is much more to remember about many things but at present my memory is sealed.

Back home, I prepare the piano for Daisy's first lesson and I am delighted when I hear a tiny knock on the door and open it to find her standing in her pretty floral frock holding out a tiny envelope with her lesson money. She doesn't smile as she enters and keeps a stern face as she sits at the piano.

She is so tiny that I have to prop her up with cushions to reach the keys. I am not sure if she is enjoying the lesson as she doesn't respond to my cheery comments, instead she stares at me with her beautiful big, blue eyes and I wonder what she is thinking. Half an hour passes and I am not sure whether she is a suitable pupil as she doesn't seem to show any kind of enthusiasm, but I decide to give it another try next week. When her tiny finger plays the last note of the lesson, I take her into the kitchen to give her a few sweet treats, which she seems to like and she smiles for the first time during our session together. I walk her back home and her Mum is pleased to see us and I agree to take her again next week. As I walk back, I ponder Daisy's reaction. Maybe her Mum told her to behave and be polite, but there is something odd about her behaviour. Her constant staring at me instead of concentrating on the notes is a little disconcerting, but I resolve to try to break through her reserve next lesson.

Now I am in the main local theatre for a mass meeting of the massive project we are about to begin.

The production team and performers are called together for the first time and the Press are invited to record the event. The two directors will address everyone and introduce people with a specific role in the production, where each one of us we will be called upon to briefly explain our role. My chosen dancers are attending and there is a great buzz of excitement rising from the auditorium.

Everyone learns that the lengthy months of rehearsals ahead are vitally important and everyone must be fully committed to the rigorous demands of the six weeks scheduled performances come rain or shine! As I look around from my position on the stage, I am impressed by the community's response and the great sense of 'togetherness'- very much like in the war years where communities looked after each other and in fact the directors have chosen to theme the whole production to the second World War. They have costumed it to that era, although my dancers are meant to be Sufi Dervishes whirling into the cosmos at the opening and it is my job to choreograph the correct moves to create this illusion.

I research the ethos behind the religious whirling to find that the Dervishes believe that everything in the universe turns and to become one with the universe it is necessary to tune into it by whirling round and round spinning in a moving meditation, which is a hypnotic form of prayer performed until a trance-like state is achieved. The Sufi Dervishes costume echoes the swirling circular motion and helps to create a wonderful spherical, hypnotic effect. The elongated tall hats represent an antennae reaching upwards to the divine force to enhance a spiritual two-way communication, where the mystical energy enters the body through the top of the head. I have about three hundred or more dancers to train, many of whom have never danced before and I am looking forward to the challenge, having been reassured by the directors that I have been chosen for the job because of my previous success with community projects. I smile at the prospective recruits of all ages and stages in life and feel humbled that they will place their trust in me. From my Sufi research I find that the spinning helps to relieve negative energy and I remember taking a dance course with Werewere Liking in Pan-African dance, where we had to spin for a very long period of time. Before the class we were advised not to eat and to take off rings as our fingers would swell with the centrifugal force.

The class began with slow turning and the drums kept our pace until the rhythm began to speed up and we had to keep on turning. After about half an hour of spinning, students were falling down being sick and our hands were swelling. I could not, like many others, remain turning and I had to drop out. Overall it was not a pleasant experience but we learnt about the sustainability of our bodies during long term turning. The turning I intended to teach was not going to be gruelling but beneficial to everyone including the audience. The word 'dervish' means 'doorway' and the whirling is thought to open a bridge between two worlds and open a doorway to an altered state of consciousness to receive God's grace and forgiveness. The irony of it all is that I do not search to enter a state of altered reality, yet I am being forced or 'chosen' by an unknown force or entity to submit to physical tests beyond my control. I am in two realities. One, where I am expected to be a leader and inspire a core of dancers and the other where the impossible drags me into a world of fear and the two worlds are so far apart that I am mentally and emotionally torn in two! My whisperers give me courage saying:

*"you are strong. You can ride through all of this. You know the power of 'love'. Take it within yourself and use it to empower your heart, your mind, your body, for it will strengthen you, protect you and guide you and in the giving out, you will receive tenfold back."*

I heed their words and feel strong. I have been placed in this position and I will do my best, for I am lucky to have been chosen and as I look at all the lovely trusting faces before me the words:

'VENI VIDI AMAVI...we came, we saw, we loved...' echo in my heart.

Yes, I am Lucky, indeed!

# CHOCOLATE AND CUSTARD

*"You are who you are, only in the moment of knowing who you are and in finding yourself in the now of the present, you exist only in that instant of infinity. Outside the ticking of time there is no moment; there is no present; there is no instant emotion; there is no diurnal round of day and night and existence is infinitude beyond imagining."*

I listen to my ancient Chinese guide whose Grandfatherly wisdom is boundless. When I have doubts, and feel worthless, when fear shakes my certainty, when panic begins to trickle into my confidence and jab at my security- I seek his council.

My now is the present of early morning waiting to feed my Chinese carp, standing by the edge of the pond watching for them to surface. I peer into the dark muddy depths to catch a glimpse of their gold and white shiny scales but there is no sign of them. Sometimes I do not believe in myself and feel alone in a dark muddy cavern questioning my ability to lead large numbers of dancers to perform a wonderful opening for such a grand occasion. Doubt creeps into my creative source and like all artists who strike out to be individual in their work, I know that once the paint is applied to the canvass, there is no turning back; so I question my ability to devise the correct picture for the task, for once the steps of the dances are set and learnt, they must remain and become second nature to the dancer. Artists of any breed are vulnerable to public discernment and answerable to everyone, as every person has the right to voice an opinion. The pressure of the responsibility for my job for the production is a heavy obligation and I seek Grandfather's advice. In my mind I see him dressed in his regal silk robes with his long white straggly beard tapering over his chest and his white doughy cheeks sagging over his jaw. His eyes are half closed as he stands peering over a dainty, red, wooden bridge looking out over a gentle stream studded with delicate pink lotus flowers and he motions me by his side saying: *"See the little fish below my child?"*

I peer into the clear water and spy myriads of tiny grey fish with minute black fins swimming furiously in the flow, all tail to tail following each other blindly with one conscious thought to find their food source.

*"See there is not one individual fish, with a single desire, other than to be with all the other fish?*

*Mass obedience to the cause is the only common goal. People can be like this! Some people only exist within the core of mass acceptance and live to follow the throng, having no original thought of their own. Now observe this-"*

He points his skeletal long fingers with yellowed, taloned nails towards the stream where the grey mass of little fishes are pushing their way forwards along the bank. I observe the pulsing mass beating with one force, until suddenly one little fish turns sideways away from the multitude and begins to nibble at the fronds of weeds waving in the ripples. The little fish is brave leaving the shoal to satisfy its curiosity and then strangely one by one, other little fishes follow its lead and begin feeding off new delicacies of underwater plants. Soon the whole shoal is gathering by the water's edge to taste fresh delights.

*"You see my child, all it takes is the bravery of one person to change the course of the masses, so do not be afraid of turning sideways to seek new outlets for expanding your Art form. Be positive in what you do and lead with conviction and strength and everyone will follow. Believe me! You see my child, 'doubt' is a conscious tool to help you seek truth. When you doubt, your misgivings lead to questions pending answers and those answers open pathways widening your scope of choices to help you make the right decision. Doubt is healthy when it alerts you to become aware of alternative pathways. But also be aware that doubt can be an unhealthy enemy when it strikes to cloud your mind with negativity and kill your creative spark, dampening your enthusiasm to search for enlightenment. So use 'doubt' as a tool and not a weapon."*

With Grandfather's advice echoing in my mind, I formulate moves to the composer's opening sequence, understanding that people respond well to 'food' words, so I create steps to the rhythm 'CHOCOLATE AND CUSTARD'. The formula works well with the dancers but the composer is not so enamoured, complaining that he has written beautiful, ethereal music and I denigrate it with the words 'chocolate and custard'. I see his point but the recipe for learning the steps works well and I am happy that even the non-dancers relate to the rhythm. The first rehearsal goes well, closely watched by the aggressive director who shouts at me when I appoint strong dance leaders to help each group, calling out to me," we don't have leaders in Community productions," so I label them 'anchors' and the women nod their approval, snubbing his interference, turning away from his oppressive glare.

After an intense and productive rehearsal, I am left in the quiet of the massive ballroom quietly collecting my music, imagining a time when the high society Regency Balls were the events of the season and stately dancing under twinkling chandeliers romantically moulded couples together under a thin veneer of respectability. The seductive thrill of clandestine eyes meeting over splayed fans, was the secret messaging code of the time and now in this present era, young girls are encouraged to send naked photos of themselves to prospective boyfriends! I sigh in the emptiness as the heat of the evening fades and feel sad for the young girls I have known who became victims of indecent photographic traps. I walk into the noisy traffic jam outside feeling very alone, despairing at the dangerous world of the young, so vulnerable to the temptations of the flesh and pressures of the mass media to comply to uncomfortable modes of behaviour. I meander across the Museum Gardens where the massive arena is being erected and an excited shiver rises in the anticipation of the grand opening of the first night where my work will be judged; but this worry subsides as a different fear and panic begins to taunt me and another insecurity bubbles, as I know I have to go home alone to face the uncertainty of what might be lurking from a very different universe. There is nothing more lonesome as leading a mass of people in the evening then returning home to an empty hallway where my footsteps echo in the hollow darkness. Aloneness is a state of being which requires good management and can be very beneficial and peaceful, but going back to a potentially scary situation and facing the menacing emptiness, is daunting. I saunter into the kitchen pretending to be confident and fearless, banging cupboards and rattling glasses as I pour myself a drink in my Bollywood bistro where flecks of silver glisten in my red granite worktops, but the party is over and silence drowns the moment. I persuade myself to take my drink into the sitting-room, which is a massive space, daring myself to face unseen watchers. The room was once a stable housing many horses and converted into a large dining area and lounge with spacious windows. The black night outside reflects an image of myself that I don't care to see, as I feel eyes are observing me and I quickly finish my drink. I check all the doors and windows before climbing the stairs. Panic simmers as I know they are coming. Rory was right…"They'll get you! They'll come for you! Escape!" I want to escape but I dutifully climb into bed with pounding heart and breathe deeply accepting my fate.

I don't have to wait long before my body is paralyzed, but my mind remains active. They are here and my fear subsides. My body is feverishly hot and my arm where they sliced it, hurts. Something is happening in my left ear but I don't know what they are doing. It doesn't hurt. Then they turn me on my stomach with the left side of my face on the pillow and I am shown an X-Ray of my skull lit up in bright red and my head and throat burn. From a distance I hear myself coughing but I am not inside my body. Why are they doing this to me? They are telling me to change my diet to help me acclimatise to a new world where food will be very different. Then I black out.

In the morning I remember the episode and I gradually sit up holding my head. I am not in pain. I think I must be going mad and try to dispel the horrific memory of the X-Rayed skull and throat.

None of the encounters make sense and it is best if I just try to get on with my life without acknowledging the terrible experiences, so I resolve to bury myself in the preparations for my long-haul expedition and deny that the night horrors ever happened. During the day battling with juvenile delinquents it is easy to forget the night assaults, as the boys refuse to listen to set curriculum texts and prefer to chat about their exploits, where I learn many handy tips about stealing into people's houses and how to get a free meal from the Pizza Palace. Stephen sly fox, as I have secretly named him, with his white- blonde, haystack hair sticking out at all angles and his slanted bright blue eyes and grinning, devious smile, tells me with pride how he has taught his Mother to steal a meal from the Pizza Palace; "ya see Miss, ya just go in and sit at a table and they take your order and you fill your plate with as much salad and extras as you want. You can take as much as you like Miss and then they bring you your pizza and you can even have a pudding. Ice cream is nice and then when they clear the plates you walk towards the toilets but there is a back door and you just walk out Miss. It's easy.

"But what if the back door is locked Stephen?" I enquire.

"Oh it's not Miss, it's never locked Miss!"

Later in the afternoon Stephen does not appear for our lesson and I am informed he has been arrested and taken to the Police station for questioning. The rest of the boys refuse to talk about it but they all know what crime Stephen has committed. After school I delight in shopping for my trip and am happy when I return home with a heavy-duty back pack, roll-up travel towel, waterproof top and trousers, and expedition mosquito repellent, not forgetting the bottle of wine I purchased with the left over change for the evening's relaxation. I line up the goods on the kitchen table wondering at my bravery or stupidity for going ahead with the longest and potentially dangerous journey I have ever undertaken. I trust to the Universe to keep me safe and my children have no doubt that my naivety will always save me from harm's way, as they say I tend to waltz through life's harshness seeing only the good in people. Well, I hope that is the case and that I am able to cope with all the journey's stresses and strains. Right now I aim to complete my first year back teaching in school and to successfully continue choreographing the set dances for the major production and try not to be so fearful of other things which are happening to me.

The next few weeks are an uphill struggle in school as the boys know they are leaving and become more obnoxious and rebellious than ever. The rehearsals somehow haven't been scheduled into the general timetable and I have to keep fighting for rehearsal space, whilst more un-coordinated women are sent to me to become dancers and the angry director continues to vent his ireful moods towards me, even my daughter who is a main dancer is appalled by his attitude and it hasn't gone unnoticed by many others. The director who appointed me to the position is entirely the opposite, always supportive and generous in his appraisal of my work, so I labour on keeping the amazing journey ahead as a carrot to work harder at everything. My night visitors have been quiet for a while but I am not lead into a false sense of security as I know their work is not yet finished.

Finally the day for my departure arrives and I am nervous and anxious. The bright morning dawns after a restful, uneventful night and I drive into York for a few last minute items. My taxi will arrive at 2 pm in the afternoon to take me to the bus station to begin the first step towards my mammoth journey and as I enter the cottage with my bags, I am knocked backwards by the smell of gas! Oh no? A gas leak? Just as I am about to leave on my adventure the cooker decides to spring a gas leak! It is 11am and time is ticking. I don't know what to do? I know it would be foolish to walk away and leave it for the long duration of my absence, so I furiously search for the gas emergency number and arrange a crisis call out. The gas company are very good and respond immediately and arrive ready to tackle the problem. I am relieved when it is sorted and calm down after my initial panic. I hope this is the only blot to the start of the journey, as all my connections with buses and flights are finely timed to get me to Cancun, Mexico? The tour advisor suggested that everyone in our little party of seven should travel light and so boarding the bus to Leeds I am proud that my small rucksack has everything necessary for the expedition. I have an hour's wait in Leeds for my bus to Heathrow Airport and am shocked to witness a pimp and his prostitutes touting for business in such a public place. One girl lies seductively across a bench revealing her inner thighs with her sarong trailing to the floor as she nonchalantly chatters on her phone in a foreign language, while another sexily paints her toenails with her legs akimbo for all to view her scanty panties. Although the display is fascinating, I decide to go inside the station to listen to the news. My bus leaves at 7pm in the evening travelling through the night to Heathrow where my American Airline jet departs at 8am in the morning to Miami and then I take another flight to Cancun. I am nervous about making the connections as I have to be in a certain place at a certain time to meet my guide. It doesn't help when my daughter's last minute phone call before I leave, cautions me that many people have been killed or kidnapped in Guatemala travelling without a guide! I assure her that all will be well and that I have no intention of going anywhere without a guide.

Suddenly a newsflash appears on the tv screen announcing a terrorist plot to bomb ten American Airline jets travelling from Heathrow! No? I can't believe it? It can't be happening? Surely it won't affect my plane? Please not my plane? I make a hasty phone call to the tour advisor who confirms that my plane to Miami is one of the suspect planes and that I should expect long delays while the planes are being thoroughly searched. I am shocked and so worried that I will miss my connection in Miami to Cancun. Travelling alone is terrifying when things go wrong and you don't have anyone to share the horror, stress, confusion and uncertainty of any problems which might arise. I try to calm my nerves and inwardly call to my whisperers and a voice in my head states:

*"Forget schedules! Schedules don't exist in Divine Consciousness. You will always be where you are meant to be at the right time and the right place, as all action is Divine action and any problems you encounter will be those you created yourself for the lessons you need to learn. Journeying is a test. Always expect the best to happen and it will be so, even when you encounter delays, disappointments and weariness, always know that the best is waiting for you - all you have to do is mentally tune into 'the best' vibration and it will be so. Taking risks and placing yourself beyond your comfort zone will increase your ability to trust and believe in yourself. Know there is always an answer to every problem. It is there waiting for you to discover it. The ultimate aim of every journey should be 'pleasure' and the highest form of learning is through Divine Joy. Remember, 'think lucky and you will be lucky!"*

The voice fades as my bus to Heathrow arrives. I board with a heavy heart trying to assimilate my whisperer's advice. This is not what I had imagined my journey to be, but I know I must accept the situation and make the best of it, trusting to the Universe that all will be well. I manage a brief sleep during the journey travelling south and try to put all worries to the back of my mind. One side of me tells me to quit now and be safe, while the other half tells me to be brave and face the perils of the journey, after all it's an escape like no other.

Arriving at Heathrow in the early hours of the morning there is an eerie, deathly silence and as I walk into the desolate dark tunnel to the terminal, my solo footsteps reverberate on the tarmac and echo around the brick walls. It is scary, like a horror movie, so I quicken my pace until I see the bright lights of the terminal in the distance. It is almost empty and completely devoid of any officials on duty. I sit down in the waiting area to pass the hours before check-in and around four in the morning people begin to arrive in drones and the quiet waiting area becomes a mass of seething, angry people demanding information about their flights and officious men in uniforms without answers, bluffing their way through explanations with glib assurances. Others sit quietly terrified of travelling on a flight that could be secretly packed with bombs and others pace on the spot making copious phone calls.

Around six o'clock in the morning, the noise and smell of nervous tension intensifies to such a pitch that there is hardly any standing room available and I have a pounding headache from the hullabaloo and feel sick with the stench of sweaty armpits and stale garlic hanging in the air. My view of the arrival and departure monitor is solidly blocked, so I cautiously squeeze my way through the masses to where I can view a screen and am relieved that I can begin the check-in process and forge my way forwards to where a harassed flight attendant is handing out plastic bags in which to place our money and passports. All other hand luggage has to be placed on the conveyor belt to be stored in the hold. I am appalled that I have to say goodbye to my handbag which contains my life for the next few weeks and I am fearful that I might never see it again. I panic at the thought that it might get stolen and all my credentials taken when I arrive in Miami. Again I remind myself that worrying doesn't help the moment and I fight inwardly to calm my fears.


I am so grateful when I finally sit in my window seat on the plane, but all is not well as everyone is shunted out again for our baggage to be taken off and thoroughly searched as another bomb threat has been issued. All the passengers are tired and irritable by this time and chunter as we exit while we wait another two hours before we board again. When we finally take-off I am sick with worry and tired beyond sleep as the loss of another two hours further compounds my fear of missing my connection in Miami. Flying to another zone backwards in time is a strange concept and having left England in the early hours of Tuesday morning, I am scheduled to arrive late Monday evening the previous night in Miami, where my flight to Cancun leaves at 10.30 in the evening, but with all the delays I am doubtful that I will make it and try to convince myself that somehow I will be helped and that I won't be left stranded in a strange country.

We arrive in Miami very late and I know I have already missed my connection but I derive some comfort from the announcement that all passengers who have missed their flights will be met by a representative who will organise another. Suddenly I realise no one knows where I am. I don't even know the name of the guide I am supposed to meet or where the meeting point is scheduled, as all the details are in my handbag, hopefully waiting in luggage reclaim. Now everything is out of synchronisation with the arranged plans and I am so worried. I pull myself together as I walk off the plane into the sweltering heat of the Miami night gasping for breath in the baking temperature. I am alarmed at what fear and desperation of the pressure of survival can do to people, as passengers fight each other for a place on the buses transporting passengers to the passport control centre.

Bags and suitcases are hurled to the ground as a herd of stampeding humans surge forwards knocking less agile folk to the floor. I am lucky to squeeze into a space next to the bus luggage rack, squashed against someone's sweaty back.

The passport control area is packed and it's like entering a beehive with drones and drones of bees waiting for an audience with the Queen bee. Suddenly I am overcome with panic and become one of the unruly strikers and run through queues of disgruntled passengers who launch insults at me and I can't blame them because I am blatantly and rudely forcing my way through the throng. I am shocked at my behaviour and very upset when I am sent to the back of the front queue because I haven't filled in a green form. I am outraged and frustrated but manage to control the tears and calmly force myself to concentrate and hurriedly fill in the form. Then once more I force my way to the front. My behaviour is so unlike me and I am ashamed to admit that I am so panicked by the thought of missing my guide that I am prepared to behave badly.

It's a relief when the stern-faced official behind the counter stamps my passport and suddenly I am freed into a hellhole of confusion. No one seems to be in charge of anything and droves of people are rushing around like crazy wilder beasts caught in a forest fire. The announcement that passengers would be met by an airline representative is a complete lie! I think all the officials are hiding from the mob in fear of being assaulted! I spy a sign to 'baggage reclaim' and turn to enter a corridor of unmoving jam-packed bodies all tightly mashed together. I manage to wedge into the throng, tightly holding onto my plastic bag containing money and my passport with one hand and in the other I carry my black poncho. Suddenly a wave of people surge backwards and I am caught up in a tsunami of bodies rolling out of the building. We are forced back through the main doors outside into the heat and I am relieved not to be crushed by the pressure and might of the wave of bodies pressing into me.

Suddenly, I am flung over a metal barrier onto the grass and land unhurt. In the turbulence I have lost my poncho but in my sweaty hand I still have my plastic bag. The night is heavy and humid and as I heave myself up off the ground, spying a soldier with a gun suspiciously glaring at me, I panic. I don't know why, but I hurriedly climb back over the barrier and run inside dodging crowds, lunging through tiny crevices in cracked spaces. The soldier thinks I am a terrorist and chases after me.

Survival has many faces and this is one of them- I never thought I would be driven to such extreme measures but I am compelled by fear. Run! Run! Legs move, heart pounds and I race up a flight of stairs with a bright blue carpet to where a tall man in a pilot's uniform is surveying the pandemonium. The soldier dashes after me and catches up just as I reach the official. I stand panting in front of him and burst into tears. I can't help it! Everything has been too much to handle. I am sure I didn't order such a catalogue of disasters from the universe? The two men unsympathetically witness my breakdown amidst the caterwauling of thousands of people shouting and screaming in the echoing terminal. The soldier realises I am just a lost passenger and leaves to return to his post, while the pilot can only offer me the use of a phone to try to contact my tour operators. The emergency number I have been given doesn't work. I try to phone my eldest daughter back home but I can't get through. I attempt to contact my other children but there is no response from any of them. Biting back more tears I thank the pilot and he assures me that in the morning things will be resolved and in the meantime I should make my way to reclaim my luggage.

With a heavy heart I walk back down the stairs and follow the signs to 'baggage reclaim'. New fears dog my mind. What if my things are stolen? What if all my documentation in my handbag is lost? I can't remember any names or phone numbers or places on my itinerary. None of this seems real.

Perhaps it is a nightmare and I will wake up safely in my own bed? The terrifying tsunami of bodies I have just encountered and the ensuing chase have driven me in a whirlwind of unimaginable terror and I am soaked in a blather of despair. Physically and emotionally I am drained and I just want to go home! I have had enough of escaping everything and I don't want to be in a sour adventure anymore!

In the baggage reclaim hall carousel after carousel are compacted with bags, suitcases and push chairs. Eventually right at the end of the hall I spy my flight details. There alone, except for a few other bags, riding around like forlorn exhibits, are my personal belongings. I dash to retrieve my rucksack and handbag like a mother racing to meet her lost children and clutching my things to my chest tears flow with heart rendering relief. There is a guardian angel watching over me after all and I flop to the floor in gratitude. I quickly search through my things to see if anything is missing and thankfully, everything is as I left it and from total despair, I am happy beyond belief. At least now I have all my papers and expedition details and I resolve to find a café because suddenly I am so hungry and thirsty.

With my papers and details intact, I am a bona fide person, complete with all I need to survive the next few weeks and I begin to be more confident about what the morning will bring. As I wander around the café areas and food shops which are all closed, I notice a small stall still open and buy a stale cheese sandwich and a can of lemonade. I am so hungry that I hurriedly eat it and feel a little sick afterwards. I am so tired, exhausted and weary. I need to sit down or I will collapse. The hall is full of sleeping bodies and Mothers with slumbering babes in their arms and there is hardly any room to walk between the dozing passengers. Luckily I see a vacant chair situated between two sleeping people, one with a tiny baby asleep at her breast. Gingerly, I step over a few bodies and plonk down gratefully into the seat but I am thrown backwards as the seat collapses and I inadvertently do an awkward backward flip waking up everyone around me. I now realise why the seat is vacant as it is broken. Hurriedly I grab my bag and make a swift departure into a large, almost empty hall. I would laugh at myself and my Charlie Chaplain mishap if I wasn't so shattered!

The waiting lounge is massive and carpeted in a purple, blue and red design which makes my head spin. I lie down in a corner cuddling my rucksack to my chest but I feel vulnerable and a little afraid.

What if I fall asleep and someone comes to rob me of all my money and belongings? I am so uncomfortable and now beyond sleep. In the quiet stillness I hear the air conditioning droning around the room and from the heat of the day I am cold. I have lost my poncho in the fracas and begin to shiver, so I fight through my back pack to find a warm jumper and begin to feel warmer, but just when my eyes begin to close, the purple thoroughfare transforms into a macabre highway of strange robotic cleaning machines manipulated by Halloween, ghoul-like creatures and I move farther down the side of the hall near, what I suppose to be a broom cupboard and curl up with my head on my knees to finally get some rest, but two men appear heading towards the cupboard. One is a policeman and the other a worker. I watch from my bent position as the two men enter the cupboard. The policeman is holding a rolled-up magazine. The rendezvous is obviously a routine habit and I shift a little closer to hear what they are doing. Somehow I am not surprised to hear rustling of paper and male grunts and guffaws of a sexual nature. Well that is it for me! I can't stand the night's interruptions any longer and sleep is out of the question. I wish desperately to be in my own comfy bed, even if the aliens subject me to unwarranted tests, it's somehow better than being stranded in a strange country in the dead of night and no one knowing where I am!

Forlornly I wander back into the main terminal. Outside it's getting light. A booth is open selling hot chocolate. A rush of memories flood my mind of whirling dancers and happy times rehearsing the opening of a massive production. The words- 'Chocolate and Custard' throb in my mind and my feet want to obey the rhythm as I make my way towards the smell of hot chocolate. I muse to myself that after all the mishaps I still want to dance... Chocolate and custard guide my feet and I guess that I am lucky- I am alive having survived horrendous events and can look forward hopefully to a more successful day ahead. The hot chocolate is wonderful, soothing and comforting and I know I am lucky. I must count my blessings, for yes I am indeed Lucky.

※◆※

# ALL PHASES ARE TEMPORARY-EVEN FOR MYSTICAL WOLVES!

*"All phases are temporary," states Grandfather wisely," a delay or detour in your journey will always enrich your experience, no matter how inconvenient the diversion- remember 'what is'- is meant to be, so be grateful for the happenstance and be joyful for the lesson learnt."*

I listen to Grandfather's wise words as I wait in line for the first flight to Cancun. The airline has been supportive and reassuring this morning, understanding my plight and making contact with my tour operator to make sure my guide knows when I will arrive in Mexico. As I wait, my mind wanders back home to all the strange alien happenings, which now seem so far away and like a bad nightmare. I ponder the chance meeting of a lady in a jeweller's shop in York, who used to attend my dance classes, saying she had just read one of my books and was fascinated by my experiences and wanted me to meet her husband who had, as a young child endured the most harrowing encounters with wolves and strange beings, living an horrendous childhood plagued by other-worldly beasts which had affected him throughout his life. Strangely, he had lived in a farmhouse, just a short way from my cottage, which in those days was part of a block of stables for the Mansion House.

Her words struck a terrifying chord, especially when she talked about secret tunnels leading from the Mansion House underground to the stables. Rory's warning…"they're underground, they're fucking underground' sprang to mind and I was curious to learn more and immediately agreed to meet her husband to talk about his nightmare encounters. She said it might help him to overcome his fears and depression by talking to someone who would understand and believe him. We set a date for our meeting and when Sadie and Walter arrived nervously one evening, I sat and listened to his story.

Walter was born in a farmhouse on the large estate owned by the Lord of the Manor and my cottage, at the time, was a series of stables for the Lord's horses. The Manor House itself, was palatial and impressive set in forest woodland.

"As a tiny baby, I would often be put outside the farmhouse in my pram to sleep, as was the custom in those days, and oftentimes large animal faces would peer into the pram and glare at me. I could smell their damp fur reeking of wet earth. Their massive faces with pointed ears and furry nostrils would breathe over me and they would stare into the pram with their glassy piercing eyes.

Sometimes they would snarl baring their sharp fanged teeth, which would terrify me and I would scream and holla until my mother came to rescue me." Walter swallowed his anguish as I asked another question.

"I suppose you were too young to be able to explain what was happening?"

"Yes, they all just thought I was a difficult child. My father who was a physically strong, no nonsense farmer, thought I was weak and sickly. My elder brother thought I was a wimp and as I grew older they all lost patience with me and became angry when I tried to tell them about the wolves!"

"Did you often see the wolves?" I enquired.

"Yes, quite often, they seemed to be always there somehow in the background and sometimes up close."

"Did the wolves ever try to harm you?" I asked

"No! But they were always menacing, always on the verge of attacking, but never did, but the fact that they were close to me and I could smell their hot breath and feel their jaws on my chest was a nightmare which I couldn't escape, especially when I was in bed when they were circling around me and lying in wait on the landing!"

I asked him why he thought the wolves came to seek him out, but he had no idea. Later after our meeting, researching the Mansion House, I discovered that the land was part of a massive estate in North Yorkshire where all the Lords were members of a secret society together with Church ministers and other high ranking officials. Locals believe that the dignitaries dealt in the occult and black magic, conjuring up packs of vicious wolves to subdue and control villagers. One of the old ladies living in a nearby village remembered her great, great Grandmother passing down stories of witches and wolves terrorizing farmers in the area. It was harrowing how Walter described the wolves in great detail and I recalled a time when I had just moved into the cottage, discovering claw-like scratches on the inside of a bedroom door as though a creature had been scrabbling at the wood to get out. I never discovered the cause of the damage.

Through my research I learnt that the original Mansion House was built in 1725 and was meant to prevent people crossing the Lord's land in order to avoid a tollgate fee to enter the city of York.

Later in the nineteenth century the house and land passed to another Lord and Queen Mary and the Prince of Wales stayed at the Manor House during a short visit to the city. In 1915 the stables where I live, became a horse hospital to nurse injured horses from the First World War, but later in 1918 the house and grounds were bought by York Corporation to be converted into a Tuberculosis Hospital and in 1923 a children's ward was added. Walter remembered, as a young child, playing in the grounds and finding a dried up well from which he and other children heard strange sounds stating: "sometimes sickening cries for help and petrifying screams would echoed up through the shaft. It wasn't just me who heard it but the other children playing also heard it. The noises from the well seemed to be coming from underground in the tunnels and we would run into the forest in fright to hide."

"Did you tell anyone about this?" I queried.

"No, never, it was a secret amongst us kids and besides the grown-ups would never believe it. To them it was kid's fantasy. My Dad was a farmer, not a dreamer and never discussed anything that was in his opinion make-believe."

"Where do you think the screams were coming from and who was making them? I asked.

"I don't know but there were hushed rumours that the mental patients were imprisoned underground and some of them were tortured and taken through the tunnels to the incinerator to be burnt. You see there was a big incinerator in the grounds and oftentimes the smell of burning flesh would waft across the forest. But it was a well-known fact that there was an underground tunnel leading from the cellars of the Mansion House to the well and beyond to a place where dead bodies from the hospital were incinerated. We often smelt the fires and the awful stench of burning flesh but we never spoke about it. Sometimes the screams seemed to come directly from the incinerator block," added Walter reflectively.

"Do you know if the tunnels from the house were built later when it became a hospital or were they created earlier?"

"Oh I believe the tunnels went all the way from the Mansion House past the stables, out by the factory and beyond to the village Church, or even further and they were created before the House was built. Some believe that black magic rituals went on and human sacrifices made to pagan gods and it was all part of the Knights Templar secret sect. It is said that the Knight of the Manor used to hunt with a demonic pack of wolves."

It was interesting that Walter thought the tunnels went under the stables where the cottages are now situated, especially with Rory's story about monsters being underground. Part of my research was to request a visit to the Mansion House, which had become a hotel and the management were very obliging, being interested in my investigation, as there were many accounts from reliable staff about strange happenings especially in the cellar. I was given an honest tour of the building and was able to question some of the staff who were very forth-coming about their strange and frightening experiences. On my visit, the Hotel manager cordially greeted me showing great enthusiasm for my research and was only too pleased to take me behind the public section to a private room behind the main entrance which had been the Lord's sitting room. The impressive, open, medieval wooden fire place dominated the living space, inlaid with carvings, statues and various symbols, which I immediately recognised as black magic emblems. For those with arcane knowledge all the signs and symbols of esoteric practice were prominent. On either side of the mantelpiece were carved wooden pine cones which are a symbol of enlightenment, resurrection, eternal life, regeneration and the practice of obscure magic. Those with occult knowledge know that pine cones represent the pineal gland, which is an organic third eye situated at the back of the head and often shown as an eye in the centre of the forehead. When I saw the pine cones I thought of the three people in my life who have actually seen my third eye in my forehead and I was reminded of my unhappy first marriage when my husband became very aggressive in bed, demanding his conjugal rights and lifted his arm to hit me when he stopped with his hand in mid- air, dumbfounded by the appearance of a strange eye suddenly glaring at him from the centre of my forehead. He was petrified and jumped out of bed, claiming I was a witch, declaring never to sleep with me again! He said that the appearance of the eye in the middle of my forehead was proof I was non-human, stating that the sight of it was horrible, unnatural and disgusting. Strangely, we were living at the time not too far from the Mansion House.

I also recall my Mother almost tormenting me with the accusation that I slept with my eyes open.

When I was a small child she would come to check on me before she went to bed. As I lay on my side she could see one eye open, declaring that it would stare at her. One morning at breakfast she taunted me with the fact that I slept with my eyes open, mockingly saying, "you sleep with your eyes open, you do! You sleep with your eyes open!" Her staunch Catholic beliefs couldn't handle my odd idiosyncrasies and she was ready to denounce me as a devil child! It was years later that I realised she had seen my third eye and on her deathbed she asked me if I could still see forwards. I told her that I could and asked her why. She replied:" because I could!" I was totally shocked by her answer and realised that she punished me because she wanted to deny her own psychic abilities. Also when I was house watching with an artist friend I had fallen asleep on the sitting room floor and he said, "when you were asleep I saw a strange blue light appear above your head and when I went to investigate. I saw an open eye staring up at me. It was scary!" As an artist he was able to draw a picture of what he witnessed and was able to describe the eye in great detail.

As I stared at the medieval fireplace I noted all the other signs and symbols indicating esoteric knowledge. There was a Baphomet goat's head carved on the right hand side of the mantelpiece, which is a symbol of the devil. Furthermore, carved on the same side was a man with a leafed garland on his head representing the Green Man, which is a springtime symbol of fertility and re-birth. Gargoyles with open mouths and lolling tongues were embossed into the woodwork on the left and there was an impressive sculpture of a large wolf near the grate. The manager pointed out that they thought it was an image of the Lord's pet dog, but to me it closely resembled a vicious, watchful wolf. Somehow the statue appeared to be another warning that wolves were a part of occult practice and that Walter, who was most sensitive, had inadvertently entered into the past where the wolves freely roamed terrorizing innocent folk.

For those who are gifted, or plagued with the sixth sense of 'inner sight', it is possible to enter a star gate into the past or future and I believe that Walter was a victim of his own gift which enabled him to be a part of the mysteries of the past. After inspecting the Lord's sitting room, I was shown into another room of that era which was equally interesting but had been turned into a conference room and did not have the same ambiance. I was then guided upstairs to one of the rooms which had been part of the hospital but had been converted into a comfortable hotel room. My psychic mind pushed past the present to the past where I saw two single beds in an almost bare room. I felt the terror and torment of two men who looked skeletal and emaciated. They were not tuberculosis patients but inmates with mental problems. Suddenly I realised I had seen the same expression on Rory's face with the gaunt, haunted eyes glazed over, hiding a secret terror within. The words of a psychic friend came to mind as he explained that it was believed in ancient times that being in contact or close proximity with wolves could cause mental illness, a nervous breakdown or even death. It is also believed that wolves protect the underworld and are brave warriors. For a few moments I was far away in the haunting, imprisoned loneliness of the two men but the manager brought me back to the present as he showed me another room in which I could psychically see had been a women's ward, also for mentally disturbed patients. I did not linger in the past and hastily followed the manager downstairs to the kitchen where I was allowed to talk to two of the waitresses.

"Go on, go on Freda; tell her what happened to you?" urged a young woman dressed in a black uniform. A shy middle-aged woman with a tee- towel draped over her shoulder stopped stacking dishes and looked at me with open eyes.

"Well, it were like this ya see, I 'ad keys ta cellar an' I were asked to go down an' get two bottles of house red. Well it weren't nowt unusual as I'd done it before, so I knew where bottles wa' an' when I got down there lights weren't working. I tried switch several times but nowt 'appened. When I stepped further inside cellar, the bloody door shuts behind me and I'm in dark. Well, I rushed ta door but bloody key gets stuck. I'm down there shouting like hell for someone ta get me out an' manager comes an' forces door open. Well those few minutes seemed like forever an' I'm telling ya there's somat down there. It's evil! I aint going down there again, ever, not bloomin likely!"

"Yeh, Freda's not the only one who won't go down there either," added the young woman, "Stephen, our young chef went down there once and had bottles thrown at him. They come at him from nowhere and he legged it pretty quick and he won't go down there alone again."

The two women said that there were loads of strange stories from locals about the cellar because it lead to underground tunnels and out to the place where they burnt bodies. The stories verified Walter's accounts of the tunnels and the incinerator building. They also told me about the ancient ice house where bones and skeleton remains had been found. All in all the evidence was gruesome and made me feel very uncomfortable about my own lovely cottage.


Walter also talked about growing up in the forest hearing strange noises coming from underground near the stables and believed that a network of tunnels went into the factory behind my garden.

"What kind of noises?" I asked.

"Well, it's difficult to describe. I suppose you might say loud bangs and explosive sounds sometimes were heard and strangulated screams and howling seemed to come up from underground."

"When did it all stop?" I enquired.

"Well, it was worse when I was very young and still carried on until I went to secondary school and then the wolves came only at certain times in my bedroom. I remember one time when the moon was so bright outside my window, it was like daylight and they came with their piecing silver eyes and filled the room with the smell of rotting cabbage and wet wool. I was terrified. I couldn't get to sleep because they were there all night prowling, but in the early hours of the morning they disappeared. I left home as soon as I could to go to work in town and my Dad never quite came to terms with my behaviour and my beliefs. My brother stayed at home to work on the farm until Dad died and Mum was taken to a nursing home where she passed away peacefully. My brother still finds it hard to talk to me because of my tales about the wolves."

"And it's affected you all your life hasn't it darling?" his wife interjected.

Walter nodded and I thanked him for his honesty and bravery for talking about his past. I don't know if anyone ever fully recovers from such horrific episodes, but I hope Walter finds some peace in his life and is able to move forwards with confidence, knowing that he's not the only one to face such shocking experiences.

From my research at the Manor House I decided to dig deeper to see what I could find and came across an old map of the vast acreage of land granted to a Knight's Templar for his bravery in the Holy Land. There was evidence to suggest that the landed gentry, Church officials, and others formed a secret sect to protect and guard the estate. From an ancient Church document, which vaguely refers to underground tunnels connecting various parishes, I realized that the whole of the area where I lived was a warren of underground, secret passageways. I couldn't find much more about the history but a certain house on the estate had always drawn my attention. It was a mini Manor House, not quite as palatial as the one near my cottage but grand, nonetheless and had a similar aura surrounding it to the Manor House. Like a magnet, I was continually pulled towards its mysterious veneer and was surprised to learn that the Soothsayer's grave- Mother Shipton, lies not far from the house. Sometimes in my dreams the house would call to me, or an energy locked within the walls would cry out and I would wake trembling. I never understood the connection and gradually the lure towards it faded, until one day I saw it was for sale. I jumped at the opportunity to take a look inside the house under the guise as a potential buyer.

Drawing up to the house I was excited and fearful at the same time, as psychically I sensed something was wrong. On either side of the impressive black iron gates perched on top of a large wall surrounding the house, were two large statues of pine cones immediately signalling to those with knowledge, that the premises had occult connections. I parked outside the gates but didn't enter through them, instead I walked around to the side of the house where two guard dogs growled a warning not to step further onto the property. I stood motionless, afraid to move until a man appeared and called off the dogs. He was dressed in army gear, like a fierce Sergeant Major.

His muscle-defined body and demeanour projected that of a trained-killer. He smiled, changing his aggressive manner when he knew I had made an appointment to view the house and called the owner. She was petite with dyed jet-black, long hair, dressed in youthful, tight, expensive clothes.

She seemed young but on closer inspection she was much older, disguised with heavy make-up. Her left eye had a squint, which can sometimes indicate that the person has undergone ritual indoctrination or black magic abuse and has attained a high level of esoteric knowledge. I immediately thought I knew her and felt she recognised me but was hiding it. Her smile was insincere and she almost smirked as she looked me up and down. As I stood on the forecourt, I looked across to a burnt black-ash copse where every tree, bush and plant was charred and gutted.

The excuse was that the land had been 'burnt' for farming purposes, but in my psychic mind I had a very different, terrifying scene playing where young naked girls were being chased through the fire by lascivious old men in a sexual black magic ritual. I had to look away from the burnt devastation to view a small wooded coppice decked like a fairy grove with a tree stump carved into a sacrificial table. My psionic ability projected an image of the mythical figure of the Green Man having sex with young virgins on the stump in a Spring Equinox ceremony, while little twinkling bells tinkled in the trees and brightly coloured ribbons fluttered in the breeze. My mind was bombarded with occult practice images as though I was remembering events.

I was then taken through a garage which was a side entrance to the house where there were three long, white chest freezers lining one wall set against bare red bricks The strange thing was that all the windows inside the garage were wired and barred on the inside rather than the outside. It was as though the owners wanted to prevent something or someone from escaping. I shuddered to see in my psionic mind dead bodies of young girls in the freezers and chained youngsters locked up in the garage. My imagination was reeling with horrors and I felt sick. Did she, the owner, know what I was seeing? She knew I was her equal but we were on different sides – she the dark side and me the white light. She grinned as she showed me into the gloomy kitchen. Did she know my prying was all a charade? The kitchen would have been well equipped in its time with its fitted dark oak cupboards and black range. The only psychic pictures that came through in the kitchen were those of high class chefs and uniformed servants busy with trays of delicately prepared food. I definitely had a notion that the kitchen staff had catered for royalty and high ranking government officials. The house conveyed clues of a high class brothel catering for the aristocracy and wealthy. We walked into the hallway painted in deep blue with silver stars scattered everywhere. Dark oak wooden panels lined the walls and stairs like a deep, dark coffin. At the bottom of the stairs guarding the entrance to the bedrooms were two huge statues of black Basenji dogs like the black Anubis god who, in Egyptian times presided over the mummifying process and accompanied the dead to the afterlife. The sight of them made me shiver as through my psychic eyes, they sprang into life baring their ferocious teeth, ready at the owner's command to tear anyone to shreds if necessary. The position of the large statues was intimidating and menacing. As I walked up the stairs, I could almost hear the sound of their panting breath threatening a vicious attack if anyone tried to escape.

The master bedroom was decorated with large pink floral wallpaper with a king size double bed and pretty floral pottery tap heads in the en suite bathroom. I didn't get any psychic feedback from the room but when we crossed over to the second bedroom I was immediately shocked by the sight of a half- naked woman in a pale pink camisole riding astride a large naked man with the iron bed-head rhythmically clanging against the wall. I had to quickly look away and clear the psionic vision as it was too disturbing. It was a very clear picture and the young woman had dyed red hair in the style of a 1920's bob. There was a child's bedroom which was decorated in dark blue with silver stars and there were paintings of a little boy sitting under the moon. I had the notion that the child was being made aware of the moon goddess Isis and schooled in esoteric knowledge. There was another bedroom which was also probably used for sexual encounters but I didn't want to linger there. Back downstairs I was taken into the sitting room and the owner didn't accompany me, leaving me to look around at my leisure. Immediately I was nauseated by a disgusting smell emanating from under the carpet near the French windows and the words came into my head... "there's a decaying body underneath the floorboards!" The smell was like rotting flesh and boiled cabbages. I shivered. I was transported back in time to a drunken party bubbling with popping champagne corks where women and men were dressed in 1920's evening wear and the women were smoking cigarettes in long jewelled holders and the men were smoking bitter cigars. I saw the young red haired woman drunkenly flirting. The scene was so real that I had to shake myself out of it and return to the present where I noted dark stains on the carpet and wet patches underfoot which squelched as I walked over them, near to where the disgusting smell was emanating. I quickly walked into the dining room to avoid the stench where there were paintings displayed on easels of the same little boy from the child's bedroom depicting more moon scenes. I didn't dally in there and hurriedly passed through into a small study and then back into the hallway where the owner was waiting. She asked if I would like to view the garden and I was shown a small pathway leading to a large open lawn. I was shocked to hear the imposing rush of traffic beyond the tree boundary heavily disturbing and penetrating the peace of the house. In my head the windows seemed to be rattling and whispering and murmuring and calling, beckoning me back inside where the body of the woman was slowly rotting. The voices were oppressive and getting louder and louder until I couldn't stand it and rushed back to the entrance where the owner and the man were waiting with the dogs. A large army vehicle was parked outside on the forecourt and they explained they were taking a trip around

Europe in the converted van. It appeared they were escaping, but maybe that interpretation was too dramatic. I swiftly made my excuses to leave, feeling shocked and certain that the house had connections with the Manor House and was involved in clandestine occult practices. It's something I will never forget and a strange remembrance of something sinister hovers mysteriously in the back of my mind but I am unable to reach its meaning.

Now I am on my way to Cancun, excited and relieved to be finally heading out to begin my new adventure. I smile to myself as I look out of the plane window at the fluffy white clouds forming shapes so dense that you can imagine stepping onto them and floating away on a frothy magic carpet. Gone is the tension and apprehension of the stressful flight, for I know, as Grandfather said, *'all states are temporary and everything is in flux'.*

Last night I desperately wanted to go home but today is another moment, another state of being, another now and I am happy to be travelling towards new challenges and experiences, knowing I am lucky to be in another time zone and I am reminded by my whisperers: *'if you think lucky, you will be lucky!'*

# THROUGH THE LOOKING GLASS

Arriving at Cancun, I am relieved to see my driver waiting to take me to meet my guide at the designated guest house where all members in our small expedition will meet for the first time. As we drive through scrub jungle and out into the suburbs, I am alarmed to witness terrible devastation and wreckage caused by tornadoes and hurricanes. My driver explains that the country is continually under threat from cyclones and typhoons and the damage is never quite restored and returned back to its original state, so many people lose their houses and jobs and there is 'mucho, mucho pobreza'.

The evidence of great poverty is apparent as we coast through decimated cities with much of the populace living in make-shift huts and under tarpaulin sheets. As we trundle through muddy tracks, which pass as major roads, I am surprised to see the occasional dead monkey splayed out on the track instead of a dead bird, or hedgehog like back home. The ride isn't too long but I am so tired after not sleeping for thirty hours and the stress of the journey begins to take its toll, so when I arrive at the small guest house everything spins and blurs and my guide, Tommy, quickly ushers me to a room at the back of the building where I collapse on a bed and fall into a deep sleep.

In the morning, much refreshed after my long sleep, I breakfast in the no frills guest house and meet my fellow travellers for the first time in the foyer, which is decorated dazzlingly in bright red, electric blue, verdant green and sunshine yellow scenes of the beach, with luscious plants dangling from shelves and various nooks and crannies. Black wrought-iron staircase railings, similar to my own in the cottage, traverse the three colourful floors. Walking into the intense vibrancy, I understand why Mexico is called 'the land of colour' and I make a mental note to one day have the courage to decorate my house in the same colours. As we tentatively sit down eyeing each other with a welcome smile, Tommy asks us to introduce ourselves and one by one we oblige. A young German boy called Hunter, introduces himself and seems very pleasant, as does a young Italian girl named Caria. A middle-aged Australian couple, who claim they are not a couple but just good friends, introduce themselves as Myrtle and Bill, while arguing down the hallway, a recently married older couple, complaining about everything before they introduce themselves as Vera and Bob, unsettle the peace of the group. Vera is about sixty years old and is a retired art teacher and is wearing the most inappropriate clothes for the journey with a low-cut sun dress, long earrings and is decked in baubles, bangles and beads. Bob, a retired infant teacher, is quietly dressed in dull grey jeans and sweater. The group mentally name them the 'complainers' before we even get to know them. I fear they have signed up for the wrong kind of adventure, carping while we all sit patiently listening to them grousing about the accommodation before Tommy has time to begin the day's itinerary.

In total, we are seven quite different people about to embark on the journey of a lifetime, with our guide, travelling across the Yucatan Province to explore one of the greatest temple locations in Central America and as we are lead to the bus station carrying our own meagre luggage, the 'complainers' trundle their suitcases on wheels and are weighed down with hand baggage and shoulder bags as though they are holidaying for a month in Malibu. We are headed to Chichen Itza in the north of the Yucatan Peninsula where the ancient Mayan temples and pyramids echo the grandeur of a past, mystical era and where the most famous of all pyramids-El Castillo waits to be explored. At sunset of the Spring and Autumn Equinoxes, a rare magical phenomenon of a vision of a serpent rising from the bottom of the pyramid to the top, spiralling up the ladder of life, can be witnessed. I am excited to see all that I have read about the Mayan civilisation and to stand in the famous ball court where Olympic grandiose games were held and the winners showered with gifts and the losers slaughtered with their heads cut off and used as footballs.

On arrival in the lowland rainforest, the thick, lush jungle scrubland surrounds us in a cathedral archway of dense overgrowth. The jungle is forever reclaiming the land, burying carved stones and decaying fallen masonry from the temples under dank wilderness and mummifying archaic statues with thick plant tendrils. Pushing our way through the scrub we suddenly step into a clearing where antediluvian stone carvings of dragon heads lie forlorn, crumbling to dust in the dark earth. Abruptly the rain thrashes the surrounding trees and a young boy appears from the bushes with a handful of plastic capes to sell to the tourists. I buy a bright yellow one, big enough to hide inside. Our Temple guide appears and leads the way across the amazing ball court, where skulls leer at us from the great wall of death, to El Castillo the famous pyramid where the vision of the snake god appears slithering from the bottom to the top and where the temple priests made ritual sacrifices to the gods. Our guide is careful to point out that film producers and mass media pundits have wrongly depicted vestal virgins sacrificed by priests at the top of the pyramid with their blood flowing down the high steps to the congregation below. He states," it is more likely that human sacrifice was made at the cenote where we will visit next. Please follow me."

The rain is lighter as we follow the guide through the shadowy jungle to the cenote, which is a massive well in the centre of the rain forest. Our party is humbly quiet, even the complainers are silent as we are lead through an opening where a vast hole in the ground appears like a giant vat of stagnant, mouldy-green slime. It is not what I thought the cenote would look like. I imagined it would be magical and pretty but the gaping rotting vegetation on the top of the enormous well is unpleasant. We stand at the edge looking down into the dank green skin on the top of the water and listen to the guide relating it's gruesome history:

"you must imagine this cenote, this well was once a beautiful, holy place for the community set in the middle of the jungle and on specific holy days it was mostly thirteen year old virgin boys who were brought here to be sacrificed."

Members of our party look in disbelief at this revelation and stare deeper into the cenote imagining the bodies of young boys being thrown below and I envisage a forsaken cemetery of innocent boy's bones, skulls and skeletons heaped in piles for the fishes to dismember. The guide notes our surprised reaction and continues:

"I know it is hard to imagine such a tradition, but you see for the people it was their religion and a child would be chosen at birth to be honoured with a sacrificial death at his coming of age.

Throughout the thirteen years of his life the child would be granted all kinds of privileges and benefits for his family and on the dawning of the sacrificial day the boy would be drugged so that he would not feel anything. He would in fact be in a state of euphoria and happy to give his life to ensure a good harvest for his people. The community would gather around this cenote, which was considered to be a Holy place, containing a portal to another world. The boy would be revered, blessed and placed on a stone altar where his throat would be cut and the blood offered to Chac Mool, then his body thrown into the cenote. For the boy, the sacrificial procedure would be painless and he would not feel a thing. He would only know glory for giving his life to Chac Mool and he and his family would be highly honoured throughout the district."

Suddenly the sky cracks and explodes with a thunderous bolt from the heavens just as the guide says, 'god of rain' and we all look up in surprise as the thunder rolls across the forest and pink streaks flash across the cenote with a cerise glow highlighting the forest in an eerie radiance. We all run for cover in the nearby cenote gift shop and the guide laughs stating:

"Chac Mool has spoken!"

I stare at the cenote from the shop window sensing the strange power of the place imbued with religious potency, authorised with a communal licence to murder young boys. I can't imagine how many young boys' remains lie at the bottom of the pit and I shiver, perhaps because I am rain-soaked or maybe because psychically I am tuning into the horrific sight of the sacrifice, which for the people would not be sickening. It would be a religious, celebratory occasion and the family whose child would be taken ,would be brain-washed into believing it was a great honour to have your child murdered in front of everyone.

I watch the members of our party seemingly emotionally unaffected by the guide's description, buying trinkets and cards and especially the complainers are displaying a voracious appetite for buying gruesome memorabilia. I venture outside under the trees to soak up the powerful vibrational energy of the enclosure and I am reminded of a strange happening that occurred before I left for my trip. It was a peculiar experience immersed with a similar kind of power and electromagnetic frequency to the cenote. I was at home asleep in the dead of night, when I suddenly woke. It was eerily quiet and as I stared into the bleak blackness, I was transported beyond my body to an unknown place, where I saw a legion of beings advancing towards me like a Roman army. The commander was fearsome. His cranium was translucent and watery clear, shimmering like a mirage under a hot desert sun. His black eyes were sunken deep, like orbs in a glass skull and he didn't have a body, only his skeleton head floated in the dark. I knew instantly he was a potent, formidable leader. He was an alien from another planet and his species was far, far superior in intelligence to humans. I was humbled in his presence feeling like a tiny ant under a king's foot and as I gazed up into his face, I knew with all my heart and soul, that I was a lesser being. Disdainfully he communicated telepathically to me that humans had been given the gift of earth to be caretakers and that the planet really belonged to higher beings who could no longer tolerate humanity's greed, violence, murder and theft. Humans ravaging their beautiful planet should be taught a lesson and soon the higher beings would return to salvage the earth and restore peace and harmony. He continued his warning saying: "Human interaction with the magic of Gaia was part of the initial caretaker contract with the higher beings, but humans have forgotten the contract and their magical potential to mingle with the natural power of mother earth. The use of nuclear weapons will have a disastrous effect on parallel universes and a day will come when the earth will tremble and darkness descend if humans do not find a way to change."

I knew that the purpose of our brief meeting was to pass on the message. Then there was silence as I pondered the meeting and as he passed through me I was left feeling strong and confident as though every cell in my body had been strengthened and healed. When I returned to my body, overhead in the still night, a huge plane or spacecraft juddered over my house shaking my bedroom like an earthquake. My stomach flipped as the bed shook and I knew it was them reinforcing their warning. Then quickly without a sound they passed. Now the wilderness is all around me and the severity of their threat lies heavy in my heart: "please let me be allowed to pass on this message, even if it be to a few!" I ask the gods in the hope that the Universe will pave the way.

As the group gathers and we walk towards the bus, the rain abates but Chac Mool, the rain god, continues his work as the trees drip their rain-soaked branches on our heads and we climb aboard the bus wet and damp from the excursion. The complainers complain about the weather and not having enough time to explore the site but as our guide points out, we have to keep to our schedule and arrive in Merida at a given time. As the old bus trundles along and the metal bar at the back of the seat cuts uncomfortably into my back, my mind returns to the idea of the cenote being a star-gate portal into another universe and I recall a piece of information sent to me by a trustworthy person, explaining how he had seen a piece of equipment in the lab where he worked, which looked like a large looking glass and was a portal to other universes. It had the power and capacity to transport anyone or anything into the past or present and could perform unbelievable tasks like that of a time machine. He also said that the 'looking glass' mechanism was a more modern, updated piece of apparatus than the time machine transporter and that by standing directly in front of the mirror it was possible to pass through the glass into another world or time sphere. I wonder if the author of

'Alice in Wonderland' Lewis Carroll, had previous knowledge of this portal entrance when he wrote 'Through the Looking Glass' in 1871? My friend also said that 'time transferral devices would be commonplace by the year 2070 with the help of superior aliens who were involved in manipulating timelines; also in 2022 scientists would discover portals in space that lead to other universes. He further explained that most people could not comprehend or see the truth of what was really happening because of the moon matrix hiding reality in an invisible veil and mass mind control held people in an illusion, to which they were solidly attached, so that the idea of time travel was only fantasy in their minds and would forever remain a dream. Having had the strangest 'time-travel' experience which was imposed upon me, I believe whole-heartedly in the possibility(further information on this experience can be found in Beyond Belief).

Now the sky is darkening as we are nearing the bus station in Merida where a new adventure awaits far from the rain forest and Chac Mool and the curious world of time travel. When we arrive the rain-drenched city is overflowing with gurgling, bubbling drains spilling into the grimy roads and foaming into grey rivulets forging down all the main roads. Lights twinkle a merry welcome reflected on the glistening street slabs and my sandaled feet are soaking, dripping blue dye from the suede.

Splashing through the waterlogged thoroughfare, I struggle to keep up with the main party as a knee injury twinges, but I fight through the pain and arrive at the hotel, which on the outside appears to be an ordinary brick house but stepping inside the small, un-hotel-like door, we enter a museum of exotic artefacts, antique furniture and unusual gigantic paintings. The place reeks of neglect, although it is obvious that at some point it must have been an amazing hotel and I sense the magic of a feminine creator, long gone. The building is deceptively massive built around an open courtyard which I have never experienced, so that the rain pours directly into the centre of the hotel where luscious palm trees and exotic plants invade the walkways. The owner, George, surprisingly, is English from Newcastle and hails a cheery welcome to us all as we wait in line to be allotted our rooms. Patiently waiting, puddles of rain water drip on the wooden brown floor from our clothes and bags as we falsely appear chirpy, except for the complainers who have lugged their bags and suitcases through the sodden streets and stand disdainfully with grey faces, dripping wet in their seaside holiday attire.

Caria and I are to share and we follow an elderly Mexican woman through the open courtyard along a series of open walkways which were once beautifully decorated with hand-crafted pots and mural paintings which have aged and are now discarded artefacts lit with tiny candles amongst colourful hammocks strung under porch ways. The smell of rotting plaster, damp cement and fresh paint is overpowering as though the owner has made an attempt to clean up the place minutes before our arrival. Eventually the woman shows us to our room, which is situated through an archway at the bottom of a long corridor. On first sight the room isn't too bad with two single beds but as I place my rucksack on the floor and take a quick glance under the bed I am shocked. Thick dust, building debris, piles of cement and garbage lie under my bed as though the place hasn't been cleaned for years! One of my phobias is 'filth' and the thought of the rubbish under my bed makes me feel ill and want to retch. I have a terror of insects and spiders and the idea of going to sleep on top of a pile of refuse horrifies me. I try to remind myself that part of the reason for my journey is to attempt to overcome my fears and this situation will surely be a test of my ability to conquer some of my phobias. The bed cover is not clean but the sheets underneath are, so perhaps things are not too bad but I can't help my physical reaction of feeling unclean and itchy all over my body as a result of the filth. The bathroom has water at least, but the smell of sewage and rotting cabbage coming up through an open grate under the sink is disgusting. I fear the air alone in the bathroom is a vat of stewing diseases waiting to seep into my veins. Perhaps I am being over dramatic but I am cold, wet, tired and exhausted from the day's travel and now I can't relax in this awful room. Caria doesn't seem to be affected by any of the mess and I try to be like her and calm my nightmare panic, while I hastily change out of my wet clothes to face the evening with the group, but at the back of my mind is the awful thought of spending the night in the dreaded room.


In dry clothes at last I walk out of the room to take a breath of air, which now in the heat of the night and after the heavy rain, is humid and claustrophobic. I leave Caria to get changed telling her I will wait outside so that we can go to dinner together but as I turn to close the door I am appalled to find that I can see straight through the wall into our bedroom. The whole of the wall is made of glass! I rush back inside the room and tell Caria not to undress with the light on and ask her to step outside to show her the glass wall. She is stunned to see, how with the light on, we can view the whole room. I tell her to go back in and turn the light off to check if it makes a difference and with the light off the bricks outside return to their normal density and we can't see inside. The room has obviously been designed for night voyeurs and I am outraged that we might be secretly watched. Here in the middle of Merida, Mexico is a looking glass wall where literally we can step inside and act out fantasies for all to view! I wonder how many other rooms have the same entertainment application and question what kind of a hotel would provide the 'looking glass' facility?


Now after an evening of light relief dancing and watching a festival light up the city streets with music and laughter, I want to go home. I want to cry. I am afraid to get undressed because of the filth and I sit up in bed with the sheet over my head because I am terrified of night crawling insects. I am a pitiful hotchpotch of raging fears and I know I have to get a grip on myself otherwise I will not sleep a wink. The light is off so I know Caria and I can't be seen but as I sit up in bed and hear noises outside the room I am amazed that the 'looking glass' effect works the other way- with our light off and a dim light outside I can see straight through the wall into the corridor where our guide has secretly brought a girl to seduce her. Little does he know that I can see everything! I am not interested in watching their passionate display and endure their intrusive intimacy until they have completed the deed. I ponder the nature of glass and how incredibly ingenious the wall has been made to resemble a real brick wall. Back home in York, which is a wonderful medieval city, where ancient glass windows were studied over time and the result surprisingly proven that glass is actually a liquid. It is amazing yet not so, considering the liquescent fluidity of the character of glass and no wonder it is being used as an element to enter portals to other worlds.

I convince myself that I have to sleep and drift in and out of light dozes as I swelter under the sheet hiding from what might be lurking under the rubble beneath my bed and between wake and sleep I listen to my whisperer's encouragement guiding me through my night terrors saying:

*"As you travel it is important to be flexible –emotionally, physically and spiritually and have an open mind to all things. A closed attitude will only bring disorientation on all levels. Be firm in your belief that 'nothing and no one can harm you' and trust in the Universe to give you only goodness and only goodness will surround you. Do not be afraid to enter through the 'looking glass' into a different reality, for reality as such does not exist and it is only you who forms your own reality. You are the one who creates heaven or hell within yourself, so to change your surroundings change your perception positively and your surroundings will reflect the change within you. Remember that when you think lucky you will be lucky and so it is with all things."*

The night closes in and at last I sleep, knowing that I am truly Lucky.

# LOST

Breakfast in the filthy hotel is not appealing, especially when the dining room is next to the open jungle courtyard and the kitchen consists of an old vending hut held together with a corrugated tin roof, surrounded by building rubble, bits of old cement and mud strewn across the dirty floor. A young girl and an old lady serve dried white bread, butter and jam with stewed tea and coffee. I am not hungry and resolve to find somewhere to eat later. We have an early morning meeting to decide who is taking the day's excursions and as I have not budgeted for additional entertainment, I make my excuses to the group to have a quiet day alone in Merida City. I watch the others busily prepare to leave for their swimming session and zoo visit, while I collect my bag to make my solo exploration of Merida. As I leave, I take a photograph of the hotel's old, faded sign hanging precariously outside the front door and step into the glaring sunshine. The heat is already rising and I understand the temperature will soar by midday. I make a mental note to remember my route into the city, as I am aware that if I get lost, no one will know where to find me and I could be gone for hours before anyone realises I am missing. I dismiss the thought lightly as my sense of direction is fairly good and walk in a straight line towards the city square with the sun burning my back. I am glad to be wearing my sunglasses, as the white painted walls of the side street blindingly dazzle making my eyes water and sting in the glaring heat. I feel dizzy from the lack of food and quicken my pace towards the city centre, where I hope to experience a long-time ambition- to sit in the centre of Merida and 'people watch' like Carlos Casteneda's character, Don Juan.

The few people I pass in the street rudely stare and I suppose a very pale, blonde-haired, foreign woman walking alone must appear unusual. At the end of the street I spy the main square where people meet and swop gossip before going to the market. I sit quietly on an empty bench under the park trees away from the glaring sun. I need an adapter for my electric plug and intend to find an electrical shop later, but now under the cool of the plaza trees I am contented. As I sit alone, I notice that old men in the square begin staring at me with contempt, as though I am blatantly flaunting their moral customs and women snidely whisper as the few become a throng, pointing and laughing behind their hands in my direction. I am uncomfortable and embarrassed by their hostility, so I abandon my plan and flee to a large bookshop opposite the main thoroughfare offering an unbiased refuge from the local mocking.

As I make my escape, sweat trickles through my scalp into my neck and drips down my forehead. It is so hot and I feel vulnerable and awkward. Taking asylum in the cool book store allows me time to breathe. Here amongst familiar surroundings I gather my thoughts and pick up a thin, soft covered book and waft it across my face, using it as a fan until I spy the manager shaking his head and I quickly, apologetically replace it, not without noticing the intriguing title - 'Time Travel In the Future'. Sometimes we are led by mysterious means to find information we might not otherwise access and I am fascinated to read the story of a man who claims to have travelled through time at least on forty occasions. I remember my own time travel experience and believe the account of a whistle-blower, a Doctor who states that in 1967 the United States of America was using time travel technology to obtain future information concerning political and economic secrets in order to gain advantage over other major countries, especially during the cold war. He further reveals that from 1976 he was recruited by the US government to help maintain and expand colonies on Mars which was called the 'Pegasus Project'. He states that many youths were recruited, both boys and girls as they were better suited to adapt to a new life and with younger minds, could cope with the planet change, whereas adults who were recruited, often became unstable and insane on their return to earth after their time on planet Mars. In 1970 he claims he was present at a lunch where Bush senior and junior were informed that they would both become Presidents from the reports brought back from the future. The knowledge and technical skill of time travel was made possible by the work of Tesla who was guided by aliens, with superior technological expertise to help him create and make time travel possible. The author further explains that there is a secret document held by the US Government which will be publicised in 2022 which testifies that Tesla came from planet Venus and was born on a spaceship travelling to earth and was sent by the Venusians to help humans develop their energy resources, as he said that planet earth was a natural generator of pure energy and could provide free power for all. A side note states that unfortunately humanity's greed for money and power outrides the compassionate needs of the people and Tesla's blueprints for free energy were filed away in a secret safe and at some point in the future will become public knowledge.

I am engrossed in the book and fascinated to read that a pilot from the North American Forces was chosen to time travel back to the last eleven days before Jesus was crucified and was instructed to only observe and not interfere or change anything in any way that might affect the outcome of the situation. In March 1973 'Operation Trojan Horse' was activated and the pilot sent back to the allotted time zone. In order to complete the mission successfully, ten tons of technical equipment was transferred to Israel with their government's permission. The pilot was successful in his mission to meet and talk with Jesus and there is a manuscript documenting the meeting proving the existence of Jesus and the events surrounding his crucifixion. The document is in the American Government's secret vaults under the title of 'Operation Trojan Horse'.

I am suddenly aware that the manager is becoming impatient and I replace the book pretending to be interested in some local art work. I am cooler now and decide to explore the city to find an electrical store. Stepping outside, the heat knocks me backwards. It is so intense- it's like walking into an oven. In the blazing inferno, people are swarming everywhere and I become an object of curiosity. I try to keep my eyes on the ground, avoiding direct contact with the invasive nosiness of the crowd and scurry up a side street holding tightly onto my bag and camera. I am relieved to find myself in a shopping precinct likely to sell an adapter and farther up the street a large yellow sign declares in Spanish and English 'Electrical Goods'. The store is modern and air-conditioned and the shop keeper very helpful. He sells me exactly what I need and I feel that I have accomplished a great feat as I leave the shop, but as I walk out into the crowded street panic strikes. I struggle to remain calm in a sea of local faces who unashamedly glare at me. I am an oddity in their midst and an alien in their society. Children stop and stare pointing with a grin. I try to respond with a kind smile but inside I am steaming, boiling with the unrelenting heat and embarrassment. The temperature in the 40's is unbearable and my jeans are sticking to my legs. My cotton blouse is limp and wet. I turn back towards the main square in a muddle as I weave my way through the swarm of bodies heading in the opposite direction. I hadn't realised how difficult it was going to be walking alone in a strange city with very different moral ethics to my own. On reaching the main plaza everything looks different and I don't recognise where I am. I even question whether I have reached another central square but I know there is only one. A cold fear shivers through my burning body and I feel sick. I want to hide and vomit. The heat has got to me and the lack of food is making my head spin. I can't even remember the name of my hotel! In my panic I steady myself against a wall and close my eyes. I will not accept that I am lost. I will not be lost. I cannot be lost. No one knows where I am and I don't even know the name of the street where the hotel is situated- so how can I find my way back? I tell myself that I am becoming delirious in a fever of doubt and I have to stop. I am totally alone and don't know what to do. Taking deep breaths, I open my eyes and in my mind call to my voices and they respond saying: *"you are never alone. Help is always closer than the air you breathe. Be calm you are not lost. No one is ever lost. It is not possible to be lost, for wherever you are, you are meant to be and never doubt for one moment the Universe's plans for you, which if you allow to unfold, you will learn very powerful lessons. It may seem that you don't know where you are or where to go, but in those few moments of uncertainty you are liberated-freed from imprisonment and the entanglement of time. Immerse yourself in that precious notion of 'nothingness' for it is a spirit gift and will not last long before you are back in the quagmire of existence."*

I quietly listen to their advice in the midst of the throng and try to blend into the wall away from questioning eyes. I understand the lesson but I query how I am going to get back.

*"Have faith! Believe what is truth, for everything in the Universe is made of atoms which are pure energy and energy is consciousness. Consciousness has an electromagnetic field which is a frequency vibration. All your thoughts and feelings exist in an energy field whether good or bad and that which you choose determines the frequency on which you operate. The energy in which you surround yourself is a magnet for drawing into yourself the same kind of energy, so if you are negative then you will attract negativity. Similarly if you are positive then you will attract positive energy. Gratitude has a positive effect on vibrational frequency and dispels negativity. So if you are grateful for all life's lessons you will be encompassed in positive vibrations."*

I listen and realize that I have slipped into the quick-sand of negative thoughts and know that I have to heave myself out of the hole that I have dug and I must think positively, because in clearing my mind of negative energy the situation will be resolved. A voice echoes in my mind:

*"remember there is a solution to every problem and a cure for every illness and for every negative thought there is a positive."*

I smile and sigh for I know all will be well trusting in the Universe and I am grateful for all lessons learnt. Suddenly, I remember the photo I took of the hotel as I left and realize the answer is on my camera. I search and find it, laughing out loud with relief. My confidence returns and the dizziness disappears. In the crowd I spot a policeman and ask him in broken Spanish how to get to the hotel in the photo. He tells me there are two in the city with the same name and I ask directions to the nearest and he gladly points down a side street. I almost run across the road to a set of shops I recognise and just stop myself singing with joy and walk into the nearest restaurant ordering three meals on the menu. The waiter looks at me quizzically, especially when I order three cocktails. I feel so liberated in the moment that I wallow in the feast that I have so far denied myself. I realize that denial is a form of negativity and brings of itself further deprivation, so I should honour myself by ordering the best I can afford. The food is absolutely amazing and as I delight in the sumptuous cuisine, I think of food in the future and how different things are going to be, especially as I have seen a film of a 3D meat printer in progress. The meat is made from a single cell from an animal and printed in layers on a slab, where inch by inch the substance builds up into a large joint which is then sliced into smaller joints. The substitute meat does not resemble a real joint but rather a lump of red tissue .Apparently by 2025 the 3D meat printers will be available for purchase.

I am glad to be in the now of the moment enjoying real food, for in the future this meal will be obsolete and replaced by synthetic imitations. Before I left for the trip I read an article stating that by 2026 there will be 3D printers making major organs such as the heart, liver and lungs to replace those in sick patients and donors in the future will not be needed. I know this because I have been shown in my meditations future healing centres where the most incredible operations are undertaken on beds of 'light' where cell regeneration and restorative surgery is performed through laser beams, taking only a few minutes to complete. The world of tomorrow is not far away, but for today I will be thankful to be safe in the now.

After my sumptuous meal I saunter back to the hotel in the heat of high noon, relieved to know that it's just down the street, contemplating how odd it is that one moment your mind can send you into a black abyss of despair and the next, with a little knowledge and understanding, your mind can alter everything. I recall Dr. Wayne Dyer's wise words-"change the way you look at things and the things you look at will change," in other words your mind can alter many aspects of how you perceive your world and if you approach life's problems with positive vibrations then the outcome will be positive.

All is quiet and cool inside the hotel and as I pass the open jungle square I notice a large cage on a pedestal with a colourful red and yellow parrot perched on the bottom rung. It flicks its head from side to side and glares with its beady black eyes but doesn't make a sound. I am not fond of birds in cages and avoid stepping near it treading on the muddy verge, which is still dripping wet from the tropical storm. I am glad we have only one night left in the hell hole hotel and wonder if our guide will appear again in the middle of the night outside our room with another amour. Sleep is difficult when you are plagued with night fears of crawly creatures and I console myself with the thought of the next day's travel to Palenque in the Mexican highlands in search of the lost city.


In the morning after another restless, humid night, I am relieved to bundle up my compact rucksack ready for the journey to Palenque. I board a small bus with the group, where we begrudgingly make extra space for the complainer's additional luggage from their recent 'must have' purchases. The bus ride to the highlands on a major road, which is merely a rough muddy pathway with massive potholes, is alarming at times, especially as the bus driver is a small man who can barely reach the peddles and struggles to turn the large wheel with one hand while he sucks a toffee lollypop held in the other hand. I am fascinated by his dexterity particularly when we swerve to avoid gigantic holes in the mud. Eventually, after trundling through difficult jungle terrain for seven hours, we reach the highlands where the roads are drier and the air cooler with the highways and byways swathed in exotic wildlife and tropical flora. Palenque is a magical place where the ruins date from 226 BC. to around 799 AD. and the site is a major classical example of amazing Mayan Art and Architecture. The Mayan's advanced knowledge of science and astronomy is seen in the incredible observatory and historical records prove their understanding of cutting-edge operation techniques, such as brain surgery. Their knowledge of the use of natural herbs and plants for medicine is nonpareil, being the forerunner of today's holistic approach to healing and their inspired, remarkable wisdom in manipulating time lines, bears great significance to today's technological advances.

On arrival, we gather together to explore a courtyard in the magnificent ruins of a temple where the remnants of drawings and statues are still visible. Although the vibrancy of the scenes are faded, enough remains to give an eerie impression of the inhabitants from the past. Our guide leads us through an arched doorway into a precarious ledge surrounding the high temple. The ledge is unsafe with crumbling masonry and little gaps in between the brickwork look treacherous as there are no safety bars to hold or guide us along the narrow edge. In England the building would be declared dangerous and unsafe for the public. One by one we step onto the tiny ridge where there is only room to place one foot at a time in front of the other. I follow Myrtle and Bill is behind me. I marvel at Myrtle's bravery as she carefully follows the others but I begin to shake. I have never been afraid of heights, but the thought of misplacing my step and falling straight down is freaking me out! I can't help the shivers shaking my body. My teeth involuntarily chatter. All my muscles are turning to jelly.

Suddenly the ledge disappears and there is a gaping hole where the brick has crumbled and decayed.

I freeze. I can't go on. I am giddy. I can't breathe. I begin to urge myself to jump off. I want to fall and end the fear but I think of my children and I am immobilised. My feet are heavy and my body is no longer mine. I have lost control. I can't move!

There is being lost physically where you don't know where you are and there is being 'lost' mentally where fear imprisons you in a black cell and you can't access your natural survival instincts. I am lost in a fog of terror and dread. All I know is I can't move. Time is slipping away. I am sweating from head to toe and my body is drifting away from me and I from it. Hands, warm hands enfold my waist.

Bill understands what is happening. I hear his voice, calmly and gently persuading me to step over the gap. He holds me tightly and I obey like a zombie. In the distance I hear shale and dry brick falling below me as I robotically step over the hole. He holds me in a secure grip all the way around until we are safely back in the courtyard.


I was lost in a distressed daze and am coming back slowly to reality. I am so grateful to Bill for his intuitive guidance and he just smiles. Simple, pure moments of joy like this are fleeting. When we face extreme danger and somehow survive, it is hard to fully appreciate our luck and how miraculous it is to return to the safety of ourselves. As I recover from the trauma, Myrtle and Bill walk either side of me towards the tomb of where King Pakal is said to be buried. There is an image of him resembling a modern day astronaut flying in a spaceship; the likeness is uncanny and feeds the hypothesis of many who believe that ancient aliens visited the planet long before humans. The picture is exciting, as in my world-wide travels I have witnessed the very same icons, statues, wall paintings, carvings and ancient signs and symbols- all identical images, which pose the question- was it the Anunaki who first stamped their mark on the planet leaving us a message of our heritage? A report was made public in 2011 by a high ranking colonel from the FBI, that interdimensional beings have been visiting earth for a very long time and are in the most, peaceful. These Documents have been declassified and released through the FBI official website. It is thought that these beings inhabited the earth prior to human occupation and can blend seamlessly into our world. It is also interesting to note that Christopher Columbus's diary, in 1492, reveals a log where he describes a strange object in the night sky which was bright as a star but much larger, which some believe to have been a UFO. The object reappears on three other occasions on October 12th,17th and 19th as recorded by Columbus. It is logged that the strange bright object in the sky affected the ship's compass needle pointing north and was instrumental in leading the ship to discover new land – America. The first UFO sighting is said to be around 780,000 years ago and it is chronicled that a strange object entered the solar system at a speed of over 20,000 miles per hour. NASA also revealed that for the first time in recorded history an asteroid was intercepted approaching earth, saving the planet from an apocalyptic disaster. I further discovered that the International space station documented a sighting of over 150 fleet of lights travelling towards earth's orbit, believed to be Alien ships travelling towards earth. It seems that strictly guarded secrets hidden for many years are now being slowly revealed, perhaps to prepare us for the future, whereby aliens freely inhabit our world and we will learn the truth that we are the visitors on this planet and that earth is the true home to interdimensional beings.

Here in the beauty and serenity of Palenque, I can believe anything because the vibration is the most pure, tranquil and heavenly I have ever experienced. The atmosphere is electrifying with invisible buzzing energy, chaste and untainted by modern stimulus bombardment. I close my eyes and become engulfed in a lost paradise connecting to the past. In a dream I walk towards the forest with Myrtle and Bill accompanying me and I see in the distance a low wooden building like a National Trust Nature Reserve restaurant built of wood. I am relieved to see it as I am thirsty from the heat and am in need of some refreshment after the traumatic experience at the top of the temple. I see some people wandering around wearing ancient clothing and I imagine they are locals employed to give some authenticity to enhance the atmosphere of the place. Just as I take a step forwards to enter the wooden building, I am hooked back jerkily by Bill and Myrtle who save me from stepping onto a major road, just missing a van travelling fast around the corner. I am shocked. I stand frozen gazing at the modern main road. I explain to Bill and Myrtle that I was about to walk into a restaurant and they exchange alarmed glances. They sit me down on a side wall by the road and whisper to each other. They think I am unwell, but I was lost in another world, another time zone, another era of Mayan life.

I know what I saw. It was real. They leave me to gather my thoughts while they go to look for water as they believe I am dehydrated and a drink will help me to recover. I know I did not imagine the scene and I can recall it easily. I sigh, almost laughing at myself to think that I have been 'lost' in another kind of situation. My mind wanders to the very strange case of John Smith who was 'lost' in space in 1973 when NASA sent him into space in a satellite and after three days in orbit the ship's orientation system failed. The experts tried to fix the problem but were unable to find a solution and John was abandoned and left to float aimlessly in space. In the year 2000 an amateur astronomer discovered a strange object orbiting the earth at an altitude of 470 kilometres which he reported to NASA who ascertained it was Smith's missing satellite and the engineers with more advanced technological expertise, were able to guide it back to earth. On opening up the capsule they were amazed to find John Smith, although unconscious, seemed to be unharmed and the cryogenic team successfully revived him, however, the John Smith in the capsule was not the John Smith that left earth. The man/creature in his place was different and had a heart on the right side of his body. Other physical discrepancies were discovered which confirmed it was not John Smith's body and his personality traits were different, so the conclusion was that the being in his place was unearthly. A few days later the being disappeared. NASA did a cover-up stating that John Smith never survived the take off and never went into space. What happened to the real John Smith? Who took over his body and what happened to the human/creature? Perhaps in the new era of disclosure the truth will be revealed and people demanding answers to unsolved mysteries such as what happened to all the passengers lost on planes in mysterious circumstances and the truth of the Bermuda triangle disappearances will be finally exposed. As we learn more about the truth of our 'reality' the more we discover that everything we thought was impossible is in fact possible and the fantasy notion that the moon matrix prevents humans from knowing and experiencing the real 'reality' will be exposed. There is further evidence to show that much of the news is fake and that the truth lies within many Sci-fi films preparing us for what really is a holographic reality.

As Myrtle and Bill return with a bottle of fresh water, I rise and smile. I want to show them I am not mad and I need them to forget what has happened. They are relieved to see I have recovered and follow me into the waiting bus to take us to our next location. Sitting next to the window, I stare across the magnificent splendour of the exotic, tropical wilderness, feeling pleased to be travelling through a landscape that I have only seen in photographs and films. The majestic beauty of the luscious green mountains towering above vast, thick forests is overwhelming and I am overcome with emotion as we set off on our next adventure. I am glad to experience raw travel, taking myself beyond my comfort zone into unchartered spheres where I have to face myself and my silly fears. I have always lived in two worlds, the one on earth and the other beyond the stars and for all the different categories of 'lost' on this planet, I know another 'lost' which is an ache, a yearning, a craving for a life in a place I can't remember. Sometimes I feel it fleetingly in a thought; sometimes I see it in a distant dream and sometimes I hear a faint, gentle vibration humming across an open meadow, leading me back to somewhere which is home, but I can't recall it in the fullness of a memory. It is a deep mourning for who I am and where I came from. One day I will return and remember all.

As the bus rumbles on, I am lost in thought, recalling a time when I was ten years old, crying out in the dead of night to my star family to take me back home. I hated earth-life and didn't fit in with my earth family. I wished with all my heart that my journey on this planet would end. A child's plea to the GREAT ONES was heard across the Universe and suddenly I stood bare foot, in my long white nightgown feeling the damp night grass between my toes, looking upwards to a steep hill under the protective gaze of a full, harvest moon. I recognised the rough outcrop of rocks where I had been practising abseiling techniques with my mountaineering club and in the bleak, lonely stillness something magical, wonderful and amazing happened. I was not afraid. It was not a dream and I had never heard of the story, 'The Lion, the Witch and the Wardrobe', so that when the most majestic, king of jungle creatures strode gently towards me with his amber kind eyes and powerful body, I was enthralled. His kindness, gentleness and overwhelming love was absolute. I placed my small hand into his thick soft fur and held onto him just behind his ear. I felt complete. I was totally safe. We had a telepathic link and through mind-communication he told me his name was ASLAN. Perhaps there is a universal, archetypal lion who exists in a realm not too far from our earth called Aslan and he is a children's champion and the author of the book channelled into the angelic realm to find him to create a wonderful, classical children's story?

As we strolled together over the hill the dewy, coarse grass changed beneath my feet to a soft, dry carpet like fresh mown hay and the black night turned into a bright sunny day in a vibrant paradise seeped in unimaginable colours and sensations beyond earth's bounty. My senses tingled with delight and I was alive again bursting with pure energy and love. I was home in a magnificent country where everything was more than it had ever been on earth. The heavenly scents wafting from glorious flowers and majestic trees filled the air with delicate fragrances never experienced on planet earth. As we strolled beneath the mountain range, I marvelled at the unusual hues of luminescent purples, blues, magenta and lilac fauna layering the mountain sides. Everything had a different colour-the sky was lilac, the lake was shimmering silver, the grass was blue. I was wholly at peace walking and talking with Aslan as though my earth time never existed. All was harmonious in the heavenly nirvana but as we walked on the air cooled, the sky grew dark and the grass beneath my feet became wet and rough. My heart sank as we returned to earth. I held tightly onto Aslan's fur but he began to shimmer and disappear, explaining that I had to return as my work on earth was yet to be completed and I had a long way to travel through my lifetime and that numerous times I would remember him through teaching and passing on his story to many children.

Finding myself back in bed, as though nothing had happened, I noticed my feet were dirty and stained with green patches. I knew my encounter with Aslan wasn't a dream. Years later when I was at college I learnt of the story of Aslan and nearly fell off my seat with shock and delight to know that he was part of other people's experiences and years further on I stood in classrooms with countless pupils watching the film of 'The Lion, the Witch and the Wardrobe', teaching students about Aslan, although I never dared to reveal my own account with him.

Now, in the moment of recollection, I am grateful to have lived my time on earth fulfilling a mission I was tasked to undertake and hopefully will achieve more to come in the light of the knowledge that I know beyond the beyond and if being lost is part of our journey on earth, then I am lucky to have been lost and found, for I am Lucky.

# CHICKEN BUS AND 007 CAR RIDE

Travelling in the raw renders you vulnerable to all kinds of sickness and disease, especially in primitive areas where basic hygiene is poor and although I have been given special medicine to tackle diarrhoea, I'm not quite sure whether my stomach cramps are dire enough to warrant its use. Ahead of us we have a thirteen hour journey to cross the Guatemalan border and a chicken bus ride to reach Lake Atitlan in the evening, so I take a little of the dosage just to make sure I am not a burden on the group and take enough to cope with the rigours of the journey. Our very early start means we have to stock up on food the night before so we can eat breakfast on the move and as usual our guide, who is always hungry, boards the bus with a massive food stash filling the cramped space with horrible, greasy trails of last night's spicy dish. The very thought of food is abhorrent to me as I battle griping stomach pains, so I sit at the back of the mini-bus where the open air vent comfortingly cools the rising temperature wafting away bad smells, as hour after hour we wind up and down through scrub jungle climbing high into the mountains and down again like a giant roller-coaster ride, until around midday we arrive at the Guatemalan border.

My research for the trip revealed that Guatemala has the highest record in Central America of kidnapping and blackmailing foreigners, so abandoning our little bus by the jungle brush where there is nothing but thick forestation, makes me nervous. In the unnatural silence, invisible eyes watch and no one speaks as we wait in the strange quiet under the baking midday sun. Our guide paces up and down checking the road for our next transport and his anxious face relays an edginess which affects us all- even the complainers are quiet. Suddenly spluttering engines with heavy clanging and banging of broken parts usurp the silence, as two car wrecks appear. We are all too shocked at the dilapidated vehicles to say anything as our guide suspiciously slinks over to the drivers and engages in heated conversation, seemingly haggling to make a shady deal. I see money deviously exchange hands and wonder if our guide is pocketing funds which should secure our safe passage into Guatemala with legitimate transport, but instead he has arranged for two taxi wrecks  probably paying two local thugs very little, to drive cars which are not road-worthy and most likely stolen from a dumping tip and the young boys themselves possibly are not licensed to drive.

The group quietly follow orders to get into the scrap heaps. No one speaks. No one dares to object, as in the middle of nowhere we have no choice. Three of us squeeze into the back of one metal shell where the seat has no springs but rests on bare wooden boards while the front seat precariously hangs off its hinges. Our driver nervously twitches, profusely sweating and constantly checks the road. The bushes rustle and I suspect we are being watched. The car in front with the rest of our small group, revs up furiously and sets off in a cloud of thick black smoke which ploughs into our wreck amidst a fog of poisonous fumes exploding from our own broken engine. We cough and splutter as we hiccup forwards following the other metal heap and I cover my nose and mouth with my hands to avoid inhaling the noxious vapour, while our backsides thud into the floor and our heads thump against the roof bouncing up and down on the bare boards as the driver scrunches through the gears to race us up a very steep mountain. I take a quick glance out of the window and gasp as the side of the road falls away to a rocky precipice below. Are we going to get out of this alive? I choke back the rising nausea, turning away, praying desperately for our safety as the car struggles to maintain force to climb up the steep slope. In my mind with all my might, I urge the burnt out engine to forge upwards and upwards.

Eventually we reach the top of the mountain skidding into a noisy town and hurtle down a side street to avoid local curiosity.

We appear to be heading directly towards a market and I believe at any moment we will turn off down an alley but the driver picks up speed aiming for the stalls. In the back we gasp and clutch our bags to our chests, desperately clinging to each other for dear life! I can't believe what is happening. It is a nightmare drive from hell which we are forced to endure and as we follow closely on the tail of the other wreck, fruit and vegetables mash to pulp beneath the threadbare tyres and apples roll like pinballs into the gutter. Down the row of stalls we thrash and crash our way through the market regardless of anything in our path as we smash into every obstacle ahead, destroying wooden crates made from simple wooden slats packed full of scrawny chickens pecking each other's backs to the bare bone. Suddenly as we scrunch into the crates, cracking through the slats, the birds are freed and fly precariously into our windscreen, wildly squawking like unleashed banshees in a flurry of feathers falling in a thick snow storm across the shattered glass and up into the air like exploding party poppers. Young boys jump out of our way as we swerve ferociously in and out of the handicraft stalls shattering home-made pots and plates. I hide my eyes as women in the distance are laying out beautiful rolls of fabric on the ground and I know they will be hurt if they don't move as we pelt recklessly into their pathway. Shrieks and screams alert the other market traders to flee as we hit colourful cotton bales sending them flying in all directions like gaily painted flags shooting through the air in a frenzied kite festival. Luckily none of the women are hurt. Nearing the end of the market we scoot around a corner just missing a group of people on their way to market and we jerkily stop in the centre of the town outside the border control office.

In the back of the wreck we are shaking from the James Bond car chase through the market place and the poisonous fumes we have inhaled. My stomach is churning and I fight back the rising sick in my throat. Like zombies we climb out of the vehicle. We are too traumatised to speak or even utter a sound. Our guide doesn't dare to look us in the eye and herds us to a waiting area outside the border control office. Our ride was obviously unlawful and the boy drivers were terrified of someone chasing them. None of us question the illicit transport and the dangerous ordeal we have just endured, as we are helpless and need to move on. Like prisoners, we are transported to an unknown destination and have no say in our treatment. We just hope to reach Lake Atitlan safely.

Border control offices and officers are well known for wielding power over visitors, extracting extra funds to allow entry into their state, especially in far out places in Mexico where the police are a law unto themselves and where bribery and corruption is the norm. This station, it appears is no different from the rest, as we are made to wait in line in the hot sun to see the officer in charge to obtain our visitor's passes. Eventually, after a tedious, arduous delay, I enter the tiny bureau and it is as though I have dropped back in time to Ebenezer Scrooge's office with congeries of mildewed files stacked high from floor to ceiling, overpowering the room with the smell of decay, damp walls, stale tobacco and pungent body odour.

The obese Officer in a tight uniform sitting behind the desk resembles a Mexican bandit from the black and white film archives, with greying black wavy hair, dark beady eyes and a bushy handle-bar moustache. He is sweating profusely and droplets of perspiration are gathering on his leathery forehead. A cigar smoulders on a tin ash tray behind a pile of papers. He pulls at his moustache as our guide hands him my passport, while a large clock on the flaking white wall, ticks monotonously in the uncomfortable silence. I am becoming impatient -how long does it take to inspect a passport? Perhaps he has difficulty deciphering my credentials? He idly puffs on his cigar occasionally looking up at me and back to my photograph as though he disbelieves I am the same person. Somehow I think it is a technique he has perfected to unnerve an applicant. Our guide shuffles from foot to foot, nervously checking his watch and breaks the silence apologetically, explaining that we have a chicken bus to catch. The Officer places my passport on the desk and clicks his tongue, sucking another puff on his cigar. He blows the smoke in our direction, which cues our guide to withdraw some notes from his wallet, secreting them under a pile of files. Almost immediately my pass is stamped and the Officer with a wide dishonest grin, motions our party out of the premises. Relieved, we cross over the border just in time to catch the chicken bus . We are lucky because sometimes it doesn't turn up or people have to wait for hours as the only transport available to the masses might have had to take a detour to pick up a sick child in the mountains where there is no emergency service. In these parts there are no set timetables for anything. I struggle to race towards the bus with my rucksack. I am so weak with the lack of food and sleep in the debilitating heat. By the roadside greasy, spicy meat is being fried and as usual our guide greedily buys two tortillas to take on board our bus. The pungent smell permeates the air with the stench of cheap cooking oil and fried onions. My head is telling me I'm hungry but my stomach cramps and nausea tell me a different story. I have a few boiled sweets in my bag and gently allow a sweet to dissolve in my mouth as I take a seat at the front of the bus. We spread out along the seats as there are no other passengers and settle down for the long haul ahead. Our guide informs us that the local buses are called 'chicken buses' because of all the livestock and dead chickens that the locals transport from town to town, but also because the drivers have a tradition of racing each other up impassable mountainous roads, challenging each other to race to the top, calling each other 'chicken' if they don't accept the dare.

The sweet offers me initial comfort and I need the sugar to sustain my energy but I am not well and close my eyes as the bus sets off telling myself…'I can do this…I can do this… I will soon feel well after a sleep.' I have been told many times by my whisperers that 'you are where your mind is' and I know this to be true, but sometimes it is difficult to put knowledge into practice when you are struggling to survive. I am living the challenge that I set myself and I know all will be well as I trust in the Universe to guide me through rough patches. Sleep affords me a little respite, but not for long as the bus begins to stop at certain places picking up locals and soon the bus is cram-jammed solid with local Indian women and children. The smell of vegetable cooking oil, damp wool, unwashed bodies and herbal hair essence permeates the cramped space. Two elderly women forge their way into my small seat and I attempt to squeeze in on the edge but it is too uncomfortable, so I stand in between a tight row of large women, squashed together like a pack of pork sausages. They are burdened with baskets and boxes from their weekly trek down from the mountain. Live chickens squawk and cackle from their make-shift cages and rivulets of blood trickle down the aisle from fresh cut meat packed in flimsy brown paper bags. To my left, a woman with a small child at her breast and two young children are wedged into a seat and stare at me, giggling shyly behind their hands.

They have never seen a white woman with blonde hair and green eyes in their part of the world. Suddenly the baby spies me and screams terrified at my presence and buries his head in his Mother's chest. His two siblings laugh out loud at his reaction and to settle the situation I ask the Mother if I can give the children a boiled sweet. She nods and the two older children take a sweet as though I have given them the crown jewels but the little one is too frightened to even look at me. I think he sees me as a white witch spirit. The rest of the local women are silent as though they are tolerating foreigners in their travelling space.


Suddenly a honking horn beeping beside us alerts everyone to the arrival of another local bus. The other driver immediately challenges ours to race up the narrow mountain pass. The women are not fazed by the terrifying situation and seem to have full confidence in our driver. I am scared! The pathway is not wide enough to take two buses and the ravine below is rocky and jagged with fallen boulders. The driver, undaunted by the side tackle of the other bus, regardless of all the passengers, forces the bus into top gear and races up the gulley. For a few moments the buses are neck and neck but luckily ours noses ahead and we throb forwards just in time to take the lead on the tiny mountain pass. The women cheer as we swerve down and around the impassable pass strewn with fallen rocks and tree debris. Little by little as the sun hides behind the mountains and a gentle hush descends, an inaudible sigh of relief is felt from the families for their home-coming as the women alight from the bus. Finally the last stop drops the little ones to the outskirts of their village and they take a final glance at the white woman who gave them a sweet. Now all is quiet as we make our final push towards Panajachel situated by Lake Atitlan nestling in the bosom of three volcanoes.

The night creeps in surrounding us in a deep black cloud and we are still travelling. It is too dark to see the shores of Lake Atitlan as we trundle along mile after mile heading towards the bustling town haloed in bright lights and zinging with a Friday night fiesta vibe. Slowly, our group wake up from our slumber, energised by the thought of exploring new territory and as we pass wonderful exotic hotels, I am stirred with expectation of staying in a lovely hotel for a change in a tropical paradise, but we drive inside a small compound where there are a series of cheap rooms waiting for us. A crazy dog tied up with chains on a rough grassy patch inside the compound, barks furiously as we are allocated our rooms. Another journey is over and we have two nights in this shoddy hovel, but I am too tired to complain and I throw myself despondently on the small, rickety bed and stare at the ceiling. I am sharing the room with my young Italian companion who is barely eighteen, is carefree and who accepts these primitive conditions without a murmur. I wish I could be less stressed and try to relax like her, but I have so many tedious phobias of creepy-crawly insects, filth, infections, food prepared in unhygienic places and grimy bathrooms with disgusting water and in this zone all my fears are tested. I tell myself it's what I bought into-challenging myself beyond reason, but right now I want to be tucked up in my own bed in the comfort of clean sheets. The person I left in Yorkshire is being stretched to the limit and I am finding it all too much!

"Are you coming out with us? It's Friday night and we can have fun!" the Italian teenager urges gently, sensing my ill-humour.

"Later, thank you, I will find you, I just need to sort things out!" I reply, mustering a modicum of enthusiasm. She nods and leaves in a flurry of energy- as only the young can conjure in such a situation.

It's hard to shake off the descending depression percolating in my mind. Maybe it's the lack of food and the state of my stomach and the disappointment of this awful compound and the dog barking furiously outside. My inner strength is crumbling. I miss home. I miss my children and I can't stop trembling. I am half way across the other side of the world in a strange land facing my darkest fears and I mustn't allow self-pity to creep into the equation. "You are where your mind is!" I repeat to myself. I can't allow negative thoughts to push me over the edge of despair when I still have a long way to journey. It would be ridiculous to give in when I know feelings are cyclical, unreliable and can change. Teachings from Dr. Wayne Dyer states that," if we change the way we look at things, the things we look at will change." Well, I can change the way I perceive this situation and in that way the situation will present itself in a different light. Determined to alter my mind-set, I haul myself up off the bed thinking a walk will raise my spirits and I dose myself with another shot of medicine to fight the gut infection and walk out the door.

Outside, the evening air is humid after heavy tropical rainfall and the wild dog strains at his leash to get to me. I am tempted to stroke him but I have been warned never to pet any stray animals for fear of being bitten, especially when there is the possibility of contracting Rabies. Before I left I paid for a special anti-Rabies injection because I would be travelling in primitive areas far from a hospital, so it was wise to take this precaution. Panajachel town is popping and pulsing with a holiday verve of Friday night exuberance which helps lift my mood and I turn down a side street towards the Chichi market, which I have been told is a 'must' to visit. I am shocked at the muddy shanty-town conditions. Images of gold-diggers in the Klondike from cowboy spaghetti western films springs to mind as I step onto corrugated rusty iron tin paths laid out down the muddy cobbled stones.

Wearing my hand-made poncho that I bought in Mexico city, which dangles casually over my blue jeans, I am a character from a Clint Eastwood movie, minus the cowboy hat and smouldering cigar.

Stepping gingerly through the muddy Klondike, the local Indians are preparing their stalls in little wooden tin shacks set out in rows leading towards the lake. Friday evening trade promises to be good as every stall is beautifully prepared with multi-various colourful goods, hand-made clothes, creative pottery, hand-crafted gifts, exotic fruit and vegetables together with cooking utensils and kitchenware. I am amazed that some of the shacks are mini restaurants and bars where the locals wave a friendly welcome and smile as I splurge past their shanty town shacks trying to navigate the mud, wearing open-toe blue sandals which are my only shoes for the journey which have bled their colour through to my feet when I was tramping through the rainforest, and now all my toes are blue from the dye.

I am tempted to buy some of the hand-woven clothes but there's no space in my small rucksack for any extra items. Eventually at the end of the long line of huts I reach the lake lapping gently over the pebbles at the water's edge. A gigantic silver moon smiles in the black, cloudless night sky. It is too dark to see the extent of the lake but the silver glazed beams light up the stones below my muddy feet. I walk further into the tepid water, washing my worn sandals and blue feet and I am grateful in the moment to know life. Children are playing, laughing and jumping across stepping stones. When they spy me they race towards me and with expert, silent, pleading, they smile and I can't resist their polite, quiet appeal. So I search my purse for spare change handing out a few coins to each child.

Their trained silence erupts into squeals of delight as they take their bounty and scurry off to spend their treasure.

Alone in the stillness under the watchful eye of the moon, my homesickness trickles back. Tears well and I can't stop a sorrowful cascade dribbling down my cheeks. There is no one around, so I allow my private outburst to flow. I gaze at the moon knowing my home is there and she has always appeared when I needed her protection, even as a small child I sought her shelter. I told my children that if anything happens to me and I don't return, search the magical light of twilight and wait for the moon to signal her secret rays and you will find me. They suppressed their embarrassed doubt, thinking Mum as usual is being dramatic, but I know the moon. The grey dusty, arid satellite is not the real moon which is portrayed. The earth's atmosphere tempers the light from the moon making it appear silver, but especially on the far side of the moon there are forests, lakes, mountains, and untold beautiful landscapes where it is easy to breathe without any artificial aid. New evidence is mounting from the confidential files that have been released by NASA which have been kept secret for many years regarding what really is on the moon and the truth about the first astronauts landing on their initial visit. Now with powerful new scientific equipment ,satellites and telescopes, photos reveal that the moon is very colourful and has many inhabitants both human and a great variety of aliens and strange creatures. There are special areas which have been allowed to be developed by the host aliens to major countries such as America, Britain, China and Russia so that exclusive, unique minerals and elemental metals can be mined, but only under the aliens control and supervision. Whistle-blowers are coming forwards to reveal top-secret information which has been concealed from the public about the truth of the moon's origin and by 2070 the earth, the moon and sun's true history and purpose will be revealed. I know all this because I am shown by my whisperers, who inform me of many incredible details and facts which can be verified.

Now in the melancholic moment of home-sick yearning I am comforted by the thought that I will be given a chance one day to divulge all. The future gives me hope and I know I must sidestep the great ache in my heart to see my children and focus on the present. My whisperers tell me that to be close to my children I must envisage my essence, my spirit energy travelling towards them and enter the kernel of their souls to encompass them in a Mother's love. Energy will always travel, like electricity and they will feel and know my love like a soft pink blanket wrapping them snuggly in loving energy.

As I make my way back through the Klondike squelching mud between my blue toes, I begin to feel hungry and the smell of exotic food entices me towards a tiny shack with a few tables and chairs outside precariously balanced on corrugated tin slats. Inside the minuscule hut a couple more tables are set out in front of a tiny bar. As I walk inside, a friendly waiter takes my order of 'whiskey e Sprite' as I think a dram of whiskey will help my stomach. I ask to see a menu and am amazed at the variety of food on offer as there are no great cooking facilities visible, only an old stove behind a shabby wooden counter. Gradually the tiny space fills with locals and visitors ordering food which magically appears from nowhere and I order another whiskey which seems to be doing the trick of settling my stomach. Through a jostling and bustling of tables a flurry of people appear carrying musical instruments. I watch in disbelief as in the tiny area a full band sets up in front of the only toilet. A little boy sits at a nearby table ready with two spoons to drum on the cracked wooden surface to accompany the band. Suddenly Santana's 'Black Magic Woman' strikes the air, pulsing the unforgettable Latin rhythm, setting every fibre in my body zinging and beating with the beat. I want to dance but there is no room and so I dance in my mind singing along with the intoxicating melody.

The sound is incredible as though the band 'Santana' themselves are playing. I marvel, that here in Panajachel's Klondike, in a wooden tin hut by the side of Lake Atitlan, half way round the world, far away from my little cottage in Yorkshire, the best live music transports me beyond the stars to a musical heaven. It is the most stirring vibration, mentally, physically and spiritually I have ever experienced. The music lifts my spirit and I am alive in the moment, not despairing or despondent but alive! I sit and listen enrapt in the music for a couple of hours, unable to drag myself away but eventually, the whiskey and the medicine and the long day with its traumatic 007 car chase through the market and the chicken bus ride take its toll. I manage to eat a little pizza but dare not risk the lovely local dishes and so I slowly make my way back to the make-shift compound.


All is quiet and the noisy dog has disappeared. At the reception a young girl sits and reads a book and I bid her 'Buenos Notches' and she graciously replies. I ask her what happened to the dog and she answers in broken English, understanding that my Spanish is poor; "El pero, he loco! Loco, you know, Rabies…they take him!"

"He had Rabies?" I question astonished at the information.

"Si, si, Rabies, is very common aqui !" she replies nonchalantly biting into an apple and resuming her reading. I nod, gulping back the shocking information and walk to my room feeling relieved and lucky that I didn't attempt to stroke the dog. I had never been so close to a rabid animal and shudder to think what might have happened. As I close my eyes with the sound of 'Black Magic Woman' resounding in my mind. I am grateful to know the highs and the lows of this existence, for we never truly know one without the other and I am lucky to have experienced both extremes, for I am Lucky.

# MAXIMON THE MIRACULOUS SMOKING DEITY

Lake Atitlan nestles in a crater under the watchful eye of three volcanoes – Atitlan, Toliman and San Pedro and are known locally as the 'three giants'. The lake is the deepest in Central America and is acclaimed to be one of the most beautiful and spectacular lakes in the world and so our scheduled trip in a little open boat around the lake visiting local islands is an exciting venture. After the whiskey and medicine imbibed last night I feel a little better but my stomach is still not good. The thought of the new adventure is stronger than my queasiness and so I put on a brave face and step carefully into the small boat as it rocks precariously beneath my blue feet.

The sun is already scorching, scattering a jewelled veil across the azure- blue lake, set amidst tropical trees and lush vegetation in the near paradise Guatemalan highlands. Our group remain quiet as we glide peacefully towards the first island-San Antonio, where on the top of a hill an imposing church spire, like a lighthouse beacon, welcomes all visitors. As our driver steers the boat towards a primitive, tiny harbour encrusted with small, hand-made, wooden fishing boats packed with empty corn husks, children run down the hill excitedly shouting a welcome and women dressed in beautiful hand-woven costumes stand ceremoniously waiting to greet us with a view to selling their wares to gullible, rich pilgrims.

As we climb out of the boat the children jump up and down enthusiastically, eager to take us to their little co-operative shop built next to their rudimentary school where the women's skilful woven handicraft work is neatly displayed on wooden shelves. The children's art work and pottery are displayed on a rickety wooden table. The poverty is overwhelming but the people's dignity and pride shines through in a united front creating a powerful sense of community. I am moved, not sentimentally but emotionally as a little three year old girl with a dirty face and sincere dark eyes implores me to buy some friendship bracelets. I can't refuse and I want to pick her up and cuddle her as she reminds me of my Grandchildren, but I refrain and give her what I can in exchange for a few colourful strands of cotton woven into small bands. She is very happy when I hand her the money and grins as though she has won the lottery and allows me to take her photograph, which in some of the hill stations is taboo, as it is their belief you steal their soul when the camera clicks and in some villages we have been warned to hide our cameras as the locals will smash any they see.

Inside the shop I wish I could buy many goods but I don't have the cash or room in my rucksack and purchase a lovely little pottery chicken bus made by the children. I fall in love with a beautiful yellow, orange and green mat woven with little Lama motifs and buy it for a small price and a packet of home-grown coffee. The complainers buy many goods as usual, always ready for bargains, but this time I am pleased because it helps the villagers to support their meagre existence. Outside in the sweltering heat a young mother opens up a conversation with me and I am able, with my smattering of broken Spanish, to converse with her. She wants to know about my life beyond the lake and is keen to learn what the outside world is like and to learn about women's role in the society where I live, which is so alien to her and her lifestyle. As we talk she dares to get close to me and touches my expensive crystal earrings, which their crystal energy I believe, helps to heal and fight infection. She investigates the crystal droplets and caresses them with such longing that I am compelled to give them to her. I can't help myself and as I place them in her hands, it is though I have given her part of me to treasure for life. She is so grateful and happy and her joy spills into the moment and will remain with me as a wonderful memory. She strokes my hair and takes out some colourful strands and begins to plait them into my hair forming a long braid which trails over my shoulders. She smiles and nods in approval when she has finished and our brief encounter ends as our group climbs back into the boat. She stands on the quayside and waves. I will not forget her and I hope the gift of the earrings brings her pleasure whether she keeps them or sells them.

As we sail towards another island I quietly ponder the women's life with all the challenges and difficulties they face daily without hospital care or medicines and with basic food rations and a limited supply of clothes, most of which they make themselves and I wonder how they would cope in our modern society with all our electrical domestic appliances and all the goods, food and medicines which are readily available. I think of how the Church, the school and the little store on the Island are mostly built of bricks but the houses are made of mud and straw as bricks are expensive. As I walked past a row of small houses in the tiny hamlet, I managed to glimpse inside a living room. It was dark, plastered with religious pictures on the walls, with the smell of burnt wax wafting through the door. The tiny village mud houses had no electricity and very primitive sanitary conditions and I am grateful to have witnessed another way of living, having taken for granted all the basic energy which fuels and heats our civilised homes. I recall a strange vision I was shown about life in the future. I close my eyes for a few seconds and suddenly feel someone rubbing cream into my shoulders. I turn and see Madam complainer smiling saying that my fair skin is turning red in the hot sunshine. I thank her for her kind gesture as the sun is getting hotter by the minute and we are all sleepy as the boat rocks us gently to the next island. I return in my mind to the dystopic vision set way into the future where I find myself following a young woman. I don't know who she is or why I am following her or how I came to be hovering over her – I just am! She is about twenty four years old with short dark hair and a pretty face, dressed in what appears to be a yellow floral 1950's type dress. She is walking across a flat marbled square where there are a few other people dressed smartly in the same style of that era. The weather is perfect- not too hot or cold, as it is moderated and controlled under a lidded, artificial sky from a computer base. Everyone appears happy and contented, purposefully engaged in their lives. She is walking towards an unusual building which seems to hang in mid-air without any support, almost like some of Gaudi's extraordinary buildings in Barcelona. As she walks towards the fascinating structure it moves as though in recognition of her approach; but I think I am imagining it. A voice inside my head informs me that the building is a living, breathing, A.I. Robot. I am stunned. The voice seems to be a guide allotted to me for the strange visit into the future. I question the validity of the information and my guide says:

"All humans live inside Robots. All species reside inside a controlled environment!"

My invisible guide pauses and waits for my next question as I float above the woman about to enter the building and watch, astonished as the front glass doors twirl and greet the woman by her first name – "good morning Miss Dorothy and how are you today Miss Dorothy?"

"Oh I'm fine Robert, just fine," she replies perkily as she steps through the rotating doors.

I am amazed at the way the building responds to her and my guide explains-

"Inside the building the intel system recognises her and scans her body, as part of her brain is connected to a computerised file which monitors all her needs, her health care and her life expectancy span. No unauthorised person or being can enter the apartments. As you can see the building itself is a living, breathing, artificial biochronic machine looking after all the people living inside. Every person is like an organic cell inside a body existing inside the Robot and each person is connected to the main vein or artery of the bio mechanic workings."

I am shocked at the concept of living inside a Robot and being physically and mentally attached to its A.I. system. I follow her into a silver lift where the walls whirl and twirl like a kaleidoscopic tunnel making and creating vivid flashing patterns of colourful images which reflect her electronic connection to the main system. My guide explains that the lift acts as a monitoring system which scans the occupants mental and physical requirements for the day and the computer adjusts the colours of her apartment to alter the ambience for her well-being. The temperature of her living quarters is gauged according to her health plan, together with dietary needs and supplements which are organised for the day. The atmosphere is tempered and adjusted to suit her mood, so that as she enters her apartment everything alters to suit her needs. As the door to her apartment liquefies, she is engulfed in a Caribbean paradise complete with a white sandy beach, palm trees and gentle rolling white waves on an aqua blue ocean. A sun bed waits for her together with blue and pink drinks concocted in fancy cocktail glasses and exotic fruits are laid out on a wooden platter. A half-naked man of her choice appears and they begin to embrace. I am astounded at the intricate detail of the scene and wonder if ever the A.I. system misreads a person's needs creating an opposing scene to the desired one. My guide softly laughs and states:

"the system is never wrong. It is designed with a failsafe mechanism and is self-replicating and will never break down. It is the same for all A.I. systems in the future which can never fail and never be wrong or destroyed."

Now back in the boat everyone is stirring as the little island of San Jose appears in the distance and we prepare for our next visit having been promised by our guide to witness something magical. He tells us that we are going to visit the amazing deity- Maximon a Guatemalan god who resides in the body of a wooden effigy. He is a god who is fond of drinking strong liquor, womanising, smoking cigars and chain-smoking cigarettes and it is expected that we give him offerings of tobacco, money or expensive watches and jewellery in return for him answering our questions and for his future predictions. He is greatly revered by the people of the region who take turns to house the statue for a year to look after him and in return receive gifts from visitors. During the Spanish conquest Maximon made his appearance as a god to shield and defend the people, representing both light and dark.

As we draw closer to the bay, the sky darkens and the humidity increases as a mist descends from the mountains like a sea fret veiling a beach. We climb out of the boat and follow our leader up a steep grassy incline towards a small settlement of wooden huts on stilts. The small sheds resemble chicken coops with little wooden ladders leading to tiny wooden doors opening into a single dark room. There is no electricity and all the small huts seem gloomy, especially as they are protected from the elements by black plastic sheeting nailed down over the hen houses creating a dark, bleak underworld. We trek through the covered walk-way trespassing into tiny dwelling spaces strewn with modern pots and pans and plastic containers. Some hutches have a few make-shift wooden shelves where they store their cooking utensils, but many pans lie forlorn in the dirt. The prevailing smell of a chicken farm is disgusting and I cover my mouth and nose as we trample past the dwellings spying the villagers rushing inside their coops not wishing to be seen by strangers. Their living conditions are insanitary and there are no toilet facilities or running water. I am appalled at the primitive living quarters and am nervous about where we are headed.

We approach a small hut in the centre of the settlement and our guide leads us up a tiny rickety ladder into a dark, cramped space smelling of hay, cigarette smoke and candle grease. As my eyes adjust to the murky light, I make out a large wooden table enclosed with bench seats where we all sit in a squashed huddle. I am at the end of the bench and as usual my fear of creepy crawlies and spiders torments me in the dark as anything could be lurking, waiting to pounce! Three large candles on the table, highlight a strange effigy in a golden halo seated opposite me. It resembles a grotesque mixture of an old Guy Fawkes dummy, a tattered scarecrow and a wooden puppet dressed in a dark suit and poncho with a trilby hat, wearing black sunglasses. Three men sit next to the 'thing' poised like Mexican bandits dressed in traditional gear and are peering ominously at us as though we are being held for ransom. I gulp and swallow my rising fear in the scary silence.

As the candles spread more light and the darkness dissipates into the squalid corners of the shed, I turn my head to the left and just stop myself from screaming. I clutch my mouth in horror as my heart races and nearly pounds out of my chest. I am sitting next to a glass coffin with a dead man lying inside. I dare myself to look again and am relieved that the man is a life-sized statue of Jesus wearing a long-haired wig which trails over his shoulders. His bright blue eyes are open staring heavenwards and his flesh and skin tones are so real, especially in the candle light, that he could easily be mistaken for a real human. The bizarre coffin is resting in the room supposedly to give strangers an added religious experience. The three men address us in Spanish but their dialect is strange and I can't understand a word they are uttering. Their greeting is translated by our guide and we are told that Maximon is happy to see us and will perform his miraculous feat of chain –smoking.

We all watch as one of the bandits lights a cigarette and places it in Maximon's carved wooden mouth and smoke coils from his nose as though he is smoking the cigarette. I have to stop myself from laughing out loud as it is so obvious that one of the men is working the puppet from behind.

The rest of the group play along with the game. On the table lies money, watches, cigarettes, cigars, a transistor radio and even an electric calculator. We are asked to make our donation and we all obey placing money on the table. I have a few coins to offer but nothing more. We are encouraged to ask questions to the god but no one dares to speak, then in the absence of a query, one of the men explains how Maximon is put to bed every night in the loft and taken care of with such pride and diligence. Immediately I have a vision of one of the men throwing the effigy carelessly up into the loft and I smile at the bluntness of his lie. Then a few banal questions are raised and the miraculous meeting draws to a close.

We are all eager to escape from the tiny chicken hut and hurry out into the dismal dark underworld of the chicken coops housed under plastic bubbles. We follow our guide who winds his way through the congeries of pots and pans heading back to the boat for our next visit to the island of San Marco.

As we board the boat back at the lakeside, the intense heat of the sun is relentless and I am thankful to leave behind the dark, dank world of the chicken-hut people and their dishonest, primitive magic tricks where they take it in turns to house the effigy to earn money from visitors.

I am tired and close my eyes wishing I had brought a hat to shield my head and face from the sun and find myself drifting off into a strange recollection of one of my remote-viewing episodes. I have always had the ability to take myself off elsewhere to view landscapes, people and new places and as a small child, I never thought the skill was unique or special as I often entertained myself with the ability to be somewhere else. I was surprised to learn that 'remote viewing' is an ability which many people own and foster especially for clandestine purposes, to which end, the American Military during WW2 had a special division dedicated to promoting the skill and technique in order to gain secret information from the enemy. Sometimes I seek to 'remote view' and other times it happens involuntarily without any pre-warning. When I enter the state of 'watching' it is unlike any other experience. It is not a dream-state, for the feeling is much sharper and clearer; it is not a memory that the mind conjures- it is rather a state of being present in the 'now' where everything is enlarged as though looking through a magnifying glass.

As I lock out the rest of the world and remember my strange journey to Mars, I am aware of the gentle lap, lap of the water against the boat and allow the memory to unfold. It was not my first journey to remote view planet Mars, as I had journeyed there before and been surprised at the many bases built by major countries since the early 1950's. The occupation of planet Mars is now well documented and accepted, along with Elon Musk's task force mission to provide public transport to Mars to colonise the planet giving people the chance to escape earth and like pioneers forging a new life in the Wild West, will make grave sacrifices in order to start a new life. On this occasion of remote viewing, I automatically found myself standing in front of a field in England facing a broken iron gate lying twisted on the grass, with long fronds of rusted iron prongs dangerously sticking out at all angles. I had no idea why I was there, but then I was suddenly transported to a heavy, red/brown atmosphere where I was staring at a huge block of steel. It was a massive metal rectangle which had a human head lolling down at the top centre. I was told it was a robot with a human head attached which had been severed from a human with the brain upgraded into a high-tech sensory detector. It was an absurd sight to see a human head perched on top of a piece of steel, like a victim's head on a medieval execution pole. There were a number of these gigantic blocks sporadically gathered together in the desolate terracotta desert. The strange robots didn't have arms but had side indentations where steel blades could shoot out to disarm the enemy.

Suddenly the blocks began to move and stand side by side forming an impenetrable wall sealing off the vicinity. Once the wall was in place the human heads mechanically shot up surveying all around, sending information back to a computerised system through eyes which had once belonged to a human being.


Behind me in the dusty, dark red earth came the sound of moving machinery and I turned to see massive, giant wheels in motion leaving deep tracks in the soil like entrenched railway lines. The wheels were so high that I couldn't see the finished vehicle and I quickly moved to the side to avoid being mashed to pieces. I remember seeing photos of mysterious tracks found on the moon very similar to the ones formed by these huge machines and guessed that they were military vehicles.

From there I was whisked inside what appeared to be an old, disused tin mine or maybe it was for some other unfamiliar mineral. There were signs that it had been abandoned quickly, perhaps during some terrible disaster as there is now evidence that Mars suffered some kind of planetary holocaust wiping out many life forms. Strangely the deep mine reminded me of the cotton mills in Lancashire, England, in Victorian times where rows upon rows of noisy shuttles shot back and forth in rhythmic spasms across wooden frames in a damp, dismal factory. Dusty machinery lay forlorn with bits of metal left half formed in the process. I didn't like the feel of the place and I needed to get out quickly and was transported into an open area where the atmosphere was heavy, dark and had a red glow. I saw German soldiers wearing tin helmets like in WW2 and was told there was a Nazi base close by which made me feel unsafe and uncomfortable. I moved forwards and was told that there was a French base, a British camp and a New Zealand base also nearby, but I didn't see them. The whole area was heavily industrious and smelt of iron.

I don't know why I was taken there or for what purpose, perhaps that will be revealed in future visits, but strangely the next morning on my computer was photo of a Martian landscape and there was a post from Laura Eisenhower, Dwight Eisenhower's Great Granddaughter, stating that she had been contacted and asked to go on an assignment to Mars to an established quarter. She had even been targeted by a man who was employed to become emotionally involved with her in order to influence her to take the mission. When she discovered this deceit she finished the relationship and refused the offer of the operation. On reading this, I was even more confused as to the purpose of my remote viewing visit and still do not know what the experience meant. Now in the now of the moment that recollection seems so useless and far away. Here I am on a small boat in the middle of Lake Atitlan surrounded by three volcanoes, sailing towards the island of San Marco having just experienced a ludicrous event of a Spanish deity smoking a cigarette – life can be so bizarre at times, thankfully!

Arriving at San Marco, I realise it is the island that had advertised 'Creative Writing in Guatemala' which had originally spurred me on to book the expedition across Central America, which I am currently experiencing and walking onto the very island which promised a spiritual and enlightening paradise. Sure, it is beautiful and an exotic retreat but I sense a pseudo religious cult organisation lurking behind the happy hippy veneer. I watch from a distance the false welcome extended to all visitors by the floral bedecked owners standing in front of their mock pyramid, designed to enhance meditation and I am relieved that I was not tempted to sign up for their course, but instead booked an outlandish expedition into the unknown. While the others enjoy a fruit cup in the hippy compound, I venture through the lush overgrowth disturbing clucking hens, squawking their disapproval as they scurry into the brush jungle. Through the tall grass, I spy a clutch of shops and houses and head towards them noting an amazing tree growing out of a house in the middle of the settlement, or rather the house has been built around the tree. Seated underneath the ancient tree is a little boy about six years old engrossed in a school book. He looks up at me and smiles and I ask to take his photo but he says-"no, you can take a picture of my homework!"

I laugh and agree but somehow I manage to snap him too and I give him a few coins. He tells me that a teacher comes to the Island once a week to give children some lessons and they have to do homework, which the boy seems very proud to complete, showing off his drawing of a little dog.

Education here is revered and considered an honour, unlike back in England where some of my students will dodge lessons making up lame excuses to gain a few hours freedom.


I wander back to the boat where everyone is gathered to sail to the next island where our lunch is booked and it doesn't take long before we arrive at the most amazing English cottage garden, set under a tropical sky. This island is so different from any of the others and much smaller with only one hotel run by an Irish couple. Walking into a familiar landscape of rose bushes, lilies, herbs, fresh lavender and a myriad of bright summer flowers, fills me with comforting aromas of home. I close my eyes and drink in the sweet perfume of mint, rosemary and thyme wafting on the gentle breeze and I imagine I am back in my cottage. As our guide calls a greeting to our hosts, I awake out of my fantasy, amazed to see a wonderful English style buffet lunch set out on wooden platters. My stomach churns and gripes. I would love to indulge in all the exquisite delights but I know it would be foolish, so I just peck at a few morsels envying the others tucking into a gourmet feast. There isn't much to see on the island as most of it is overgrown with tropical palms and scrub jungle except for the beautiful English garden planted at the front of the small hotel and we only spend an hour relaxing over the lovely spread before we head back to the boat.

I feel queasy on the lake. I fear my medicine is wearing off and I am a little dehydrated after a day in the hot sun, so I place my hand in the cool water as we glide along. The refreshing chill of the waves is wonderfully soothing and I stare into the clear ripples below making out a few electric orange fish darting underneath. In the tranquil moment my mind wanders to a strange vision I had a few months ago when I was unexpectedly taken on another 'remote viewing venture' which occurred one night when I woke up fighting a bout of acid reflux. I took an antacid tablet and tried to get back to sleep but instead found myself splashing my hand in a brown river and was then immediately transported to a military base, somewhere possibly in Iraq or Afghanistan as there was a guard on duty outside the compound who looked like a Middle Eastern soldier. I have no idea why I was taken there as I seemed to be watching an American platoon involved in secretly attempting to break into the base. I had a voice guide, which seems a usual occurrence on spontaneous remote viewing ventures, who told me that the Americans had concocted a strange tunnelling creature which had been created at the infamous Area 51 base where hybrids of humans, animals, creatures and fish are developed and where cruel, horrendous experiments take place.

The American unit was dressed in night manoeuvre camouflage with infra-red goggles to see in the dark. I watched as the men deftly carried a machine from their vehicle to pound a large hole in the ground a few feet away from the enemy army base fence. The machine was silent as it cut through the ground in one shot and made a significant hole about three feet deep and three feet wide, swiftly slicing through the earth. Then they brought out a cage from the back of the van which had some sort of creature inside. I was disgusted and horrified to witness what they called the tunnelling beast. It looked gross- being a hybrid between a large mole, and a giant flounder fish with a woman's face! It had grey/silver rubbery skin with a shiny blubbery texture. It was almost slippery when they handled it. When I glimpsed its face, I was sickened and horrified! Its feminine appearance with half closed eyes as though blind like a mole, was almost beautiful. My heart turned over as its eyes flickered in the moonlight. It had a thin wide mouth like a large plaice fish which was tightly shut.

They took it to the hole in the ground and attached a thin silver line to its neck as they placed it down the shaft where it quickly tunnelled under the fence and appeared the other side in the compound where an insider had left a pile of clothes. The creature was pulled back through the tunnel and replaced back in its cage and returned to the back of the vehicle. I watched a small soldier in a black plastic all-in-one suit scramble into the hole and push his way through the small tunnel and out to the other side where he picked up the clothes and disappeared into the dark shadows. The soldiers in the American unit quickly dispersed leaving no trace of the tunnel as another machine skilfully piled back the soil. In the cool of the night I shivered and rapidly found myself back in my bed. The horror of the night mission still haunts me because I can't forget the face of the creature. I don't know why I witnessed it- perhaps I am meant to share it? Now in the heat of the late afternoon we return to the busy market in the Klondike and look forward to a Saturday night in the tiny bar with the amazing music. A Saturday night far, far away from the York, Micklegate drinking scene. The night closes in and I am relieved to be travelling in the morning to a small town, Antigua, Guatemala's capital city which was destroyed by an earthquake in 1773 and is now a thriving outpost.

After our Saturday night entertainment, we gather together to board another small bus. The journey is long and tedious and when we arrive it is cool and misty with a foggy veil drifting down the mountains. In the distance a volcano guards the vale and the atmosphere is strangely mystical. I wander down the main street and am amazed to find an Irish bar full of Irish and English folk enjoying a pint, like it is a normal Sunday afternoon in the British Isles, yet outside sitting on the dusty pavement, the local Indians smoke their clay pipes watching the world unfold. Next to the bar is a large store selling all kinds of goods and I am curios to explore inside. The dimly lit interior with the smell of incense and strange herbs, is like an ancient Aladdin's cave with piles of corn, wheat and flour stacked in thick, rough sacks near the entrance. Beautiful pottery and handcrafted clothes made by the local women are set out on rough, wooden shelves and towards the back is another door. As I enter I laugh out loud at the sight of rows upon rows of effigies of Maximon all dressed in different suits with hats and some with sunglasses. The carved wooden face is roughly cut and is not a great work of art. I thought the Maximon we encountered in the chicken hut settlement was a rare effigy but obviously there is a large demand for his presence. I stare at the wooden puppet faces and ponder the masses of visitors yet to be tricked by the canny locals. The puppet god profusely produced is a strange sight and I suppose it's not that much different to a religious shop selling lots of crucifixes and images of Jesus and the Virgin Mary. I walk outside the store leaving behind the mass of smoking deities, persuading myself that it is time to imbibe a little dram in the Irish bar where the familiar sound of voices speaking my language is refreshing and welcoming. For a brief moment I catch a little of 'home' and tell myself I am not homesick but just a little nostalgic remembering my family and our Sunday lunches together. Here in the bar there is laughter and merriment and I know I am lucky to be experiencing a journey of a lifetime packed with fantastic memories to share, even if the smoking deity is a comical trick, for I am LUCKY.

# DAYLIGHT ROBBERY

Another place, another time, another culture blend into one passionate emotion of 'gratitude'; for I am thankful to be alive rejoicing in the moment, having travelled out far beyond my comfort zone to test myself in so many uncomfortable situations and now I am in Antigua, Guatemala. I am staying in a converted convent staring at my dyed- blue sandaled feet, whilst sitting in the community area surrounded by lush exotic plants with little boulders placed strategically on the colourful tiled floor, with bright sunlight beaming through religious stained glass windows forming colourful patterns on the indoor plants. I close my eyes as the light streams through a window scene depicting the Virgin Mary and baby Jesus. When I open my eyes I am certain that one of the boulders moves but I am not wearing my glasses and I assure myself that I must have imagined it!

As I ease into a quiet space in my mind, I realise that far away in my normal, routine life, back in York, many things pale into insignificance in the general pattern of life's struggles with mounting problems, making decisions and worrying about finances and I begin to appreciate that these worries are mere debris in the real building blocks to attaining spiritual awareness and growth. I have been told that 'deep pain opens doors if we are prepared to find the key' and that 'deep sudden shock removes us from mundane reality and gives us breathing space inside and outside of the restrictions of time'. I wish here on earth that our pathway to enlightenment was easier but it appears not to be so.

Resting in the quiet of the quasi-religious atmosphere, I am at peace but as I open my eyes, I think I see another boulder moving towards me! Without my glasses everything is blurred and I assure myself I must be mistaken, so being tired after the long journey I attempt to return to a meditative state. I breathe deeply feeling the warmth of the sun on my face and ask for guidance about a person's image and how 'persona' is perceived by others and influenced by 'behaviour'. Being in a small group of strangers we have all established an idea of each other rightly or wrongly, from our interaction with everyone and I think that I must appear aloof and unsociable, as I spend a lot of time on my own. It's not because I prefer my own company, but I can't afford to participate in the extra activities and I don't want the others to know. As I sink into a peaceful zone I listen to the voice within answering my question:

*"The way you view and hold your own mental picture carries the same image to others. Your internal image affects not only your behaviour but the response of those around you, so it is important to create the right movies of yourself in your mind. Remember moods and emotions affect actions- not only yours but those of others. We are all connected to each other in a stronger or weaker network and through this we unconsciously pick up on internal states of mind. Time, relationships, situations and happenings all have a bearing on our growth and development in a forever changing sphere where nothing stays static and it is the way you use your inner energy, your soul light, which determines which cosmic force you align with, whether it be the good force or evil.*

*Your application of your chosen force will define your final outcome when you leave planet earth.*

*Whatever label you choose to determine who you are, nothing can alter your primary essence which has been formed from your actions and mental framework."*

I am grateful for the information and open my eyes. I spy one of the boulders moving slowly across the tiled floor and scramble through my bag to find my glasses. I am shocked to discover that the little boulders are turtles freely roaming around. Now I can see quite clearly their patterned hard-backed shells and their little beady eyes peeping out of their rough, wrinkly faces. I am not relaxed with them wandering around my feet and I make a quick exit back to my room. Convent-like, the room is clean and smells of carbolic soap and the wash basin is pristine, scrubbed with hard labour of quiet Nuns. At last I am not worrying about the filthy state of our accommodation and I smile as the phrase springs to mind-'cleanliness is next to Godliness'. I lie on the bed wondering what to do next as the others are on one of their extra excursions to ride a horse half way up one of the volcanoes and then walk the rest of the way to the top. Physically I am not able to do this with the condition of my knees and hips and financially I cannot afford it. I listen to the sound of the generator in the background and remember reading that the vibrational energy of the constant noise is called 'white noise' and blocks out environmental intrusive sounds. I recall my daughter plugging in the hoover to get her baby to sleep as she said the noise was similar to that of the sounds in the womb and that many hospitals and care homes install 'white noise' machines to help people sleep and to relax them.

I am fascinated by this as everything is vibration and our inner energy sends out signals on a vibrational level. I decide to do a little research on the subject and as there is a small library in the hostel I dare to traverse the turtle trail to find it. I open a large dark oak, carved door with a shiny brass, embossed plate announcing the 'Library', to find a little lady inside dusting the shelves. She is probably a Nun left over from when the building was a Convent and I attempt to speak to her in broken Spanish but she giggles and disappears. The library is heavily gloomy and smells of parchment and incense. The furniture is made of carved dark oak and my mind conjures pictures of sixteenth century conquistadors meeting around the large polished table to discuss further conquests. The books are weightily bound in red and green leather with gold embossed titles and are mainly religious and there is nothing that might remotely shed some light on sound vibration. Just as I am about to leave, a small man enters wearing green corduroy trousers, tweed jacket, with a red scarf tied around his neck and carrying a hand-woven bag over his shoulders. His partly bald head is sunburnt and his straggly grey hair hangs limply around his ears. He squints at me through small thick-rimmed glasses and I greet him in Spanish. He laughs and says, "No need for that, I speak perfectly good English!"

I smile and apologise for my poor accent. He tells me he is from Peru and teaches in a local university.

"What are you doing in here?" he queries as though I shouldn't be there and I explain to him that I am looking for some information on sound vibration. I tell him I would like to learn more about 'white noise' and his attitude changes dramatically towards me as though he has suddenly discovered a long lost friend and asks me to sit down at the table saying; "I haven't much time as I am on my way to give a lecture, but I can tell you a little in layman's terms so that you might get the gist of things."

I can't believe my luck and yet I know when you seek information with a pure heart, the universe responds and that there is no such thing as a chance meeting or coincidence- rather it is divine synchronistic intervention.

"So what is it you would like to know, Miss?" he enquires with a smile.

I tell him I would like to know more about 'white noise'.

"Ahhh, you see, 'white noise' is a vibration released at a constant frequency and never changes. It provides, if you like an unvarying uniform resonance which can be comforting to many people as a background sound to their busy minds and can pacify and calm a troubled soul. It produces a 'shhh' sound like a baby hears in the womb and it can be quite hypnotic."

I am intrigued by the information and thank him for his time but he interrupts with:

"And you know there are other colour vibrations?"

I am amazed and stay glued to his words as he continues:

"Oh yes indeed, indeed there are ...there is a 'brown noise' and a 'pink noise' and a 'brown/pink noise' which has a lower pitch than 'white noise' and has a constant sound like the rise and fall of the sea. 'Brown noise', which is also called 'red noise' produces a rumbling sound akin to that of a tumble drier and is said to improve thinking skills." I am overwhelmed by his knowledge on the subject and find it very difficult to process the information as he fires it out so quickly. I nod trying to understand but he sallies forth on yet more data:- "There is also 'blue/violet noise' which is a hissing sound rather like a water sprinkler spraying the grass, which is sometimes used to help people suffering from tinnitus, as it preoccupies the mind with another sound other than the disturbing one in their head." I nod again, trying to assimilate the information, having got more than I bargained for, but the Universe is bountiful. I don't know his name and interrupt his flow by asking him and he looks at his watch and replies: "Oh my goodness I must fly or I will be late. It's Rodrigo and by the way there is also 'Grey noise' which vibrates up and down making a higher and lower sound. Well goodbye, I hope I have enlightened you somewhat?" I enthusiastically confirm that he has and I express my gratitude as he rushes out of the door leaving me in a whirlwind of unusual facts that I never knew existed.

I rush to my room to record everything before I forget the details. Immersed in all the information, I am surprised to see Caria my young, Italian roommate, rush in and fling herself on the bed crying. Through intermittent tears she explains that the complainers took her horse and she wasn't able to ride up the volcano. They said they had booked the horse first. I try to console her but she is furious and vows never to speak to them again. We are interrupted by Tommy, our guide who asks us to meet in the library for an urgent meeting. Caria dries her tears but does not adjust her petulant expression and we walk into the library with her darting thunderous looks at the complainers. Hunter, a well-mannered German boy, sits patiently and Myrtle and Bill enter smiling a greeting to everyone. Tommy takes centre stage and stands with one hand holding up the fireplace as though this stance enhances his authority and tells us that our journey to Flores, our next place to visit, is very far away and that we can cut down on time and energy by taking a small plane directly to Flores, but it will cost extra. I am not sure whether this is another of his money-making tactics but everyone seems to ok the idea and I remain silent working out in my head how to get the extra money from my bank account. I don't want to upset the flow if everyone wishes to take the plane and Tommy agrees to set the wheels in motion to catch a small craft from an army airfield. As everyone disappears Bill approaches me and asks why I didn't say anything. I shrug my shoulders, embarrassed at my poor financial state. "Myrtle and I know you can't afford it- please take this?" he softly urges. I look down at his handful of notes and I am overcome with gratitude and emotion. I can't stop the sudden flow of tears as he pushes the notes into my hand and I thank him profusely as he smiles and leaves me alone in the library. The meditation on 'self- image' returns and I had not wanted anyone to know about my meagre finances but to Myrtle and Bill it was apparently obvious, as I must have portrayed that image to them. Bill's act of kindness is almost devastating as I am humbled, ashamed and overcome all at the same time. The quiet, secret way in which he approached me was sensitive and kind. I am grateful with all my heart to receive such charity. I compose myself and walk back to my room to prepare for the evening with Caria and Hunter as we have booked a salsa lesson with a local dance teacher who is renowned for his speciality in the Latin genre.

As the three of us step out into the evening, there is a Friday night fiesta feeling rising amongst the locals as they congregate in the streets drinking tequila and laughing. Families are gathering together after their toil and confined routines of the week to celebrate the start of the weekend. Hunter leads the way through the clusters of townsfolk until we reach a small door leading into a tiny room with a large fan noisily sweeping cold air into the sweltering heat of the night. I am nervous and excited, longing to dance but fearful that I might not be able to pick up the steps. Our teacher greets us with a huge grin and Caria blurts out that I am a dancer and that she and Hunter are not! Domingo, our instructor nods and takes a towel from around his well-toned neck and wipes his dark, handsome, oily face. He shakes his long black hair and ties it back with an elastic band. His muscled arms fold circles in the air as he explains the rudiments of the salsa steps. I am relieved to pick up the moves easily and shimmy into the Latin style confidently, while Caria and Hunter peck at the steps with an awkward, embarrassed manner, looking uncomfortable in their young bodies. Domingo spends time with me to teach me more elaborate moves while the two youngsters practice their dance and after an hour of gyrating to the intoxicating syncopated music and sweating profusely in the oven-like heat, we feel we have earnt a drink at the local hot-spot in the town hall. As we saunter into the clammy night air, I am embarrassed that my old tee-shirt and worn blue jeans are damp with perspiration and my stained blue feet are an eye-sore, although when I was dancing in the lesson, nothing mattered only the rhythm and my body moving in sync with the beat.

As we enter the town hall night club, with a Night Fever, disco lighting rig and loud Latin rave music, I feel grossly under dressed. I have never witnessed the passion and almost violent aggression of a cock fight on the dance floor, but as we enter the night world of the Salsa battle it is apparent that combat is seriously underway. Men dressed meticulously in flash suits- 'Grease' style, cavort, whirl, spin, spiral with swivelling legs and ankles pulsing in and out between their partner's legs like cannon fire exploding from a static cannon. The men drive the action riding out like proud stallions, while the women meekly follow to adorn male prowess with colour and elegance. Farther into battle, the men surge forwards vying for the main spot on the dance floor with petulant flicking and clicking of hands and feet. We watch from our crowded vantage point as the grave process draws to a close and the winner bathes in a halo of applause. Tommy our guide joins us as we sit perched on stools at a high table near the bar and we even perform our own little salute to the Salsa cult far away from gazing eyes on the main dance floor. I watch the next round of the Salsa feud from my seat and note all the beautiful women eyeing the peacock men performing their ritualistic courtship moves. The women with their elaborate hair styles and swish cocktail dresses appear like beautiful swans in moonlight and I want to hide in the shadows in my shoddy jeans and damp, limp hair.

A memory floods back to a time when I felt humiliated and humbled in the same way. At six years old, my Grandmother had saved up her meagre pension to take me to De Montfort Hall in Leicester, far away from my tiny country village, to experience an amazing ball because dancing was my passion. It was an annual great occasion with ladies and gentlemen dressed in their finery to dance ballroom dances to a live orchestra under the wonder of magical chandeliers and bright spotlights. From a very young age I danced before I could walk and my Grandfather, who was a wonderful ballroom dancer, used to lead me on the Dance floor when I was three years old, to perform his favourite dance- the Samba. It was natural for me to be lost in the dance and I never thought it unusual to perform in front of the Saturday night village crowd at such a young age. I was not close to my Mother and there was rivalry between her and my Grandmother, who took care of me most of the time, so when my Mother dressed me for the special occasion in an itchy woollen, pink jumper, and old plaid skirt, grey knee socks and old brown shoes, I had no idea how I would appear to others. When I ran to the bus stop to greet my Grandmother, her face darkened as she said," don't you have a pretty dress for the dance?" At that moment I knew she thought my Mother had dressed me shoddily on purpose. I felt I had let her down and disappointed her, but she never expressed her feelings, but I knew she was aware of my Mother's motives. Far away in the fairy tale ballroom I was mesmerized by the glamour and the splendour of the event and when my Grandmother took me on the dance floor to perform, in my mind I was wearing the most beautiful dress like Cinderella at the ball and I didn't allow the poverty of my clothes to cloud the thrill of the moment. In my mind I carried the image of a princess and that was all that mattered.

Now, as a dancer I own the steps and through my training and years of experience I can muster a show of confidence, but when I spy a male peacock strutting towards our table I am filled with fear and panic. Caria laughs, warning me he is coming to ask me to dance, but I want to run and hide and I hang my head so that he won't see me. I feel his body moving towards me and like the other peacocks, who are infiltrating the watching audience to choose new partners to dance, he is confident of a catch. I pray he will walk straight past our table, but no, he is standing in front of me dressed in his spotless white suit and greased back hair holding out his hand towards me. I hesitate, but everyone cheers and I have no choice but to take his hand. I want the floor to swallow me whole. I look a mess in front of all those beautiful people. He leads me right into the centre of the dance floor as though he is the shining warrior dance god, dressed in white gleaming armour. The music begins and I can't move. I feel awkward. One foot does not follow the other gracefully and in my mind I am hopeless. I am sure he is disappointed in my performance and to offend me further he slows down the steps and begins to count the beats out loud. I am so embarrassed and want the whole experience to end. I know if I changed my mind-set and say to myself- "I am a dancer!" I would be able to surprise him and wipe him off the dance floor, but he is so arrogant and controlling, that I can't dance with him. As the music fades I rush back to my seat ashamed of myself but Ciara and everyone claps and I know their applause is just kind sympathy.

In the shadows Domingo has watched my dreadful performance and somehow understands my feelings. He gently takes my hand and smiles leading me out onto the dance floor where he expects me to put everything from my lesson into practice. From within I am suddenly confident. Now with the right partner and the right mind-set I passionately attack the moves with swivelling hips, heaving bosom, agile legs and arms. Together we own the floor and from the corner of my eye I see the white peacock staring in amazement, which spurs me on to throw myself more frenziedly into a Latin spin and we finish in a dramatic pose amidst thunderous applause. Domingo leads me victoriously off the dance floor and he smiles as he has restored the dancer within me and freed my inner soul. Dance partners are like people in a marriage- it takes two to tango. If there is disharmony between the couple, the steps will falter and the dance will fail. If there is harmony the steps will flow and the two will fly in a whirl of ecstasy like a marriage made in heaven.

The next morning as the others are involved in their extra activities I wander through the colourful streets of small terraced houses built on a grid system and I carefully map out my journey noting various shops and unusual signs so as not to get lost again. The sun is pleasantly warm but not high enough to be scorching and I spy a large store with yet more effigies of Maximon displayed in the window and smile remembering the smoking trick. Unlike in Merida where eyes followed me everywhere, here there is a gentle acceptance among the local Indians of foreign visitors and they do not stare or show their disapproval of my solo wanderings through their streets. I am not afraid to walk alone in strange places as perhaps, naively, I believe that everyone has a good, kind heart in the depths of their being and maybe I project this in my self-image. Also I do not flaunt wealth or try to appear superior to the locals, as I believe we are all connected to the flame of creation.

As I wander farther down the main street I hear familiar Northern, English voices chattering noisily. Three English women approach and wave enthusiastically when they see me as though I am a long lost friend. The women surround me and speak quickly with animated tones. I am flabbergasted to learn they are from my hometown- York and they are as equally surprised to learn I also live there. After the first gleeful interchange they relate their horror story. Linda, a large short-haired blonde lady wearing a straw hat and floral dress stands with legs akimbo relating her story; "We've come on a guided tour trip, the three of us together ya see,' an we weren't warned, no one warned us about bandits and the like..."I am shocked at her outburst and listen intently as her friend Susan takes up the tale: " No, no one told us it weren't safe! They never told us ya see not to take us money wi us!" Their outburst is like listening to a group of school children arguing over a playground incident, with everyone talking at once. I sympathise and ask them to explain. They tell me they were out as a small group, walking in the afternoon to go to a bar, when a youth rode up on his motorbike and stopped beside them pointing a gun, demanding their passports and money. They were so shocked and terrified that they immediately gave him everything, fearing for their lives. "I mean it weren't as if it were dark night time or owt- it were in broad daylight!" Susan adds. I am shocked to hear that women from my hometown had been held at gunpoint and their money and passports stolen. They were certain the police had an idea who the culprit was and assured them that their things would be returned. "Look, you're alone; aren't you scared that it might 'appen to you?" enquires Caroline. I smile knowing that I am not afraid to walk alone, as inwardly I am confident that I will be treated well. I laugh and tell them I have a formula which I have rehearsed but luckily have never had to put in practice. "What's that then?" asks Linda, bluntly.

"Well, I never carry much money with me and never dress in a flamboyant manner and if I were to be stopped by a thief I would tell them they are very welcome to have what little money I have, which isn't much, and if they attempt to physically abuse me, I would tell them I was dying of an awful disease and it was my duty to warn them because they would catch it if they touched me."

The women burst out laughing, thinking I am joking but I took some lessons in self- defence from a master Tai Quan Dao teacher and was told that in a sexual attack, if you can stay calm enough to take the assailant by surprise, by urging him on or saying something to distract him, you might gain a few seconds in which to run or kick him. The women think I am crazy and make their excuses to leave to dawdle into the town centre where there is less likelihood of being robbed. I am happy to continue my stroll to explore Antigua alone and to enjoy the sights, sounds and flavours of a land full of colour and surprises carrying with me an inner vision of me as a humble, fearless traveller and lucky not to have been the victim of 'daylight robbery!' or hopefully never will be because I am Lucky!

# IS REALITY REAL? IS 'TIME' A HUMAN CONSTRUCT?

Time to move on and our last day in Antigua promises to be bright and sunny culminating in a celebratory dinner in a restaurant of our choice, to honour our journey so far. We are all looking forward to visiting other amazing places on our extraordinary expedition and still have far to journey across Central America. While the others are occupied shopping, I have chosen to find a café and sit in peace to rest before our next adventure to Flores. I know my way around a few streets and decide to wander a little farther to discover more of the historic town. As I round a corner, the aroma of fresh coffee percolating from locally grown beans, entices me to follow the mesmerising smell to an unusual café tucked inside a high wooden-boarded compound enclosed inside thick wooden gates, which luckily, are ajar. I gently push through into an amazing world of art and culture unusually laid out in the open air. I have never experienced the interior of a house set outside before and I wonder what happens when it rains?

Inside the compound the garden area is prepared with tables and chairs arranged like a small outdoor café with a serving table at the side covered with a white cloth on which an old-fashioned coffee machine and some freshly baked cakes are quaintly exhibited. I don't know why, but I get the impression that the place hasn't changed much since the 1940's and has an air of a French café hiding secrets, safeguarding exploits of a Resistance group. I smile, telling myself my imagination is running wild as I stand in the centre of the yard, gazing at a sitting room decked out in the open air complete with beautiful furnishings. The most dramatic, colourful paintings are displayed everywhere. There are cabinets full of antiques, with book cases brimming with books and beautifully decorated pots and fine statues exposed to the atmosphere. From behind, a voice with a French accent asks :" Can I 'elp you?"

I turn to see a small friendly man smiling, with a greying goatee beard. There is no one else around and I ask him for a coffee whilst profusely praising the art work on display. Immediately he responds beaming with pride and preening his beard, he takes me on a tour of all his paintings. I genuinely love his work and he is so grateful for my compliments. Inside, there is a bedroom but the bathroom and washing facilities are outside. Standing in the moment, viewing all the precious artefacts and gaining visions from his presence, I see in my mind, French soldiers from World War 2 and an impression of undercover clandestine activity. I blink away the images and am brought back to the present as he introduces himself as:- "Peter or Pierre...whichever is your preference?" he adds nonchalantly. He escorts me to a table at the front of the café and brings me an old-fashioned china cup and saucer with wonderful hot coffee brimming over the edge and places a small dish of chocolate-coated coffee beans on the table. The coffee is the best I have tasted on the trip and the chocolate coffee beans have a wonderful soothing, healing effect on my stomach. I ask Pierre about them and he tells me they are very good for 'digestion' and I ask him where I can buy some but he sidesteps the question and raises his arms in the air as though he doesn't know and leaves me to drink my coffee in peace.

The sun is gentle today and I am grateful that my melancholic mood has lifted and I am thankful to the 'Great Ones' for their love and protection. I am happy in the 'now' of being and rejoice that so far I have survived the rigours of the journey and am looking forward to the next part of the expedition. I finish my coffee and offer to pay for it, telling Pierre that I have had a wonderful time and I promise to bring my friends in the evening for our celebratory meal. He wistfully nods refusing my money. I thank him and make my way through the massive wooden gates, surprised that no one else has appeared to sample his great coffee but my mind is distracted with the idea of finding chocolate coffee beans to soothe my stomach as Pierre's had a wonderful healing effect.

Unfortunately, the ones I find are not as tasty and I am a little disappointed that they do not have the same soothing and healing effect on my stomach.

Now in the evening we are preparing to celebrate our final dinner in Antigua and I manage to persuade the group to sample the food at the café where I had the lovely coffee early in the morning. There is a new air of acceptance and excitement among us and I am happy and proud to be able to lead the way to the restaurant. We walk down the same street that I explored in the morning but as we round the corner, things look different. I am a little confused because when we arrive outside the tall wooden gates they are locked and barred as though the place has been abandoned for a long time. The wooden slats are enmeshed in a lush overgrowth with a tapestry of jungle plants growing out of cracks in the wooden casing. Old menus are visible hanging precariously from timeworn wooden planks and a large decayed painting depicting fine dining is a sad sign of what used to be. The gates are locked with a thick rusty iron padlock and there is no sign of life inside. I furiously rattle the gate in a frenzy of disbelief and Bill sidles a look at Myrtle whispering:

"Come on dear, let's find somewhere else?"

"But it was open this morning, honestly, I was here, I know it was here...!" I scream pitifully.

The others look at me in dismay and turn away embarrassed by the situation. I stand alone for a few moments outside the padlocked gate, utterly devastated by the reality of the dilapidated building. I know it wasn't like this earlier and I know what I experienced this morning. I know it was real and yet when I look back things don't add up. Why was everything that should have been inside, outside?

Why did I get the feeling I was in a 1940's movie? Why was a I given healing beans? Was Pierre real or was he an illusion from the past? I have experienced walking into different time zones before but this was so real- but then I question 'what is real?' Are our life events really real or an illusion? Do we exist in a holographic universe? I am sad, sorry and bewildered not knowing how to explain to everyone what happened. I am feebly quiet as I follow behind Bill who finds an amazing restaurant and I am grateful he has saved the day-yet again! Soon everyone forgets my blunder and revels in the wonderful food and wine, while I try to forget the incident, but somehow I can't shake off the mystery and I don't think I ever will! I question whether the experience actually happened.

Scientists explain that to claim something as 'real' it must possess a set of properties which remain constant, even when no one is looking. It must be immovable and unchangeable in its own element.

I know it wasn't a dream and dreams are not real because they can change in substance and do not remain, usually, constant. It was not a vision as visions can represent a reality but can also change and do not remain constant; so was it a slip through time, a blip in the holographic game? Did I step into a time gone by where the topsy-turvy world of the inside of the place being outside, should have given me a clue that I was not in my own timeline? I can't shake off the enigma and decide to question the restaurant manager about the café. I catch him in a quiet moment when everyone is eating and ask him about the old, locked up building and he looks at me quizzically shaking his head, saying; "I do not know Madam, it was closed down before my time and has never been occupied since I can remember." He moves away busy with drink orders and an elderly chef creeps into the bar to eye the customers enjoying his cuisine. I take my chance to ask him about the strange café and he shrugs and smiles saying his Grandfather knew the owner a long, long time ago who was a French artist and a painter who had fled from France during the war. He said-" There were stories about the Frenchy and his gay partner who were involved in hiding resistance fighters but who knows, who cares…it was a long time ago. Excuse me…"

I sigh and return to the table to eat the delicious feast, feeling content that at least the history of the place fits in with my experience.

The night has been a success and we all retire early as we have a 3am start to catch a plane. I am tired but I can't sleep as I need answers! I close my eyes and drift into a zone where I normally take off on a remote-viewing escapade, but this time I allow a story to unfold, rather like watching a film with a running commentary accompanied by a whispering voice saying:-

"You entered the café through a portal. Just as you rounded the corner you stepped into a vibration pulsing from another era. It sometimes occurs when inner energy coincides with an outer energy vibrating on the same frequency that the two merge."

I watch as the film plays and I see myself step into a watery, shimmering veil, as though I am pulled through a glass doorway. I watch as I enter the café, which is set inside the building, not outside as I previously experienced. I ask the voice why I encountered the scene outside rather than inside and the voice replies:

" That should have been your clue to be aware that you had left your own time zone. Sometimes when you walk into the past, your energy is not strong enough to recreate the whole picture and some of the scene gets left out or appears a little different to the 'then' reality."

I understand and observe as I meet Pierre and ask the voice why he was not shocked to see me and the voice replies:

" Pierre and his partner were and are very special beings with the power to harness energy to help people. Many refugees at that time passed through their portal to safety from a war-torn country and when you entered the portal by chance, Pierre recognised you were from the future and gave you special healing beans for your stomach."

The film fades and I am content to understand what happened. I have stepped into the past before and believe all the possibilities the universe provides- it's just a little difficult at times to accept, especially when it happens unexpectedly.

An early start at 3am to catch the plane to Flores cajoles us into action as we board the bus to the Army airfield where we wait sleepily for the small craft to be loaded. On board we are given hard boiled sweets to help alleviate the pressure in our ears upon take-off. The short flight is pleasant and allows us to cat-nap to catch up on lost sleep. I close my eyes and allow my mind to drift to the concept of 'time'. Ever since I was a small child and able to travel out of my body at will, I have known that beyond earth, time does not exist. From the moment of our birth we enter a prison of habitual ritual obeying the clock which dictates when we eat, when we rise, when we sleep, when we work and when we play. We dance to the rhythm of the tick- tock stop watch, as the ring master whips the round of ever-lasting routine into shape, turning day into night in the diurnal cycle of existence. Counting sheep, counting days, wishing away nights to reach important dates with landmark birthdays, fritters away a life time expectancy. Earth time beats us into submission as we enter our allotted life span where the time of our first breath is recorded as is our last. Birth to death is time bound on earth but not beyond. I recall Einstein's take on 'time' stating that:

'the distinction between past, present and future is only a stubbornly persistent illusion'.

The illusory tentacles of time hold us in a fixed mode but on understanding this, it is possible to bend time. I have been able to achieve this only in situations of dire necessity and I find slowing down time easier than speeding it up. Bending time requires great power like potent electricity from the heart, and the force of love is the most powerful of all energies. When my daughter was very young and I was in the middle of a difficult divorce she was very upset by the upheaval. Friends were good and tried to help and one Saturday afternoon she was taken to the cinema with her little friend and I agreed to collect her at 7pm. I lived twenty two miles away from town and it usually took about half an hour to get into the centre, depending on the traffic. I was at home with my son when I realised the time was 6.55 and there was no way I could make it into town on time. I was frantic not to be late for her, so I quickly entered a trance state, watched by my son who knew what I was doing, and took myself out from earth's sphere to a deep black hole where everything is vibration. Tiny tentacles like pieces of string, hover in the atmosphere connecting everything like microscopic energy formed in fibre optic light. The now prevalent String Theory depicts the Universe as a cosmic symphony of strings vibrating from earth and echoing across celestial space to multiverses beyond.

These microscopic organs reach out from the earth's atmosphere and it is possible to vibrate energy into a floating antennae to slow down the force of time. It is like sitting on a tightrope and bending it in the middle! Keeping this energy flowing I raced to my car and drove rapidly along country lanes and out onto the motorway heading into the centre of town and parked the car. Miraculously, I arrived punctually at 7pm to see my little one come out of the cinema beaming with her little friend.

I was so relieved to get there on time and although this concept is hard to believe it is understood by eminent scientists and people who have access to classified information. Many people believe that time only moves in one direction –forwards and cannot be reclaimed, but from my own experience this is not so. I have been unwittingly thrown back in time and have proof together with a witness, but now there is no time to recall this as we are landing and our new adventure begins.

Flores is a magical, tropical island in Guatemala's northern Peten region on Lake Peten Itza and is known as the gateway to famous Mayan temples and ruins. From the air strip we travel by bus to a lovely place, which is the first proper hotel we have so far experienced on our journey and it is a joy not to be staying in another hostel. My little Italian friend is again my room-mate and we have a lovely view from our room overlooking the skyline of the town. The strange tall, round buildings with thatched roofs highlight the skyline in a mosaic of electric blues, reds and yellows and are unlike anything I have ever seen. The straw roofs are medieval and I can imagine a Shakespearean cast acting the prologue to 'Two Gentlemen of Verona' in the street below.

The hotel has a lovely pool and our group naturally gravitate there to relax. We even order drinks like normal tourists, instead of making haste to catch another bus struggling with our luggage and battling through crowds. Here by the pool the weight and stress of the journey slides into oblivion as I watch people unwind ordering lunch and smiling. I have left my tawdry blue sandals in my room, allowing my feet to air. I hadn't realized how swollen they are underneath the awful blue dye. I sit by the cooling pool and massage them, feeling peacefully at ease and beginning to feel 'me' again, not having to supress my anxiety about so many trivial things, allowing my inner confidence to trickle back with a little self-praise, even congratulating myself for not having fallen to pieces under the duress of the journey's demands. Here in our holiday mode, time has a different perspective, for there is no pressure to be on time to travel from one place to another, meeting schedules and racing against the clock. The only time allotted slot is to meet for dinner this evening to eat at a lovely restaurant. Lying on a towel in the shade I allow thoughts to drift into a safe, comforting zone, sailing back to a time when I choreographed a solo dance for my M.A. degree entitled-' I, ME, MYSELF' where I addressed the three different aspects of the 'self' and composed music to accompany my ideas. Modes of addressing the 'self' are unique parts of the whole, like the facets of a diamond and it is so wonderful, awesome, terrifying and yet comforting to know that each 'self' and every aspect of the 'self' are totally exclusive to each person. I hear a voice whisper on the gentle vibration drifting from the lake below in the rising heat, in the deepening stillness and quiet of the noonday sun, I listen to the words drifting into my consciousness:

*"The concept of 'I' is the strongest expression of the 'self' and is a reflection of the Great "I AM" of ALL BEING, so be careful when you express negative feelings stating- I am unhappy; I am angry; I am sad, because you are deflecting the true essence of the light that surrounds you in pure love to a destructive dimming. When you state –I am happy; I am contented; I am grateful, your vital energy blends with your true nature and you feel whole and in harmony with the Universe."*

"Yes, thank you but what if I'm not happy or feeling sad or feeling angry, how do I express myself?" I query. A soft tinkling laugh responds and the voice replies:

*"Of course you are allowed these emotions, indeed you are human and have a whole gamut of feelings which you vent, but if you are experiencing negative reactions to situations, there is always a way to turn things around but it takes practice and a deep understanding of the law of 'giving' to put it into action."*

I listen to the words and try to understand the meaning of the message and ask- "What about the 'me' aspect of a personality?"

There is a pause as I have to move farther into the shelter as the rising heat of the day intensifies and with it comes a silence, a sleep time, a too hot to move time and I open my eyes to see most of the group are asleep under shady umbrellas or have retired indoors. I smile thinking -'I am happy in this moment' and close my eyes to resume my whisperer's teaching:

*"The 'ME' of the self is a selfish mode. It is learnt first as an expression of the self as a baby who demands...'me, me, me...! 'and it is only until later as a toddler the term 'I' comes into use."*

I nod to my invisible teacher understanding the lesson and eagerly listen to her final words-*"Now you want to understand the term 'MYSELF' which is not used so commonly as the other expressions, as it usually refers to the 'self' removed from immediate action. So when a person says, "as for myself..." it is a way of not taking direct ownership or responsibility for something, but rather deflecting the issue. But please tell me why you are being so philosophical on such a hot day?"*

I smile as tears flow. "I don't know?" I reply whispering the words. The voice is silent while I gather my thoughts.

"Maybe it's because in this moment I have stopped struggling and fighting with myself. I know all these aspects of me are inside of me but what happens to all those facets when we leave the earth?" I silently question. The voice sweetly and calmly replies:

*"All is one as one should be and is and forever will be. There are no distinctions beyond."*

Silence folds as the heat increases and rivulets of sweat roll down my back and forehead. The voice disappears and the air is almost too hot to breathe, not even in the heat of the Monsoon in India did I ever experience the scorching air burning my nostrils and the back of my throat- no wonder everyone takes refuge indoors until the torrid heat of the day subsides. Indoors the air is cooler and there is only a skeleton staff on duty and I look at the notice board stacked full of tours advertising visits to the nearby famous pyramids and temples. I am excited for our excursion tomorrow to visit Tikal, which, it is claimed to be the most 'Spiritually empowered place on earth' and interestingly is featured in the 1977 Star Wars episode-A new Hope. Tikal is located deep in the Guatemalan rainforest and it is important to have a local experienced guide when travelling there. Our new adventure begins late in the evening tomorrow and we are to climb the highest Temple in the jungle to witness the dawn creeping over the forest. I know it will be an amazing experience to remember for the rest of my life.

The heat subsides and I take a walk through the small town spying a lovely little clothes boutique at the end of a row of white painted shops. In the window along with many other lovely items is a pair of cheap white cotton trousers, so I decide it is time to treat myself and wear something nice for the evening. I am disappointed that they don't have my size but the lady states that her sister can make me a pair within half an hour! I am pleased with myself for finding the shop and am lured towards the lake to wait, making tracks through a thoroughfare of small houses. The water is so blue, so turquoise, so azure with all shades melding into one glorious lagoon under a powder blue, cloudless sky. The blueness is overwhelming and the colour vibration peacefully work its magic on me with its calming influence. The colour blue can soothe troubled souls and is often used in prisons, mental hospitals, swimming pools and surgeries as it has a positive effect on both mind and body, especially as it tranquilises the nervous system.

In between the houses there isn't much shade and I am relieved to reach the water's edge where a few wind-worn trees provide a little shelter. The heat is still intense but not so scorching and from the lakeside, movement from humble dwellings stir. A small band of fishermen are gathering and untangling their black thick nets and throwing them into two small boats ready for the evening's fishing. My legs are tired and my eyelids are heavy. I stretch out under the ancient branches resting on a convenient rock that has stood the rigours of time, allowing the blue vibration like a stringed lullaby, to rock me to sleep. Into the blueness I dive in my mind, whirling and swirling in an hypnotic symphony of aquamarine bubbles sinking down and down into darker water and now I can't see above or below me. Dropping aimlessly into the blackness I stop breathing. Now I am floating in nothingness. Is this like the stillness of death? Is this the calm portal to another world of existence? I relax and accept my fate. I am not afraid. Suddenly I am encapsulated in a large rubbery, shiny bubble like a space helmet and begin to breathe as silver hands pull me down, guiding me beyond the confines of the lake. Down through the darkness I am propelled and although I can't see my helpers I feel their friendly presence.

I am entering a black tunnel and in the distance I spy a spark of white light growing larger as I sail forwards propelled by an invisible force. Closer to the light, I can see around me in the clearer water three beautiful beings carrying me through the watery glade who nod, smiling to reassure me that all is well. I stare at the creatures, these water spirits, the Mer people who have the same shaped bodies as humans but they are covered from head to toe in sea world patterns, the most glorious I have ever seen. The closest to these creatures I have witnessed on earth is the beautiful lycra, full bodied costumes of Cirque de Soleil performers, whose creators must have been divinely inspired. These mer- bodies are hairless and their heads are smooth and shiny, glossed in shell patterns and floral sea anemone configurations. The two masculine beings are bigger with muscled limbs rippling in the water like sea eels. The feminine creature is so fluid and graceful like a willowy ballerina with lighter designs on her face similar to a collection of smooth shells intertwined with delicate fronds of seaweed. The three gliding through the swirling water are beautifully camouflaged against the interchanging blues of the eddying flow.

The journey is quickly over and my feet rest on a sandy platform inside a large magical cave where crystal stalactites and stalagmites glisten. A gentle symphony of gurgling, dripping and whooshing of the sea against the rocks echo a briny melody. An old man/sea-creature sits on a boulder. His body is bent like an old man and his skin is a shiny, blue/grey colour. I watch him arch his spiny back and suddenly morph into a lithe dolphin, disappearing into the pool inside the cave. The three who escorted me sit on rocks and motion me to do the same. Exquisite Mer children gather round exuding a high pitched trill vibration like the joyful laughter of young ones. Suddenly all is still. Heads turn to the centre pool where below an explosion of water boils to the surface as it rises, spurting a fountain of blue sea water over the congregation. Through the bubbling cascade a figure appears. She is Aphrodite, stunningly magnificent and regal- yet she is Medusa with curling, coiling sea snakes in her hair; she is also Neptune, ruler of the sea as she turns the other side of her body towards us. The King/Queen is all. For a few moments she/he rises above us in a glistening cloak of vapour dripping salty droplets on the crowd. Each salty drop tingles as it touches my skin, sending quivering shocks through my body. Everyone responds to the Presence humming harmoniously like a Bach choral hymn, creating a celestial unearthly frequency which rises and rises to an incredible pitch as the deity descends back into the deep sea below.

In the damp air for a few moments, no one stirs and as the last bubble beneath the waves disperses, communal mind chatter breaks free. Deja vue images curl in my mind as I know the Mer people from the past from somewhere locked in my memory. They exude a wholesome feeling, unlike anything on earth. A female adult telepathically says: "We are glad you have joined us. You come from our people...do you not know?" she says with a beautiful soft voice. I shake my head in disbelief replying, "I come from the Moon, my people are there."

"Yes, that is so, but there are Mer people on the moon, in fact the first microbes from the moon came here to create our Mer people and we are descended from them. When the primary Mer people were created, some explored life on the surface of earth and developed legs and stayed on top never to return. Your essence and being is Mer, believe me?" she states soothingly. "But I am not a swimmer and I don't like to put my head under water and I am afraid of the sea, although I love to look at it!" I blurt out defensively. She laughs and a golden echo bounces off the rocks as she holds my face in her long, slithery hands stating; " remember when you were little? What food did you crave? What did you love to eat and couldn't get enough of?" I listen to her words and try to remember but I am silent. "You loved all food from the sea. You loved sea snails and whelks and crabs and prawns and cockles and oysters and all fish. Do you remember?" I smile. I do remember and it is the food I still crave. I must have seafood to survive and love sushi and all manner of raw fish. I love seaweed and anything remotely fishy but I never connected this with my origins from the Mer people and I am not sure whether I am comfortable with the idea. She understands and smiles as her face slowly fades in a watery veil drifting farther and farther away until I wake to a soft gentle breeze wafting over my nose and rustling my hair.

I slowly stand trying to assimilate my dream. My mouth is dry with a salty coating and I need water to soothe my throat. The dream seemed so real and I find it hard to accept the message pertaining to my origins. They told me that there are Mer people living in deep chasms below earth all over the planet and that one day everyone will know and accept their existence. I walk slowly back to the shop to collect my trousers in a daze, trying to understand why I was given the vision, pondering the purpose of the information. I force myself to be in the reality of the moment as the shop keeper is delighted to see me and warmly greets me holding out my package. The trousers are beautifully made and I am thrilled knowing they have been made just for me. I am so lucky in the moment to be grateful for all I have, for all I know, for all that I am and for the lingering taste of a strange seaweed in my mouth. Yes, I am indeed Lucky.

# BREATH OF THE SEA

Another morning dawns offering fresh experiences in a different time zone, amidst a magical paradise of colour and lush, tropical vegetation. The day ahead will be spent in nervous anticipation of a midnight trek through the rainforest to climb the highest temple in Tikal to witness the sunrise over the jungle. Now in the early morning, the hotel is quiet and as I am not hungry, the meagre breakfast is adequate. With a slice of toast, I wander outside by the pool to collect my thoughts.

Here in Flores time feels different- maybe it's because we have stopped travelling for a while and are resting before our major adventure this evening. Also this place marks an ending of half of our journey, affording us a brief pause to reflect on what has been and what is yet to come. I sit down to admire the view of the lake pondering what 'endings' and 'beginnings' really mean. Einstein said there is no such thing as beginnings or endings as time is an illusion and past, present and future run simultaneously folding into each other and that it is only humans who differentiate between life's phases.

I close my eyes to contact my whisperers to connect with their wisdom and a gentle voice in my head responds to my questions saying:

*"An 'ending' of any kind is not just stopping- it takes a firm letting go, in order for the expiry to reach its true conclusion. Riding out the exit is not easy on any level as life is a series of chapters and how you fade in and out of each stage becomes the challenge of your personal journey. Every chapter of your evolvement is like a phrase in music or choreography and each must be allowed to rise and fall naturally and to peak and decline in its own unique way. Sometimes in life you reach a*

*plateau where you either remain where you are, or risk jumping over the cliff to pursue another terrain. All action has a consequence and every thought an effect, so do not expect to pass through a phase without repercussions, albeit good or bad. From birth to death your life takes you through many doors and as you pass through each one , they will close behind you, never to be opened again.*

*Each room you enter has its own matchless emotional, purpose, flavour and colour until finally, you settle into the last chamber, your last chapter, which for everyone is different and created to meet your unique cosmic destiny."*

I open my eyes as the voice fades feeling the truth of the words, accepting the universal, celestial meaning of the message, understanding a little of how destiny leads us from one junction to another as life unfolds in a complex tapestry accompanied by the music of the universe. I am reminded of Stravinsky's adage –"music creates a common order between man and time," and I am so grateful my life is, has been and will continue to be influenced by the life-force of music. I remember an occasion in my music lesson, when I was fifteen years old, listening for the first time to Vaughn Williams 'Fantasia on a Theme by Thomas Tallis', where immediately the atmospheric first few bars detached my mind from the classroom, propelling me into a deep emotional medieval tone poem, to witness the rustling wind through quivering grasses whilst gazing up into the high walls of a castle. The music transported me into the past and shot me forwards into the future at the same time. From the past the castle unveiled a heart-rendering love story and in the future amidst the dilapidated ruins of the castle walls, I saw myself standing alone. I will never forget that experience.

Years later I stood alone on the same spot, gazing up at the castle ruins which I envisioned in my music lesson, amidst the quivering grasses by the moat in the grounds of Sherriff Hutton Castle, where I lived for a short while. The scene was exactly the same as I had witnessed in the classroom all those years previously, with the glory and dark secrets of the fortress hidden in the music. In reality, 'time' does not shoot in straight lines; its true essence outside of earth's boundaries is liquid, fluid and transmutable.

The sun is already quite high promising another scorching day and I plan to relax for most of the time in preparation for the night's trek ahead. I have no idea what awaits us or the dangers involved in such a daring mission. I am afraid of jungle creepy crawlies, especially in the black void of night and I secretly question my physical ability to climb a high temple with my worn out knee, which I am beginning to suspect is my disintegrating hip after years of dancing, leaping and jumping. Also I am scared of jungle animals which might be lurking in the undergrowth and bushes. The group have been warned to cover up as there is a possibility of leeches attaching themselves to our exposed skin as we push our way through tropical vegetation. The thought of a leech sticking to my body terrifies me and I intend to make doubly sure to cover up .Also the deadly, Malaria carrying mosquitoes will be in force in the humid jungle at night and so we have been advised to use jungle-strength anti-mosquito cream. Airing my fears to myself, is helpful and I am convinced I will be fine, trusting to the temple guide to safely lead us on our challenging quest. As some of the others gather by the pool, I take comfort in the fact that they seem very relaxed and confident about our expedition and I think that if the old, retired complainers can do it-then so can I!

Most of the group spend the day resting in preparation for our night trek and the hours soon slide by and it doesn't seem long before we are gathered together just after midnight to silently tramp over the uneven cobble-stone streets to board our mini bus. Just as we are about to climb aboard, our guide realizes he has forgotten to ask us all to bring a torch. I have never had much faith in him, proving incompetent on many counts, so to neglect informing us about the torches is unforgivable. I am relieved a professional guide has been employed to lead us through the jungle. It is despicable that between seven of us there are only two torches. Hunter has one and Tommy, our incompetent guide has the other! Our ride from Flores to Tikal is quite short and as we turn off the main road and enter the rainforest scrubland my stomach churns with fear and anxious anticipation of what lies ahead.

Through rickety overgrown paths we arrive at the warden's hut. As soon as I step from the bus into the dense blackness, the deafening jungle cacophony blasts the air with unfamiliar squawks, howls, screeching and continuous mumming and buzzing from hidden insects lurking in the bushes. It is terrifying! I don't know why I expected the jungle to be quiet, but I am shocked by the din. However, I am pleased to meet our new guide, a jungle warden who is very tall, wearing military gear and appears a fit, jungle-wise guide. He introduces himself as Carlos and assures us of a magical adventure. He is a little concerned that we don't have torches and asks us to stick close to him.

Something screeches past me in the blackness, howling viciously. I feel its breath on my face and I scream. Carlos laughs and says it's only a 'howler monkey' and that they are not vicious, but they make the most terrifying yowling which echoes throughout the jungle.

The incident is unnerving and I cling onto the end of Hunter's jacket as we begin our terrifying trek.

Poor Hunter doesn't complain and like a small child, scared in a big kid's playground, I stay close to his side as he has a torch to light the uneven ground. I pull my hood up tightly around my head to keep out the leeches and in no time I am sweltering under my gear in the intense humidity. I try not to imagine snakes, spiders and the prowling jungle predators scrutinising us as we tramp through their territory. Rising panic creeps through my feet, into my lungs and feverishly pounds my head. I can't breathe! I can't even see my hands in front of me as the blackness is total. My heart pounds so hard I fear it will jump out of my chest. My mouth is dry. I am deliriously thirsty. My legs are trembling. I am crying inwardly as fear takes hold. I don't think I can go on? It is hard to breathe.

Another howler monkey screeches. I pull my arms away from the bushes, feeling the monkey's presence close to my head. My legs fold at the knees and my feet are heavy. Terror unlike any other dread swallows me whole. I am a gibbering wreck within. My teeth chatter involuntary as I desperately cling to poor Hunter, who is patient and kind helping me to stride on. The desperate darkness hurls my mind to a time of abuse in a Catholic school as a frightened first year and a victim to pain from an evil teacher and I fight the scene with all my heart to place my hurt into the hands of the Universe. I want to forget. I need to forget. I can't see the night sky. I can't see any stars. Only blackness engulfs us all and I surrender to the nothingness and plod on relentlessly until we finally reach the base of Temple 1V. Hunter is relieved to be free of his burden and I thank him profusely for his help, but my next fear stands in front of me and I am alarmed at the horrendous immediate trial.

I am stunned as I had not expected to climb two hundred and thirty feet up a rickety ladder with only one hand rail on the right side without any safety holds on the left, leaving a gaping gap into the night air. Perhaps I should have done my research more thoroughly to discover how dangerous this mission is but now it is too late and I have no choice but to follow up the narrow stairway to heaven!

I tell myself to focus on the person's legs in front climbing one step at a time and not to look to my left. I refuse to acknowledge the shooting pain in my knees and will myself upwards. As I climb, I mentally recall the information from Wikipedia written about Temple 1V to keep my mind occupied, remembering that the pyramid was built around 741 AD. and was created to celebrate the reign of the twenty seventh King of the Tikal dynasty. It has seven stepped levels-I wonder how many levels I have climbed so far? My legs ache and my breath is becoming short and tight as my asthmatic lungs fight the challenge. I cannot stop as the people behind are willing me on.

Now the night sky has stars and the blackness has faded into a navy- blue blanket studded with silver jewels. Higher and higher we climb and I have a sudden urge to spread my arms like an eagle and fly into the open air, but I quickly bury the idea and concentrate on reaching the top. Suddenly the climbing stops and I face another horror. The ladder ends! A terrifying climb up crumbling rock with no safety rails to reach the final ledge is required. My tiny legs can't stretch that far and I don't know how I can haul myself up. I pause, feeling this might be my last leap of faith and attempt to hurl myself up the ancient rock face. I manage to reach up the ledge to grasp the grainy texture of the stone with my sweaty palms and scramble my legs behind me. Abruptly from below, hands push my bum sharply so that I am propelled upwards and land on my chest, face down on the upper strata. I quickly scramble to my feet, gratefully thanking Carlos our professional guide for his prompt action. He laughs saying 'it has become my speciality!'

At the very top I am surprised to find a flock of people of differing ages from many countries, waiting patiently in the sacred hours before dawn. I expected our group to be the only party to experience the magic of dawn from the top of the highest temple, instead we are sharing it with a congregation of strangers. Amongst so many, attending this special, sacred moment there is a strange quiet, like worshippers in silent prayer. It seems everyone is anticipating a miraculous dawn with some kind of spiritual awakening. A few are sitting cross-legged with eyes closed holding candles lost in deep contemplation; some are silently watching and waiting and others are having a picnic like the sharing of the fishes and loaves with Jesus near the sea of Galilee. Individually, we are all expecting a kind of holy encounter. I nudge past a small gathering to perch on a convenient boulder which is terrifyingly near the edge, but also awesome in its magnetic pull towards the deep chasm below. I fight the urge to stand precariously on the ledge, wondering how many people have succumbed to the taunting dare of flying into the night sky and perhaps how many human sacrifices have been ritually slaughtered from the top of this temple? The thought is too horrific to entertain, so I concentrate on soaking up the hallowed ambiance. It's difficult as I am hungry and very thirsty and I blame Tommy again for his ineptitude to organise the trip. I tell myself I am very lucky to be here in the serene uncertainty of a unique event.

Waiting! Waiting! Watching! Watching! Feeling drowsy and bum-numbingly achy on top of the world in a dream-like haze with more waiting; more watching; fighting sleep, until suddenly here it is. We all rise to welcome the magic of the moment as the first streaks of light flash across the tree-tops. It is not as I expected. It is not white, or golden or pink but electric blue! An electric blue beam sweeps across a deep green ocean and with it comes the breath of the sea. A strange sigh echoes through the trees breathing life into the planet. It breathes in for the count of four and exhales accordingly creating the rising and falling sound of gentle waves rolling on a ribbed seashore. The breath of the sea will never leave me, for in this moment the earth and sea are vibrating as one elemental force creating life itself in one fell swoop of deliberation. Time was then when the pyramid was built as it is now, nothing has changed. The day dawns, the night closes in, then the day dawns and the night follows. Breathe in/ breathe out- the universal breath of the sea sustains all. The life cycle wakes each day to transform the world and in a dying breath fades at night where we sleep to wake on a new beginning and in this fresh day we arise and are lead into the next phase of life. All birth brings death-all death breathes life and so the breath of the sea never ceases, never changes and forever will be.

After the magic of the moment, the bright blue beam fades into a grey mist folding over the forest and I turn around to see clearly in the new daylight everyone's faces. It is back to stark reality again and the magical reverence dissolves as the fatigued crowd disperses like a tired cinema audience after a late night show. Our group waits patiently to descend the terrifying ladder and across from our temple is another pyramid not quite as high as ours, where a group of people have also spent the night waiting for the dawn. I spy a little agile man in a red bobble hat jumping across boulders like a young spring goat with circus antics so bold and daringly performed on the top of the temple. His courageous feats amuse his group who clap and cheer at his clowning tricks. Now I must muster my courage to tackle the descent.

The first unaided step down isn't as bad as going up and I am helped by Carlos to get my footing onto the first rung of the rickety ladder. Being able to see where I am placing my feet helps the descent go by quickly and soon we are all safely back on the ground after our fantastic adventure.

Just around the corner is a vendor selling snacks and drinks in a clearing and I spy the little agile man with the red bobble hat laughing with some of his group. I gather that he is their guide and his handsome, winning smile is infectious as peals of laughter ring out through the bushes. I stand with Myrtle and Bill enjoying a well-deserved cold drink and I am happy to tuck into a packet of dry biscuits. Overhead colourful parakeets fly squawking through the trees and I am keen to snap a photograph to show my children. Hopping ungainly through the bushes with my camera angled up towards the trees, I attempt to capture them in flight but suddenly my camera is snatched from my hands and I stand aghast at the little man with the red bobble hat running through the jungle following the birds snapping shots of them with my camera. I am offended and angry that he has dared to snatch it and I run after him and snatch it back, but his smile is so winsome and mischievous that my anger dissolves and I find myself attracted to him, especially when he introduces himself as 'Alvaro-tour guide and taxi service' and grins teasingly. He tells me of strange caverns beneath the temples which intrigues me and as we walk back to my group I hear myself accepting his invitation to explore the underground caves.

Myrtle and Bill are not happy about the little man and caution me not to go with him, but my naïve belief in his credibility overrides their warning; besides I am curious about the caves and perhaps a little flattered by his attention. With firm assurance that I won't be long, I saunter by his side and we talk freely about the beauty of nature and the mysteries of the pyramids. Through a rough clearing he finds a small patch of grass and motions me to sit down where he hands me a chunk of delicious chocolate explaining how it was first discovered by a group of nuns who used its miraculous properties as a healing agent. Also the 'real' cacao is used in meat casseroles for a special dish prepared for the ritual celebration of the Day of the Dead. The information is fascinating but I point out to him that I don't have much time, so he takes my arm and escorts me to a temple where I spy a small strange entrance leading to a dark ominous tunnel where he leads me inside. I am suddenly fearful as his hands pull me towards him in a forceful embrace. I wrench away and he is surprised at my response as I stupidly realise he wants more than to guide me to secret passages, especially when he demands a 'pubic hair'! I am shocked and defiantly shove him away in disgust and run as fast as I can like a silly school girl back to Bill and Myrtle. They are sympathetic but not shocked by the guide's behaviour and gently remind me that they did warn me. I feel stupid, gullible and deeply regret my rash, reckless conduct. I suppose I was flattered by his attention and inquisitive about the underground caves and was foolish enough to be duped by him. Bill explains that in the region there is 'black magic practice' and the taking of hair, nails or body sample is often used in rituals to enslave a person. I shudder to think what might have happened and desperately try to obliterate the encounter as we slowly make our way through the jungle to our transport to return to the hotel.

Back at the hotel everyone retires to bed for the day to recoup after our night's adventure and to prepare for our next long journey to Xunantunich Archaeological Reserve on our way to Belize.

Somehow, even though my encounter with Alvaro was irresponsible and shocking, I have gained some inner strength from the incident feeling that perhaps I might still be attractive and not yet on the dung heap of has- beens! The trek into the jungle at the dead of night has made me face some of my innermost terrors and the fact that I accomplished the mission has given me confidence to face other fears. I decide after resting to wash my hair and wear a skirt and put on some make-up which the others notice as I join the group for our last dinner at the hotel. Some make complimentary comments and others smile and I am pleased I made the effort to reveal another aspect of myself.

Before I sleep I dive back into the memory of the dawn striking across the jungle and recall the 'breath of the sea' gently breathing with the rhythm and I realize that after about four times repeating the breathing exercise I float into a deeper alpha state of consciousness feeling my body totally relax. I have been given a gift from the Universe to share and vow to use this technique as a meditation skill to help people achieve a deeper level of contemplation.

In the morning everyone is packed and ready to tackle our next bus ride to Xunantunich Archaeological Reserve. The drive is long leading us up and down and around mountains and forests, through small villages and farmland where we occasionally catch glimpses of the Mopan river which we will cross by a primitive ferry to visit the reserve. When we finally reach our first destination I am surprised to find armed guards by the simple ferry, which is basically a block of wood attached to a rope which is pulled across the brown, muddy Mopan river. Large iguanas scuttle through the long grass and one dares to stop and stare at us as we board the make-shift ferry. The site is a little disappointing as the temples are not as high or impressive as the others and after a couple of hours loitering and eating our packed lunches we are ready to make our way to the border control into Beliize. The heat of the day is making us all sleepy and as we drive through more scrubland jungle, many of us take the opportunity to nap.

When we arrive at the border control a gentle welcoming breeze blows through the black corrugated iron tunnel and I am grateful to breathe in the cool shade. As I hand my passport to the officer he smiles and gives me a wonderful compliment-"Eden, like the garden, you are beautiful!" I blush bright red and don't know how to react. I can only think that I am wearing my new confidence with conviction and smile shyly. It proves that if we project assurance from within with positive energy, then others will respond accordingly. I take my passport and enter the new world in extreme bright sunlight as though I have stepped into centre stage under the spotlight and as my eyes adjust to the dazzling glare, I am shocked to see Alvaro standing by his taxi wearing a different uniform and looking serious. I smile a brief greeting and he purposefully walks over to me explaining he had gone to the hotel to apologise for his behaviour and that he had waited for over an hour to see me, but I had gone to dinner with the party. He asks me where I am staying in Belize but in all truthfulness I do not know and he shrugs his shoulders and slumps away like a disheartened school boy. I don't know why my heart flutters. I tell myself I am stupid to feel this way, after all I am sure he is a con-man, so I follow the others into the waiting bus and quietly sit pondering our unexpected meeting.

As we drive through this new zone I am amazed at how different Belize appears after long haul travelling through Guatemala. People look totally different and even walk with a free, more zingy gait and although many live in dire poverty, they seem to override their difficulties with a grin and a 'happy-go-lucky' attitude, even amidst the heavy presence of armed soldiers. Flavours from many different cultures mingle and it is apparent, as we meander through the market on our way to our next billet, that the merging of Mayan, Mestizo, African, European and Asian cultures can live peacefully side by side and thrive on meagre supplies during hard times. The farm produce in the market is generally substandard, dry and old. I wonder how the vendors manage to eek out a scanty profit from such poor quality vegetables, but the Saturday afternoon feeling of weekend celebrations has begun and as music blares across the stalls, young boys and girls laugh and dance, pounding the dry earth with their bare feet in unified rhythm.


Out across from the market and along the edge of town, evidence of hurricane devastation lies everywhere. Straw, cane and mud hut dwellings half decimated by fierce tropical storms lie in heaps, yet people still continue to occupy the remaining wreckage. Elderly people sit in ancient rocking chairs under the shade of congeries of rubble and smile as we walk past. It seems a long way to our next location and I wonder if it's one of our guide's cost cutting exercises to make us walk when we could have taken a taxi. Out of town we stride and into the jungle where we walk in single file through a well-beaten path. My little Italian friend and I loiter at the back of the line carrying our back-packs lazily in a stubborn manner, but a shout of 'snake' from upfront alerts us and we quicken our pace. When we reach the snake, we find that someone has squashed it in the middle of its wriggling back and I almost feel sorry for it. But we leave it in its last defiant battle to survive and trundle on. We wearily trudge through the jungle as the late afternoon sun begins to slide behind the trees and somewhere in the distance, disco music booms incongruously amidst the forest trail.


After a very long hike we reach a curious encampment with charming straw mud huts built in different shapes, sizes and colours perched high on stilts amidst the dense bushes. We are welcomed into the compound by the caretaker who unlocks very high bamboo gates and escorts us to our individual little huts. Caria and I are shown to a delightful, square, sea blue hut built like a quaint children's summer house, complete with red gingham curtains. It is a relief to be staying for a few days in such unique little shacks, the only aspect which makes me uncomfortable is the close proximity of the jungle with all kinds of insects and creatures crawling around, including snakes and iguanas taking shelter under our wooden floor boards.

The canteen is a large hut, not on stilts, in the centre of the compound and is beautifully decorated with all kinds of tropical flowers including large-stemmed birds of paradise blooms. There are no walls and the gentle jungle breeze flows through the restaurant furniture fluttering the table cloths like coronation flags. As I scurry to the canteen, afraid of the hiding iguanas, the sun suddenly dips and darkness closes in as though someone has flicked the 'off' button in the sky and we are thrown into total blackness. The lights in the canteen are welcoming and delightful, shining brightly as we sit down to a reasonable simple supper. Our spirits are high after enjoying our food and we settle down to chat. Myrtle picks up a small drum and begins to beat out a rhythm. Gunter takes some spoons and drums on the table and for some reason we all burst into song-singing...."in the jungle, the mighty jungle the lion sleeps tonight." It is so joyous and spontaneous, ringing out across the darkness with... "whim-away-a-whim-away...ooooh" and no matter what we have experienced or felt about each other on our incredible journey, these few minutes of sheer, unified, uplifting singing will remain in my heart forever, like the magical breath of the sea and the electric blue light pouring across the dawn jungle. I am so blessed and lucky to have experienced such wonders- for I am Lucky.

※

# NAT KING COLE AND FRANK SINATRA ARE ALIVE- CROONING IN THE JUNGLE!

It is early Sunday morning and we wake in our quaint doll's house on stilts in the middle of the jungle, where squawking exotic birds echo through the compound, beating their wings like wet sheets flapping on a washing line. It is strangely invigorating, and an unusual wake- up call. I suddenly remember the iguanas scuffling under our floorboards and hastily make ready with Caria to jog down to the canteen where a lovely breakfast awaits. In the canteen everyone is busy discussing activities, offering different ideas about how they want to spend the day. I plan to walk into town to visit the bank and play the tourist card. Caria has similar plans but the complainers are not satisfied with the lack of direction from our leader and decide to book a taxi to drive them on a picturesque tour of Belize. Hunter and the others are open to suggestions but will probably spend the day resting.

As Caria and I set off lazily walking into town through the jungle pathway, we step across the dead snake smothered in black ants tucking into an easy meal, alerting us to be cautious of any other creatures which might be lurking in the brush, so we quicken our pace. When we arrive on the edge of town, a lazy Sunday morning mood hangs in the air after the party fever on Saturday night. Most shops are closed but a few cafes begin to open. Caria wants to go in the opposite direction and as I need to head for the bank, we part company planning to meet later. When I arrive at the bank, I am greeted by two armed soldiers on guard and although the main bank is closed, they allow me to use the machine. After negotiating my way through several languages on the screen, I manage to get some money for the next part of the journey. Walking back into the bright sunshine after the dim booth, the morning has lifted its sleepy head and the streets begin to buzz with local traders preparing their stalls for Sunday business. In the square a very unusual restaurant sports a bright yellow Chevrolet car balanced on the roof and I imagine it is photographed by many visitors- myself included. The locals are friendly and cheerful. Delightful children follow me, calling out a whole series of questions- where do I come from? What I do? Do I have children and if I want to buy trinkets? Eventually when I make it clear that I do not want to purchase anything, I am left alone to wander through the streets. So the morning gently unfolds until I begin to feel hungry and make my way towards a massive open-plan food hall with a corrugated iron roof, offering all kinds of street food. Large wooden trestle tables with benches are laid out in neat rows for families to sit and eat together. The place caters for all kinds of cuisine and I am careful to avoid rich, spicy food which might upset my stomach for the next day's travel to Belize docks, where we are to board a boat to Kay Calke, a tiny island set in the Caribbean sea. I order a plain burger and take it to eat in a corner away from the jostling crowd. The burger is fine and I am entertained by a sweet little African girl dancing in the sunshine, lost in her own little world. She reminds me of myself as a small child where dancing and music were my everything, always lifting me out of unhappy times. A shaft of sunlight halos her head in a golden haze and I snap a quick picture as she gazes skywards. As I inspect the photo, I am intrigued to see that she is encapsulated in an ethereal aura of light. I know she is a very special little spirit placed on earth to shine and give light and life to others and I am reminded of a similar kind of light energy called 'ectoplasm', which is a spirit-elemental mist, often displayed when a being from beyond enters earth's magnetic field. I remember a very strange incident which was witnessed by my class of adult women dancers. It was a Thursday evening and I was about to start my adult jazz dance class. I was sad because it had been my favourite uncle's funeral that day and I was not able to attend, as I had many teaching commitments and running the school alone, there was no one else who could step in. As we began our routine, my mind wandered to him. I told him I was very sorry not to be at his funeral and I heard his voice plainly reply, "don't worry me duck, I know, I know, you don't have to tell me!" Then the voice faded and the strangest thing happened.

The dusky evening light in the hall grew misty, as though a veil of thin smoke was blowing through the gym and we all momentarily paused mid steps, wondering what was happening. Then the lights went out and the large iron fire doors swung open and cold air filtered in. We all stood perplexed by what was happening. Then the lights came on and I hurriedly closed the fire doors and went to turn on the music, which had mysteriously stopped. I was shocked to find that the music player had been turned off at the mains, which was impossible, as no one had been near it, yet it had been physically turned off! I showed the ladies what had happened and they couldn't believe it! We resumed the class, pondering over the mysterious incident, but I couldn't forget what happened. I remind myself that sometimes spirits, newly passed over, have the ability to use electrical energy to contact the living by manipulating electrical devices. I firmly believe that it was my Uncle Terry, assuring us that he was still with us and all was well and he wanted his children to know that his love for them would continue forever.

The food hall is filling up with families breakfasting, enjoying a lazy Sunday break from the routine drudge of everyday chores and I am grateful to be observing their world, experiencing a different style of living in a less affluent part of Belize. The atmosphere generated from such family gatherings is wholesome, especially in such a harmonious community. My voices explain;

*"All is energy. All is vibration. The vibrational current is of itself neither good nor bad; it is the source of the flow which dictates the direction and mode of the energy, whether it be evil or good. A virtuous soul, like your Uncle was able to use the electric current to communicate in a good, positive way but equally, the energy can be manipulated for evil purposes. The earth is a planet where choices are freely made. It is part of the unspoken test, which everyone undertakes when they enter human form. Everyone is free to choose their pathway."*

I listen to their wise words, remembering a terrible ordeal from an evil spirit lingering in an old farmhouse cottage which had been used for black magic child sacrifice. Black Magic embedded in satanic rites is a powerful tool and uses the same 'energy'. Karmic law dictates that anyone using this kind of power to harm others will be punished by the same evil force which will return to them ten times more vicious than their original intention. I was taught this karmic rule by my Grandmother-in-law who was a world renown healer in India who, when she sacked her cook for stealing, he retaliated by poisoning her with black magic datura snake venom. As she lay in bed at night contorting in pain she realized what was happening and knew it was the cook who had poisoned her, so she sent the energy back to him. He died that night in terrible agony, whereas she quickly recovered. I look around at the happy faces preoccupied with their Sunday feast, enjoying their favourite food and laughing with friends and I am comforted by the all-encompassing goodness of the gathering. I shiver when I think of my silly mistake with Alvaro and the thought of what might have happened. I wonder if he will show up again? I felt eyes watching from afar as I walked through the town this morning, but perhaps I imagined it.

In the now of the moment the sun is shining and happy Sunday music is blaring from the loud-speakers, but my mind returns to the evil energy locked in the farmhouse in a small village in North Yorkshire where my first husband and I bought a beautiful farmhouse cottage. After living in a small flat in London, we were looking forward to moving to our dream house. I was heavily pregnant with my first child and the plan on the day of the move was for my husband and his friend to drive up to Yorkshire in a van with all our furniture and goods. I would travel by train and take a taxi to the house with our little dog to wait for them. The cottage was enchanting with a beautiful garden and it was wonderful to be making a fresh start in a village far away from the London scene with the exciting expectation of a new baby on the way.

I arrived at the empty house amidst glorious sunshine with my little Shitzu dog, Cheeni, who loved running around her new-found playground with a freedom she had never before experienced in the confines of the flat. I picnicked on the little food I had brought on the well-kept lawn, in full confidence that my husband would soon arrive with food supplies and all our goods. As the afternoon wore on into early evening, the light strayed behind darkening clouds and I went indoors to wait for their arrival. I locked the conservatory door and waddled into the dimly lit kitchen entering a strange emptiness I had not previously encountered. My little dog followed close at my heels with her tail down. The brightness of the sunny afternoon faded leaving a dull, chill in the air and the sound of my steps on the tiled kitchen floor echoed as though we had entered a darkened tunnel. Suddenly the phone on the wall rang connecting me to the outside world. Up until that moment I was not bothered that I knew no one and was totally alone in a strange place, but I was so relieved to make contact with my husband, as I had begun to feel vulnerable as night closed in. The phone call was brief as he explained that high winds on the motorway made it unsafe to drive the van, so they would arrive in the morning. I was dumbstruck by the news and suddenly felt so alone, cold and afraid. Cheeni curled up on my feet as she sensed my unease. Momentarily, I held onto the phone as though clinging to a lifeline and kept my back turned against something lurking in the shadows. Whatever it was, I knew it was smirking as though I was meant to be stranded alone in the house. Suddenly ,my baby kicked inside me and like a tigress with her cub, I turned purposefully towards the unseen enemy, with rising protective anger. I was determined that something sinister was not going to destroy my happiness. As the sun began to set, a flash of glowing orange struck something gold on the kitchen wall and I looked up to see a crucifix hanging over the door. I had grown up with the icon and thought that I had escaped my Catholic upbringing, but I remembered that it was also used as a symbol for protection against evil, like the time my Father bought me a white plastic crucifix with a silver Jesus hanging on the cross and placed it over my bed to protect me from the so-called fright-mares, which continually plagued me, but I knew they were not dreams but real horrors. I was upset because I wanted a dolly not a crucifix!

I walked into the dining room and spotted another crucifix hanging over the door. I entered the sitting room and found another hanging above the entrance and a sense of knowing suddenly washed over me with a terrifying understanding that the crucifixes were placed in each room as a source of protection against an evil force. A thought flashed across my mind urging me to get out of the house and run, but there was nowhere to go and I didn't know anyone. It was growing colder and I had no idea how to switch on the central heating and there was no firewood to make a fire. I pulled my cardigan tightly around my shoulders and heaved myself down on the floor, sitting with my back to an old radiator with Cheeni on my knee for warmth. The house was empty without any curtains, so the blackness of the night seeped in and my reflection in every window glared back at me like distorted mirrors at the fair. I was on show for all to see with a dark presence lurking, watching and waiting.

I decided there was nothing I could do but try to endure the night and perhaps sleep, although there was nothing to sleep on and no blankets, but going upstairs to lock myself in the bedroom seemed a good idea. I waddled back into the kitchen and turned off the light by the hallway door but as soon as I had flicked the switch off, it turned itself back on again. My heart jumped into my mouth and I gasped in horror, sensing the evil presence close by, defying me. I was determined I was not going to be beaten, so I brazenly turned off the light again, but it boldly turned itself on. It was open war! I turned it off and awkwardly marched through the door into the hallway with Cheeni before it could retaliate, but in the quiet, echoing emptiness beneath the stairs, the sound of the switch resounded with a hollow 'click' and the light underneath the old wooden door shone brightly, challenging me to turn around, but I hurried up the stairs as fast as my pregnant belly would allow.

Escaping the thing below was my only thought and I was so relieved to close the empty bedroom door behind me and lock it.

Uneasily, I lay down on the carpet with my little dog curled into my chest and spent a terrifying night with sounds of clanging steel on steel as though I was in the middle of a medieval battlefield with swords and shields clashing. I told myself it was the old radiators retracting in the cold, but I knew it wasn't. After the initial baptism of terror that first night, the onslaught intensified and became a nightmare for the next five years revealing terrible insights into an unbelievable world of evil and psychic events which I and other people witnessed.

But now in the sunshine brightness of wholesome goodness, the past has no place to distort the present and there will be another time to recount the happenings in Pear Tree cottage. Finishing my delicious burger, I decide to wander back to the compound, as the food hall is now heaving with families and stroll back in the lazy, Sunday sunshine. I pass the spot where the snake had been killed but there is nothing left of the carcass except for red stains in the dry earth. As I wander through the scrub bushes, strains of music drift through the trees incongruously blending with the jungle cacophony and I feel blessed to be experiencing the strange symphony of sounds. As I near the compound a taxi takes off into the distance and I wonder if Alvaro is snooping around, but when I arrive at the bamboo gates guarding our little hut haven, all is quiet and I find my little Italian friend in our hut, lying on her stomach on the bed pouring over a book.

"Oh 'allo, did you know dolphins sleep with one eye open and that butterflies taste through their feet?" she states knowledgably.

I flop on my bed and laugh replying, "no I did not? What are you reading?"

"Unusual facts about insects and animals-it's to improve my English" she earnestly informs me.

"Well, did you know that in the Shanidar caves, researchers found the remains of flatbreads made from unleavened bread, which proves that 70,000 years ago Neanderthols had a more complex diet and methods of cooking than was previously thought and ingredients like nuts, pulses and seeds were used to flavour their food?

"Really?" she replies, taking in the information with her head on one side pondering the words and then asking," what's a Neanderthol?"

I laugh explaining a little about the theories on humanity's evolution but I think it is too complicated for her and she changes the subject by telling me that in a few days it will be her eighteenth birthday and it will be the first time away from her parents and she will be alone to celebrate it. I place my arm around her and assure her that she will not be alone and I resolve to arrange something for her with the rest of the group.

"But please no embarrassing me?" she pleads.

I promise not to embarrass her, knowing from experience how, at her age, so many things can be humiliating to the awkward teenager.

"You do understand me, don't you?" she queries, dolefully rolling her big brown eyes. "Have you ever been embarrassed?"

I laugh, assuring her; "Oh yes, many, many times!"

"Tell me? Tell me?" she cries jumping up and down on the meagre bed.

"Well one terrible time, I will never forget is when, I wasn't much older than you!"

"Yes, yes!" she eagerly sighs, kneeling on the bed with excited glee.

"It was my very first ball at my college and I had been invited by a very smart young man from the College of Estate Management, which was a very prestigious college for privileged young men; in fact, many of the young ladies from my college were aristocratic- like the Queen's cousins, who sought dates with them. So I was considered to be very lucky, especially coming from a working class family, having lived in a small farming village and not having experienced glittering dance balls. Of course at that age I had no idea of the importance of my first ball, but I knew I had to look glamorous, so I spent all of my first term's money on a special outfit for the occasion and had no money left for food, but such is the vanity of the young."

"What did you buy?"

"I bought a beautiful, white, Swiss lace fitted blouse with voluminous sleeves and black silk, flowing culottes and beautiful high heel black shiny shoes from the prestigious Biba store. In those days I had very long hair down to my waist and had a very elaborate hairstyle created by a good stylist."

"I bet you looked very glamorous?" she teases cavorting around the room pretending to show off an invisible ball gown, " and ...?"

"Well when we arrived at the entrance there were many young people stepping out of large limousines in their finery and making their way down a very grand, red-carpeted winding staircase into a magnificent ballroom. We joined a small queue and when it was our turn to appear on the staircase and make our entrance in front of all the select people, I put my foot onto the first step and my high heel got caught in my long trouser leg and I went tumbling down from the top of the stairs all the way to the bottom, rolling and gathering momentum on each step, until I crashed and landed in a pool of spilt beer at the bottom. I remember the fall seemed to take forever in slow-motion and the silence was deadly as I fell and fell. Red-faced and with a soaking bottom, I stood up and pretended it hadn't happened. Then the crowd returned to their polite conversation and I stood against the wall most of the evening to hide my stained backside.

"What did your boyfriend do?" she asked sympathetically.

"I'm afraid he was so shocked and embarrassed that he disowned me and went off with his best friend's sister!"

"Oh no? I am so sad for you?"

"Oh, don't be! It was fine. It was for the best. I am glad we didn't become an item. You know often when you think things are bad, it turns out that a much better chance is waiting around the corner."

"And was it?"

"Oh yes, but the embarrassment of the moment is still sharp in my memory and I will never forget it! But you see 'embarrassment' has a purpose of teaching us a life lesson. In that moment of sheer humiliation we have no defence against the world and we have to come face to face with our own naked self. It teaches us to be humble. Have you heard the phrase…'pride cometh before a fall'?"

"No, what does it mean?" she enquires.

"Well it means that if you think you are the best and are above the rest, something will happen to bring you down to size and make you realise that you are not better than anyone else. Like me when I thought I looked so marvellous and I fell like a clown in front of everyone."

"Tell me more, tell me more?" she implores.

I decline although there are many amusing, embarrassing moments to share but it is time to make our way to the canteen to meet the group. As we amble down I look at her young expectant face, so innocent and naïve and I am moved to give her some advice-"You know Caria, catch your dreams before thy slip away. Dream big and don't let the world get in your way. Travel is a great teacher as you are discovering. I have found that exploring is a terrifying, electrifying way of taking the lid off of my head to find out what is truly inside. To challenge myself and to dissolve fears and inner inhibitions, I deliberately take myself where I am afraid to go. When you expose your mind to greater possibilities, the small worries and problems get put in their place as the bigger picture expands, the universe listens to the bigger picture." Caria just smiles. She is young and I don't expect her to understand.


When we enter the canteen everyone is assembled and Tommy stands at the front ready to inform us that we will eat at a cheap roadside café, where the food is good and we can decide afterwards what we want to do. We collect our things and follow him into the hot night and trek along the jungle path watching out for snakes, trudging out beyond the town to a little, dingy cheap take-away van. The air is greasy with sweet, economy oil and dust clouds from the busy traffic, leave grainy, sticky, deposits on the thin metal tables and chairs laid out on the side of the highway. We look at each other in dismay. The complainers have the money to leave immediately in search of a good, reputable restaurant, but the rest of us are obliged to accept Tommy's lead. The fatty food is disgusting and the little I order is unpalatable. I am left feeling hungry and cheated again. Sitting by the roadside with motorbikes and cars hurtling past, with their headlights glaring into our faces, we hastily finish the congealed offering. Bill and Gunter try to lighten our mood by enthusiastically raving about a special Karaoke place they found hidden in the jungle and the others fire up a keen response. I hate Karaoke but follow the others who, heartily are willing to make the most of a disappointing evening.

Gunter and Bill, enthusiastically lead the way, followed by Tommy still munching a greasy burger and the rest of us, pleased to escape the glaring traffic, trail behind. A full moon lights a white, bright pathway through the bushes as we file through new terrain. The pathway seems to lead to a wide opening in the jungle, where for a few moments, Bill and Gunter debate which way to go, but soon decide straight on is the correct way to forge ahead. Farther along we hear sweet strains of old ballads leaking through the trees in a hushed tone as though we are entering a secret world of the villagers. We follow the music until we spy, hidden in the jungle overgrowth, a large concrete rectangle covered by an iron corrugated roof. There is a door, but the rest of the building is totally open to the world outside. Villagers and youths sit on the open window ledges silently listening and watching the karaoke videos played on a tv perched on a make-shift stand with an electric cable running into a small kitchen where the leads are fed off illicit electric lines stolen from an unknown source. As we walk inside the dimly lit space, we pay a small toll to a man at the door, which we think is a little funny, as everyone peering in from outside are entertained for free. One single lamp on a stand lights the way towards a few rows of wooden trestle tables and benches where we sit. In the brightly lit kitchen beer and lager is on sale. I don't like beer or lager but the others jovially imbibe whilst perusing a song menu. After a short pause in the proceedings a man walks forwards from the dimly lit audience and chooses to sing Nat KIng Cole's 'Old Black magic'. I listen to the introduction sceptically, but as soon as the man opens his mouth and sings, I am totally shocked and awed by his amazing voice. If I close my eyes I would swear it is a recording of Nat King Cole! The tone, the phrasing, the timbre of his voice is an exact replica of the famous singer. Such talent is incredible, especially in the middle of the jungle, on a Sunday evening surrounded by poverty-stricken Belize villagers who are mesmerised by the singer's gift. 'That old black magic has me in its spell, that old black magic that I know so well…' rings from the rafters and fills the air with rich tones from a lost era. At the end of the song, applause erupts like a stick of dynamite exploding in a disused mine, scattering the moment with harmonious joy.

As the applause fades another local man takes the stand and chooses Frank Sinatra's-'I did it my way.' It is a tough powerful song to sing and to croon it in the style of Frank Sinatra is very difficult, but as soon as he sings the first note, Frank Sinatra's voice entertains the masses. I can't believe the talent of these people. The flair, the gift, the aptitude and genius of the singers is astonishing. I don't know how they create the sound of such famous singers and I feel sorry for them that they don't have the opportunity to show their talent to the rest of the world. They have something to be proud of, something unique unto themselves, especially as our crew can't sing and make a mockery of Freddie Mercury's-'I want to break free!' We spend the evening sharing the villager's fantasy realm of a glossy, fake world where glamorous models and handsome men pose in a dreamscape of idol images on the screen. I will never forget the stunning singing of the local people and am lucky to have experienced the living voices of two incredible singers of a bygone era.

Now the morning brings us a new adventure as we board the bus to take us to Belize docks where a boat waits to ship us out to a tiny island-Caye Calke, in the Caribbean sea. Just as I step onto the bus the young waitress from the canteen runs up to me with a message, saying that a man called Alviro is looking for me. I thank her and hastily climb on board. I am a little flattered but also relieved not to see him, knowing I luckily escaped his amorous intentions. I sigh as I gratefully take my seat next to the window, feeling lucky and blessed to be experiencing a new challenge, for I am both- Lucky and blessed!

# THREE SECOND QUANTUM LEAP
# INTO THE FUTURE

Now having left Belize docks, sitting on the deck of the boat, looking down into the ocean below, a gentle breeze ruffles my hair and my face is moist with a salty mist spraying from the playful waves lapping below. Exhilarating, after the dense, rainforest humidity, the expanse of clear blue ocean under a cloudless baby-blue sky, is thrilling as the watery world goes on and on forever. I relax and embrace the peace, while the undulating rhythm beneath my feet and the swishing waves, sigh a sweet lullaby of serene calm under the Caribbean Ocean spell. I take a deep breath of briny, crisp air- so refreshing after the musty forest terrain and want this moment to go on and on, but all too soon the island appears and we slow down to dock. It is strange that the Island doesn't have a beach and there is no sandy approach as our only access is across a wooden platform built on stilts in the sea. Strains of reggae music pulse across the boardwalk as I disembark and a hint of ganja sours the clean air as I step into a new Caribbean domain.

Entering a new world where the tempo of living is slow, slow, slow- feels peculiar after the non-stop hectic, merry-go-round of rough travelling across Central America. Here the lazy, hazy haven is a little eccentric paradise tucked away from the rest of the world. Our group follow our guide through tiny sandy paths and as there are only three main streets on the Island, it is easy to navigate our way around our new location. There are no cars, only bicycles but the tour guide for the island has a little electric buggy like an open golf cart, to ferry tourists around. We soon arrive at our hostel where we are greeted by the owner, who hails from Essex, and is a left-over Hippie from the Woodstock era, who travelled to the island with his wife many years ago and never left. It's easy to see why, as his laid-back life style encapsulates the 'pot' culture of the island where no one rushes, or is tied to the clock. It's too hot to worry about trivia and time belongs to no one and everyone.

Again I am sharing a little room with my Italian friend who will be eighteen tomorrow and I have a plan for us all to celebrate together, but I need to find a good restaurant to host our party. Luckily there is one Italian restaurant on the island, which makes my mission easy and the proprietor is happy to book a table for our party. As I amble along in the dry heat, almost every house and shack resounds with the reggae beat, except for the Latin quarter where the salsa tempo pulses like an eternal party. I wander down to the 'Split', which is where a piece of the island was severed into the sea during a raging hurricane and the locals established an open air bar in what was left of the land for everyone to congregate and sample fruit cocktails. I sit sipping a fresh pineapple rum special, whilst dangling my legs in a small rivulet of burbling sea water flowing from a gulley, where tiny silver fish are nibbling my toes and it is very tickly. The sun is high and scorching hot. I am glad of my large, floppy sun hat to shield my face and bare shoulders.

Cooking on the island is mostly barbeque grills and for a change, the group lunch was quite wholesome and healthy with salad and barbequed meat and fish. For once I feel satisfied that the meal was value for money. Now after resting at the Split, I explore the front street. The streets are known to the locals as 'the front', 'the middle' and the 'back', as there are only three main streets on the whole of the island. The air is cooling and a few locals are around lazily wasting the day chatting with neighbours. There are a few tourist shops on the front and although there is no beach as such, there is a sandy strip with weather-beaten tables and chairs set out for picnicking. I spy an old man sitting in the sand with long grey and black Rastafarian ringlets draped over his multi-coloured kaftan. He is wearing a striking, round tribal cap which matches his flowing robe and his bare feet resting in the sand, are worn and calloused. His eyes are shielded by a pair of modern, fashionable sunglasses with bright blue, light-resistant lenses, through which the dusty sand peers back at me in a golden haze. A young girl, about ten years of age, wearing a simple cotton pink dress, with long black, curly hair tied in bunches, stands close by. When she spies me, she immediately takes the opportunity to entice me over to talk to her Grandfather. "Come Lady, come. My Grandfather can give you news. He is blind but he sees all. He can see the past and the future. Come, come Lady and speak with him. He knows you are here."

I approach cautiously as I am not sure what I might get sucked into, as I have been cautioned not to give away money to locals who will take advantage of naïve tourists.

"Come Lady and sit with us," she urges.

It is very difficult to walk away and refuse the invitation, so I awkwardly sit down next to the old man who takes my right hand and laughs. I ask the young girl what he finds so funny and she replies:

"He says you can see forwards also like him!"

I nod and take my hand away. He then burbles words and sounds which are completely incoherent, but the young girl is willing to translate his messages for a small fee. I knew there was a catch in it somewhere, but I negotiate the fee for a reasonable price, as I am curious and fascinated by his magical presence. When we are all satisfied with the arrangement, the old man takes my hand and whilst chanting a ritualistic mantra, he shakes my arm in time to incoherent warbling. The young girl explains that he is looking into my energy and preparing himself to 'go under'.

"Go under?" I question.

"It means he is meeting with the spirits of another world," she states calmly.

I nod and wait for him to pause before retrieving my arm. He listens to invisible beings as he responds with grunts and loud clucking sounds. Then after a long silence, when he is completely still, a rattle of sounds spurts forth from his mouth like a machine gun spewing bullets. The Granddaughter listens intently and when all is calm she translates as the old man, spent from his ordeal, limply hangs his head on his chest as she speaks softly:

"Grandfather is going forwards in time. He sees a young girl with long dark hair walking in a dirty alleyway with a young man by her side, who is her boyfriend. The alleyway is at the back of some sex shops and fast food cafes. The air smells of cheap food and stale perfume."

"How far into the future is this?" I query.

"Shh! Don't interrupt Lady! The young woman with long dark hair tied in a ponytail is dressed in a bright, shiny green jump suit and is walking in an alley full of dustbins, with trash strewn all around. She is taunting and teasing her boyfriend, who is a target for the mafia. She is the daughter of the mafia leader and her assignment is to kill the young man. She has hidden in her purse a heat ray gun which seeks out the target through heat recognition. The victim's details are coded into the gun which pursues the victim anywhere, even around corners and into buildings. The ray bullet will not stop until the target is reached and the subject killed. On her wrist she is wearing an object which looks like a watch. It is a teleporter device. On the dials inscribed are - seconds, minutes, hours, days and years. The user may choose the amount of time to be teleported into the future or the past. It enables its user to take a quantum leap into the time of their choice. She has estimated that she can shoot the ray gun, throw it in the trash and hurl herself into the future for 3 seconds before appearing farther down the road walking towards her boyfriend's body as though she is just witnessing the scene. She will catapult over the bullet and travel faster through time before the bullet strikes its target. She chooses a spot that is hidden from the big-brother cameras to shoot him but will land further down the street in full sight of the surveillance cameras to make it appear that she has nothing to do with the killing and will fake running to the spot where he is lying, feigning her horror at his death. She believes she, and her Mafia family have planned the perfect crime.

I listen amazed at the information and before I can ask questions, the old man recovers from his rest and begins babbling again at a rapid rate until he flops exhausted and his Granddaughter takes over interpreting his ramblings.

"This is unusual, Grandfather says he has three pictures to show you taken from the same scene but from different angles. The second scene shows a young man wandering down the same sleazy street taking photographs on his new camera, which is the shape and size of a small matchstick. It has amazing technical facilities and can capture images beyond the picture itself. It has a 'roaming' device which can wander into buildings and record what's inside or expand a shot down to its miniscule detail. It can present a panoramic view instantly up to a mile in radius. He is playing around with his new toy and hears a strange noise further up the street and as he peers ahead he inadvertently takes a photo of the scene. He hears a crash as a young man falls into a trash can spilling a pile of filthy food waste over the rancid pavement. He runs towards what looks like a body lying on the floor. As he stands shocked at a young man's body lying face down on the ground, with blood pouring from his chest, he is aware of a young woman dressed in a bright green jump suit, screaming and running towards the body. Suddenly, he is surrounded by police and flashing lights. They take over the scene and ask him to accompany them down to the station to make a report on what he witnessed.

The old man comes up for air and gulps. The sea whispers in the distance. Then he rests his chin on his chest in repose. I open my mouth to speak but the young girl says, "Wait he is not finished, there is more." I watch as he begins to breathe heavily and spouts out more sounds which seem to tumble from his mouth like a scree avalanche rolling down a mountain. When he finishes, his Granddaughter assumes her translator role and I wonder what all this information has to do with me.

"Now for the third picture." She continues." In the background the young woman in the bright green jumpsuit is smirking with her Father and two other hit-men. They believe they have successfully engineered the perfect murder. In the forefront is a scene at the police station where the young photographer is being questioned and his camera scrutinised. The young man relates his side of the story and it seems with the big brother surveillance evidence, the young woman is in the clear, until a tech engineer rushes over to the detective's desk. After thoroughly scrutinising the camera contents, the technician spies a splash of bright green in a corner of the lens and because the camera has special apps, he is able to zoom in on the bright green shadow. As he closes in on the flash of bright green spilling into the picture, a woman's body comes into focus appearing to be floating over the top of a ray-gun bullet. She is travelling rapidly through the ether, faster than the bullet. It appears she is flying to a spot further down the road. The Detective inspects the evidence and from his experience of the new technical device, he can see it is clear that she shot the bullet, then transported herself forwards at an estimated time of 3 seconds before the bullet entered its victim. Using the evidence, which cannot be tampered with like in the old days, when video evidence could no longer be reliable or used in court because of the ingenious skill of photo-shopping someone's identity on top of another's, the up-to-date technology cannot be faked. The police arrest the young woman along with her Father and two other mobsters."

The old man recovers and raises his sunglass eyes to the sky. He smiles. The young girl claps her hands and pats her Grandfather on the shoulder. I am speechless. I don't know what to say or think.

I find myself saying out loud-"Why me? Why was I shown this? What am I meant to do with the information?"

The old man stands and leans against a table and states in perfectly good English:

"The future holds many secrets. The knowledge of which will open many doors today. You will write this, will you not?"

"Why yes, yes I will!" I reply, somewhat surprised at his perfect accent.

"Then you will inform. You will show the world what awaits. To be informed is to be forearmed, is to be ready, is to be aware, is to make informed choices. Knowledge is the key to all understanding. Understanding leads to truth. Truth is the final frontier of all that is." With those last words he moves carefully away aided by his Granddaughter who steers him towards the main street.

The sea whispers and brings peace along the breeze. I ponder the meaning of my meeting with the old man and sit on a bench at one of the old rickety tables. A young girl runs out from one of the shops and asks if I want a drink. I feel obliged to order a lemonade and she smiles as another girl runs towards my table to take an order, but she is too late! The iced lemonade is refreshing and I break one of my travelling rules by drinking it. Ice in a foreign place must be avoided at all costs, as you never know the source of the water and drinking it can lead to all kinds of stomach bug problems. My stomach has not fully recovered from my time in the rain forest but in the lazy heat, I take cool comfort from the drink.

In the tranquil moment, I watch a local fisherman skilfully tugging and twisting a line as he throws it in and out of the sea. His moves echo a dance; a dance of survival; a dance of simple living; a dance of exertion and purpose. He laughs as he lands a catch. It's a medium-sized grey fish with shiny purple scales glinting in the sunlight. I clap the catch as he wanders over holding his prize, which he has humanely killed. He tells me he was a policeman in Belize but his passion is dance and playing the drums and is a member of the Belize Dance Company. He also sings African Folk songs and I ask him to sing one and he happily obliges by choosing a romantic ballad about a pumpkin and watermelon. His voice echoes across the gentle rolling sea, as the white tipped waves wash against the boardwalk. I am touched by his sincere performance. I do not want to cave in to the temptation of accepting his offer to cook the fish for us, so I walk away. He is a lovely man but our chemistry does not match and soon I will have to prepare for a surprise birthday meal.

I am pulled towards the 'Split' where people are gathering for late afternoon cocktails. I love watching the children splash and chase around the whirling inlets of water gushing from the sea into small ponds where the silver fish play. Some children are calmly eating their tea on the banks of the mud streams, licking the tomato sauce from their lips as they munch into their burgers freshly cooked at the bar. A young African man who is the tallest person on the Island, I am told, and hails from the Masai tribe, is diving off the split into the sea, splashing and playing with the children, ducking and rolling through the waves as the young swimmers try to catch him. I sit dangling my hot toes in the cooling surf tumbling towards me. The young man smiles as he surfaces from the brine with his long Rastafarian locks dangling over his shoulders. His pearly white teeth gleam in the sunlight and his athletic, lean body glistens like a Greek god rising from the deep. I turn back towards the bar where the bartender is slowly unzipping a ripe banana for a cocktail and everyone is relaxing in the shade. The young Masai warrior heaves himself up onto the boards to sit next to me. The heat of his wet body seeps into mine as he edges close. His name is Ezekiel but friends call him Zek.

We talk for a while and time is sealed in his sunshine haze. I am young again in his gaze. His black wet hand taps my milk-white fingers as he playfully says, "Come I will show you the Island. Are you afraid?" I laugh as he pulls me up dripping droplets of sea water onto my shoulders.

Don't judge me, for I am not judging myself- I only know that the island is our last stop after intense travelling and the relief and emotional release of the safety of now is overwhelming. The heat is intoxicating and common sense has flown out beyond the ocean. The alluring magic of an all-embracing smile is liberating, freeing me of my silly anxieties. It is like randomly discarding all my clothes to jump into a thrilling sea. We walk closely, our bodies occasionally touching and as I only come up to his ribcage, I have to peer up into his face to see his expression as he points out flowers and herbs naturally growing in the hedgerows. For a giant he is gentle and caring, not overpowering in his strength and vigour. We walk towards a ramshackle shack which has been decimated by the latest tornedo. No one rushes to repair the ruined damage. There is time and there is time. There is tomorrow and tomorrow. Living for the present is all in this isolated nirvana. His home is all he has and although meagre, it is sufficient for his needs. I cannot prevent the inevitable and why would I want to? I have lived in an emotional desert for so long, in a dry, arid land of nothingness and now soft tender kisses caress my shoulders and I succumb to the lush, fertile oasis where sustenance is found and given. I want to always remember the feel of soft, black locks bouncing on my breast.

Now in the early evening, I wash and dress ready for the birthday party. The abandoned joy of the afternoon lingers. Everyone sensing the closure of our long-haul expedition enjoys the party and wallows in friendly nostalgia of the highs and lows of our travels together. Late in the evening we depart to our quarters and farther down the street Zek is sitting on a bench waiting for me. It is awkward as my little Italian birthday girl and I are walking home together. He senses this and departs. The next day our party have booked a Ganja boat ride in the late afternoon which sails out to sea until the early hours of the morning and I look forward to the new experience.

The next morning I walk around the island expecting to see Zek, but I am told by one of his friends that he is working on another island gardening and so I take the opportunity to explore the place, unaware of the watchful scrutiny of a green-eyed goddess. Later in the afternoon as I sip a pineapple cocktail at the Split, Zek appears and asks me if I want to take a walk. His friendly, all embracing smile is hard to ignore, so I agree. We saunter through sandy bushes where illicit electric cables feed and supply many homes with illegal energy. He shows me the football ground and a school and I briefly imagine what it would be like to give up everything and teach in the school, but I know I could not leave my family. We walk to a make-shift shack which is a shop and he orders me a fresh orange juice served in a used plastic bottle and orders for himself a toasted sandwich, which after seeing the bottle, I decline the food. The orange juice, surprisingly, tastes very good despite the container and I thank the young girl serving us, who eyes me suspiciously through a false smile. The afternoon wears on lazily and we enjoy each other's company before it is time to board the Ganja boat and Zek grins as he waves goodbye, knowing what's in store for me.

The six o'clock rum boat sets sail out into the deep blue ocean with all our group on board, eager to party, as we watch two young men prepare and slice fresh tropical fruit to place into a large plastic bucket, then pour bottles of rum over the top. After allowing the fruit to soak up the rum, they scoop the cocktail into small plastic cups and hand everyone the special concoction, which is mighty strong. Only our crowd is on board, together with the Captain and the two young sailors, so everyone feels at ease to let themselves go and fully embrace the experience. As we sail far into the distance, the sun sets and more and more rum punch is emptied into our cups. Out beyond nowhere the boat stops and the smell of weed permeates the salty air. The milky way is sprinkled with silver dew drops in a velvet black cloak and the boat becomes dotted with little red and orange beacons, like fireflies fluttering in the breeze, as everyone is handed a lit Ganja roll-up to smoke.

I am not use to the rum or weed! I suddenly feel sick as the boat rocks to and fro. Vomit gushes up into my throat. I hang my head over the side, but my stomach is not relieved and I just flop helplessly overboard, floating my hands in the cool water. After a short while, I begin to recover and look up into the great expanse of the universe and am struck by the vastness and incomprehensible possibilities of all that is beyond all understanding. Suddenly I am blubbing, wailing and sobbing, crying my heart out and I don't know why. Bawling into the night with chest and stomach heaving into the open ocean with my throat sore from the howling, I am suddenly embarrassed by my ridiculous outburst and look around, but the others are so far gone in their own trips that they haven't noticed the din, set against the loud reggae music blaring from the deck speakers-"No woman, no cry, No woman, no cry!" Bob Marley croons as I begin to sober up a little and refuse another cup of rum. I want to go back. The rum boat has been an unforgettable experience, but I am wrung out emotionally and need to sleep. Eventually the boat judders beneath my feet and we set sail to return back to the island.

In the morning, I wake up late and surprisingly my head is reasonably clear. The hostel is quiet as I make my way out towards the front street to get some breakfast. Zek is away working on another island and there is a gentle peace among the locals as they slowly saunter through their routine chores. I decide to walk to the little shack shop, where Zek took me to buy orange juice to buy another, which I figure will be healthy after the Ganja boat ordeal. The girl behind the counter is happy to serve me and in a strange way is unusually cordial whilst handing me the juice in another used plastic bottle. As I leave, I detect a sly smirk on her face, but I dismiss it, as I walk into the bright sunshine, eagerly drinking the refreshing juice.


The day wears on lazily and Zek doesn't appear. It is our last day on the island before we leave the next morning to travel across fifteen official borders to arrive at Playa Del Carmen- our final destination. I busy myself packing and preparing for the long haul travel overland. As evening seeps through the last golden rays of the day, I decide to take a stroll around the island to say my last goodbyes. I walk along the pathways that Zek and I trekked, until I come to the children's playground, where there is a basket-ball match between local teams. I pause to watch as I spy Zek scoring a goal. He notices me but does not respond. I figure he is too focussed on the match to say goodbye. As I walk on, eyes watch from every angle, from every bush, from every doorway and in the distance the drums beat, while the moon watches weaving her warning of deceit. A man appears out of the bushes to tell me something, but I don't understand what he is saying. I thank him and walk on. My body aches and my throat and tongue are sore. I just reach my room in the hostel before the poison in my body takes hold. Everyone has gone for a final meal together, but I am too ill and drag myself to the bathroom to face a night of hell in the searing heat. Lying on the bed is uncomfortable especially as my head and hair are drenched with sweat and my pillow is wet and soggy. My body heat is rising and a yellow stain seeps through my sweating limbs. I realise the orange juice the girl gave me, was poisoned. Through my delirium, I make sense of the man's warning telling me that Zek's girlfriend is out to take revenge and now I am paying dearly for my stolen pleasure. I can hardly stand but keep hauling myself to the bathroom and when poor Caria finally comes in, she is appalled by my state and the smell in the room. All night long the poison works its way through my body and in my head everything falls into place. The girl's attitude and her smirking smile as I left the shop was because it was pay-back time for her in a used plastic bottle! Around five o'clock in the morning I fall asleep, weak and exhausted.

Somewhere in the distance I hear voices..."What are we gonna do? How will we get her on the boat? Do we need to get her to hospital?" I open my eyes to a small crowd gathered around my bed.

Tommy is peering over me and Bill is holding my hand. Somehow they get me to stand but I am too weak to walk. Bill calls for a bicycle taxi to carry me to the dock, while Caria takes care of my luggage. Lying on the side of the boardwalk on the bare wooden planks, looking out to sea, like a waiting corpse, is not how I envisaged leaving the island! I don't know how I am going to cope with twelve hours on a rickety bus? To travel in this condition is going to be hell! Tommy gives me medicine and a sachet of special salts to hydrate my depleted body. As everyone arrives to board the boat, there is a strained, strange silence as people try to be kind and considerate, whispering around me like I am already dead! Hunter and Bill carry me into the small boat where I can barely sit up, but I lay my head on Bill's shoulder. Every bounce, every roll, each motion of the boat hits me in the stomach and I want to retch, but there is nothing left to vomit. My greatest fear is that I will disgrace myself in front of everyone, but hopefully the medicine will take care of that.


The nightmare boat ride ends and I am carried to the bus where I am placed next to Caria. I lie back and roll my poncho over my head so I am hidden from the world outside. All I want to do is sleep.

"Please take me out of this horrendous situation," I cry to the Universe. My head throbs, my stomach feels like someone has taken a scouring brush and scrubbed my gut clean. I am so sad and disappointed not to see all the wonderful scenery that has been part of our expedition across Central America, and to relive some of the magical times, but I am too ill to sit up properly and am best slumped under the canopy of my poncho where I can sleep in the dark. Hours pass and we stop at the borders where I am too ill to move, so Tommy takes my papers and money to organise all the official documents. Later in the morning I surface a little and take a sip of water, but I am too weak to speak. Somehow, the Great Ones take care of me and shelter me in their protection. I sleep and sleep as in a mini-death, until finally the bus pulls into the station at Playa Del Carmen and I am stronger and better, which is good, as everyone rushes off the bus leaving me to fend for myself, even Tommy has left me to my own devices and I struggle with my back-pack towards our final accommodation.


Checking into a lovely beach hostel is a great relief and the room Caria and I have been allotted is a delightful round hut with a straw-thatched roof set in a lush compound of exotic plants and flowers.

I am too weak to join the others for a meal, so I take to my bed and sink into lovely fresh white clean sheets. The fever returns, but I sleep through the night and wake to find the pristine white sheets stained with yellow from my fevered sweat. But I am better. I am stronger and have survived a terrible ordeal. Now it is time to return home.

I am well enough to enjoy a celebratory meal with everyone and although it is sad, it is jubilant and victorious. We have all come through a tough journey. Afterwards, I walk out into torrential warm rain and enjoy getting soaked. I revel in the glory of the storm knowing that tomorrow I will be elsewhere, I will be going home. I dance in the rain whirling and twirling in the middle of the empty road, rejoicing to be well and alive. Passers-by cheer and shout out greetings as I cavort towards the bar, maybe I still have a fever? Taking hold of my senses, I walk sedately into the tavern, drenched to the bone, but I don't care. My long, now curly hair is dripping over my shoulders and I order a whiskey and sprite. As I sip the golden nectar, I am watched by a handsome man sitting on a stool opposite and I openly flirt with him until he plucks up the courage to sit next to me. I am empowered with strength and nervous energy from my recovery. I could conquer the world!

Sometimes you fleetingly meet someone who is in time with your rhythm and the magnetism flowing between you is overwhelming. I know that if we had met another time, in another place we would be together. The time we spend together is precious, but I am aware that I have booked a taxi in the early hours of the morning to take me to the airport. He walks me back to the hostel and I decline his offer to make love on the beach. The clock is ticking and I am eager to be ready to face another life. We part with a sweet sadness, but it is beautiful to kiss, to feel, to know another's caring in a strange limbo of paused time.

Back in the room I cannot sleep. I wonder about Caria who has waited all night to go dancing with a young bar-tender, but I fear his intentions are not honourable. Around two 'clock in the morning she appears and is very upset. The bar-tender did not take her dancing! I am sorry for her distress and like a mother hen I try to console her. She is also sad to say goodbye to me for we have shared many strange times. As she curls up in her bed, I am sad to leave her, for I know we will never meet again. I watch her fall asleep but as I creep out of the door she sits up in her bed and calls out to me.

I kiss her and walk out of the door. I am on my way home.


An overwhelming sense of relief hits me as I ride the taxi back to Cancun and I feel lucky beyond all comprehension, but then, I know - for I am Lucky!

# 'IS THERE LIFE ON MARS?'

(David Bowie)

Bitter-cold wintry rain hammering the windows from grey skies is my 'now'. I miss the heat and humidity of the rain-forest. I miss the hot sunshine blazing across the Caribbean sea. I miss warm rain showering exotic trees. Here in the grey days, all is stark and bleak. Travelling far, daring to seek myself in a land beyond my comfort zone, was recklessly testing, but now back home, where routine is dull and gloomy, I am restless for new challenges. The anti-climax after untold rigours of daily adventure, hangs heavy. I seek resilience born out of freedom- now lost in tedious monotony.

Rain, rain and nothing but rain with leaden, overcast skies is my nowhere of today. Where are the endless blue skies? Where is the ragged excitement of survival in the unknown? Here the grey lid never falters, or alters and early morning doesn't differ from late afternoon. The watery, pale canopy confuses all sense of time- only the clock has the answer. The sky has lost its 'skyness'. There are no clouds, no breaks in the endless grey, just a steely saucepan lid sealing in the simmering world below.

Back at school, the gloomy humdrum curriculum dictates the day's mood and I endure unreasonable, lacklustre boys, who would sooner be plotting their next theft than studying Shakespeare. The syllabus is not designed to meet their needs or interests and even Sherlock Holme's antics, unfortunately written in a style of English beyond their comprehension, disrupts the whole class with guffaws and crude laughter when the word 'ejaculates!' is read out emphatically by one of the street-wise boys and another shouts across the classroom-" he said,' ejaculates' Miss; he did Miss! What does it mean Miss?" I tell them it simply means 'said' but the disruption is endless and it is hopeless to try to steer them back on track. I stare out of the window into the overcast, rainy scene. A little robin is hopping along the grass searching for sleepy insects and I smile at the thought of Christmas looming ahead -something to heave me out of this colourless depression. Since my return I have not had any Alien experiences, except that every night in the right hand corner of my bedroom a round circle, within another circle of red and white light appears when I turn out the light. I have searched every inch of the room to trace a light source, but I can't find anything. I suspect it is being beamed across the garden from the factory opposite. Each night it appears accompanied by a strange monotonous drone, the kind of sound used to hypnotise someone, and every night I fight it and try not to look in that direction, but I am hypnotically drawn to the circle and then fall asleep. I struggle to ignore its presence, but so far have failed at the attempt. I don't want to admit that it's all part of the same Alien game and push that thought away. In the meantime I wait; wait for the inevitable intrusion of mind and body from who knows where?

The bell releases the class without my permission, as the mob race out of the classroom, screaming, banging bags on desks, and punching each other as they fight to be the first out of the door. It is the end of another school day and a strange quiet descends as the last detention pupils escape through the main gates. It is still raining and the ashen sky has remained constant throughout the day and the same watery-greyness, which seeped through a silver dawn, has lain unaltered, like a stage-painted backdrop. I wonder how the natural atmosphere can be altered without irreparable damage to the ionosphere for future generations. I want answers! Deep within my mind I search for a reply to my questions and close my eyes. Breathing deeply to sink into an alpha state of altered consciousness and through my third eye, a figure appears at the back of the classroom shrouded in a luminescent bubble. He is tall, well built, with long blonde hair and looks Scandinavian. He does not speak but his voice appears in my head. He tells me that the information he will reveal will not be understood or accepted by the majority, until later in the future, when humanity has passed through many stages of change. He explains- *"My race comes from your species, but we have evolved to a higher level. We wish only to assist planet earth and seek those who can help to raise the higher consciousness of humankind. You are one of many, whose purpose in your incarnation, is to promote awareness and educate the masses to awaken to their true spiritual nature. We give you information to pass on to others."*

His presence is unlike that of a human, whose body is dense and anchored to the ground, instead he appears like a shining mirage in the desert, fluid like a floating bubble. I ask him about the rain and why it is constantly flooding the countryside for days on end. I question the distinctive qualities and dynamics of the rain and ask why it differs from the showers I experienced as a child. I describe, how recently, I have seen many different types of unusual rain- some so fine like misty dew in the early morning; rain hurtling from the sky like a waterfall crashing from the clouds and patchy regions of sharp showers confined only to small areas. He understands the question and his voice echoes clearly in my mind as he states:

*"Your rain is manipulated. Your weather is modified and controlled by a central AI SYSTEM which affects changes to the seasons."* (I remember the prediction of Nostradamus who said in the fifteen hundreds,' there will come a time when the seasons will not be recognised except for the nesting of the birds!') He continues-*" the installation of 5G signalling is part of the great plan to acclimatise earth in readiness for the planet to be inhabited by many other alien species. Aliens, hybrids, mechanised humans, transhumans and ordinary humans will live side by side under a lidded dome where everything is controlled. 5G electromagnetic signals are harmful to humans causing all kinds of illness and radiation sickness. Humans cannot take the full blast of 5G, so to dilute it for a time until humans become acclimatised to it, water has to be pumped into the atmosphere to dampen down and thin out the electromagnetic effects. The extra moisture in the atmosphere helps people to breathe through the dryness caused by 5G. The rain has been*

*devised with different types of humidity to help control the radiation leakage, that is why you have witnessed many different varieties and densities. Those in control will gradually introduce 6G, which will eliminate many people. The metals pumped into the atmosphere from chemtrails, intensify with the heat of the sun and the additional 5G force amplifies the temperature, so it is necessary to flood the skies with moisture to counterbalance this. The different types of rain and dynamic variations are created to address imbalances in the ionosphere. Soon the technology of 'cloud seeding' will become commonplace, which is a technique whereby capsules of silver dioxide are shot into cloud formations to squeeze out more moisture causing unnatural rainfall. The misunderstanding and misuse of this method will cause great flooding and many problems in dry desert countries."*

His voice fades as he disappears into the ether through the back wall just as the cleaner, clattering her mop and bucket, barges in apologising for any disturbance.


Back at home in the heavy silence, I pour myself a drink. I am given so much information from beyond and I need to act responsibly to share my knowledge, but I know that I will be ridiculed. I argue with myself that life would be much easier if I just dropped all the incredible, dystopic, other-worldly data and forget my mission, but I can't because I know in my heart, everything I am told is the truth. Sometimes I just want to fall off the edge of the universe and dive into the unknown, but that is not an option. Sitting at my computer, just for the hell of it, I research evidence of unusual weather conditions thought to be the cause of many disasters such as- unstoppable fires; strange volcanic eruptions; flash flooding; the impossible drying up of rivers and lakes, plus the extinction of some species of birds and animals, together with the disappearance of certain plants. Irrefutable data points towards the fact that something is causing cataclysmic events around the world and it's not fake global warming propaganda. Flocks of birds have been found dead, washed up on shores without any sign of what caused their unusual mass fatality and I am not surprised that a new movement is evolving to encourage a mass exodus from earth to terraform Mars. Folk are being lured into the idea of becoming the first pioneers on Mars, but little do they know that Mars, already is inhabited and mined by many nations!

I finish my drink and close down the computer, whereupon oppressive stillness descends, engulfing me in an isolated bubble. I am acutely alert to nothingness. I am alarmingly conscious to the 'no sound' stillness, which coils through the house like sly smoke infiltrating through every crevice. The emptiness echoes under my feet and is overpowering. I cannot breathe. I know I am being watched. Something is waiting. The inevitable will happen and I cannot escape. I force myself to make my way up the stairs, folding into a pretend bravado of confident strides, marking out each step and with pounding heart I prepare for bed. With the light on, there is no sign of the hypnotic circle, but as soon as I turn the light off- it appears! I turn the light on and it disappears. I search the spot for anything which might cause the effect, but there is nothing. I can't play this silly game all night, so I resolve to turn the light out and go to sleep and not look at it- but I do! Immediately the circling drone envelopes me and I fall asleep. It is not a normal sleep, but like a lucid dream, where I am keenly conscious of everything more real than real, I find myself in another dimension.

It is dark and I am riding in an army truck with soldiers. It is an American army truck and the soldiers are both British and American, men and women. We are silent as the truck bounces along rough terrain. I am perched near the opening curtains of the vehicle and can see rugged, red terrain below as the flaps blow open in the slight breeze. 'Martian soil' I say to myself as I dare to peek through the khaki curtains at the red/purple sky. The guy seated next to me whispers, "You new?" he questions, sensing my apprehension. I can't find my voice and just nod. He grins with a knowing smile and says, " you get used to it. You know here on Mars, our days are longer than on earth?" I nod again and he continues; "back home folks just wouldn't believe it, no Mam, they just wouldn't!"

I look into his black sincere eyes and his ebony, shiny face is welcoming and friendly. I want to ask so many questions but I am afraid to open my mouth in case the dream turns into a nightmare. "I'm Carl, by the way," he states as he holds out his hand and I shake it sheepishly, but I can't say my name and he quietly laughs, saying, "sometimes it takes a little while before you find your voice, when you first arrive." I am grateful for his understanding. A woman opposite takes out a packet of gum and offers some to those around her adding, "there are whistle-blowers back home who are leaking information concerning life on Mars, you know, some Astronauts have admitted as much."

"Yeh, Elon Musk is looking for volunteers to come and start a new colony!" perks up a soldier further down the truck. Everyone groans, and moans at the idea of infiltrators into their colony. "It's not yet safe for civilians and it would cause sheer chaos!" states a man rubbing his eyes and everyone agrees.

"Did you hear the latest news?" he laughs, speaking in a posh affected tone of a newsreader; " soil extracted from the surface of Mars shows that there is a distinct possibility that life existed on the planet, until a massive cataclysmic tragedy, such as a falling meteorite caused total mass destruction and devastation of any civilisation which may have existed there." Everyone laughs and jeers. "Someone ought to tell those mother f...ckers the truth man!" Pipes up a young, tough private." I mean, when they gonna tell the world that travel to Mars has been ongoing for longer than I've been alive?" Everyone agrees.

"Look, brothers and sisters, who's gonna believe we're all super soldiers heh? Serving in a secret army, trained since we were little, chosen to do this work and sent back after years of service, but reprogrammed so that it appears we've only been gone for a few minutes?" "Yeh! Yeh!" the troop sniggers." I remember one time when I was little and my Mom told me not to wander outside the gate and when the core came to take me for training, my Mom thought I had been kidnapped and called the police. When I appeared a few hours later she whipped my butt so hard, I couldn't sit down for a week and when I told her the truth she whipped me again for telling lies!" Everyone laughs sympathetically, having experienced similar happenings.

I look at Carl sitting next to me and ask shyly, "I'm sorry I'm new to all this - how come secret travel to Mars is possible without flying in a rocket?" He grins and replies," My oh my! You are new! How did you get here?" I shrug my shoulders and he clicks his tongue, disbelieving my ignorance, continuing: "You surely heard of a dude called Tesla?" I nod again. "Well he discovered that you can bend space time through portal tunnels and wormholes making travel from 'A' to 'B' almost instant!"

I thank him, not really grasping the concept and our conversation is interrupted as we stop abruptly and everyone jumps out ready to undertake their assignment. I watch Carl disappear with his platoon and stand gazing up into massive structures, unusually sculpted, unlike anything I have ever seen, except for Gaudi's amazing architecture in Barcelona, where the buildings appear like magic to be suspended in the air without support. Large opaque windows float unsupported by normal bricks and mortar, but are sustained by a jelly-like substance which expands and contracts to accommodate different spaces. Above me gently gliding in a murky-aubergine sky, is a flying object in the shape of a Zeppelin plane, made of steel and glass. Inside I view strange shaped office desks and a person inside browsing through floating data on an invisible screen. A voice says- "they call those' Transoffices". I turn and see Carl standing grinning by my side. "They told me to show the new visitor around, so here I am Mam, at your service, now I think you had better tell me your name!"

I chuckle apologetically and say, "Lucky, I'm Lucky!" He laughs adding, "Well you sure as hell are, when you've got me to show you the ropes!"

I ask about the 'Transoffices', and he explains that they move from one base to another where information is requested and he points out that underneath the floating Transoffice is a large round shape like the lid of a screw-top jar, which fits directly into a round hole in the base of a building, securely anchoring it to its foundation. As we watch one land in its base, other Transoffice vehicles take- off in different directions and Carl leads me behind the main building to a ginormous metal construction, housing a massive indoor city, where people from different countries occupy specific zones. He guides me inside and we walk towards a large tin structure made of layer upon layer of shipping containers built to house British Soldiers. "It's called the 'Canister' for obvious reasons and nicknamed the 'can'," he states, "do you wanna see inside?" he asks. I nod and he shows me one of many small rooms providing basic accommodation for the single British soldier.

After inspecting the billet, we wander into the bright, buzzing thoroughfare. I notice the absence of colourful clothing and individual styles. Carl explains that everyone wears a uniform to depict their country and rank. Wearing vibrational bright colours is considered dangerous and unsettling and that crowds are easier to control if everyone is uniformly dressed in sombre colours, preventing encouragement of individuality and dissent amongst rival factions.

I marvel at the vast city with its enormous shopping mall with every kind of store you can imagine, except for clothes shops. Every shop is enticingly colourful and exciting but you can only buy goods according to your rank and credit count. Merchandise is paid for by a chip implanted in a person's wrist, which stores all personal details and Carl proudly displays his chip. Near the 'Can' is an amazing library. It has a massive glass frontage but no books, yet it contains every conceivable volume ever written, supplying the source of all research and up-to-date data on any subject. "Come on , let's go inside," urges Carl enthusiastically. As we enter the space-tech, futuristic honeycomb of learning, a holographic librarian appears. He looks like a human but is a biometric humanoid robot. I am not prepared for his question-" and what specifically are you looking for?" he enquires. "Alice in Wonderland" I reply without thinking and immediately Lewis Carroll is displayed on a screen in front of me with hundreds of different illustrated and non-illustrated volumes including videos, musicals and other related articles. I am aghast at the depth of information and the humanoid asks if I would like to peruse the information in a booth. I nod and he flicks his hand in the air and the lights in the building change, illuminating many people in the establishment, all studiously transfixed to screens in small booths lined down a long corridor and on different floor levels, so high that I can't see the ceiling." Follow me if you please to booth four. I think you will find everything you need and more. If I can be of further assistance, please press the black button. The green one will start your journey."

The lights return to an opaque veil blotting out the other customers. Inside the booth all I ever wanted or needed to know about my chosen subject is at my fingertips but Carl is impatient to show me more of the indoor city and we leave to walk a little farther down the street to view a massive 'experiencer' entertainment dome, called the 'Hyperdome'.


The Hyperdrome is a bizarre blur of fairground, altered reality rides, feely-touchy films, hi-tech interactive games, horror walk-throughs and virtual reality experiences. Entrance is free for all soldiers as it is a great source of entertainment and stress release. Carl explains that you can order any kind of sexual encounter in any desired situation, but it is a virtual experience, labelled 'Robotica Erotica'. You can spend a whole evening exploring your deepest desires and fulfilling your whacky fantasies. "Would you like to try it with me?" questions Carl, teasingly placing his arms around my shoulders. I am surprised by his request and shrug off the invitation. Carl apologises for his silly remark and we walk on in silence.


Farther up the road in this maze of thrilling entertainment is the 'Symphonium Suite', which houses all kinds of music in a massive stadium with holographic music concerts, a historical music museum, music laboratory, disco dime and anything of a musical nature. Carl, after regaining his polite self, explains that If you want to sit in a concert hall with a live audience to listen to a symphony, then the experience can be virtually created. Any type of music is available accompanied by different mode situations in which to enjoy the event. Colour vibration can be added to any encounter in order to enrich the occasion and you can wander through the 'Rainbow Dome' to feel the power of different energies from all the colours. "It's like taking a colour holiday," adds Carl shyly smiling, commenting- "of course all these facilities are available to most density beings, although the higher density sixth and seventh upwards don't usually participate in such activities and the lower densities, third, second and first frequent the bars and brothels just outside the city."

"What do you mean?" I enquire, not understanding the concept of a 'density being'.

"Well, in the Universe, this Universe, there are many different levels of existence. I am told there may be as many as fourteen different layers or hierarchy in this sphere. Your status depends on the frequency of your vibration which emanates from your inner being. So to put it simply, if you are a very, very good person your inner vibration will be bright and stronger than a person who is not so enlightened."

"It's a very simplistic concept," I add.

"Well, that's the best I can explain it and after all, planet earth is a kind of university which we choose to attend to expand our spiritual growth."

"And here on Mars?" I query.

"It's an extension of earth but different, as here there is no 'death' and no 'aging'".

I am surprised by his matter-of-fact comment and he laughs at my naivety saying, "aw come on! You don't think that highly trained super soldiers are gonna be allowed to die in battle do you? That would be such a waste of time, effort and money. No, we have special units which restore limbs, parts of bodies and give life to the lifeless and also cloning facilities, together with soul migration techniques."

He reels off the information like it is totally normal to be brought back from the dead- the 'Lazarus Effect' as he calls it is common place on Mars. "You wanna see?" he questions, and leads me to a massive construction situated next to the Hyperdrome.

We walk in silence towards the huge building made of blue glass, metal and a pliable substance which changes shape according to the needs of the moment. REGENERATION and RESTORATIVE CENTRE is displayed in huge blue neon lights on the front of the structure. There are no doors on the glass frontage, but as we stand looking at the amazing architecture, a glass and metal shuttle in the shape of a dart, flashes through a large glass frame which liquefies as the shuttle approaches, allowing it to glide through and dock at the entrance.
I gasp at the amazing technology. Carl laughs at my childlike incredulity as I watch a corpse carried and dispatched by robots, to a waiting lift which transfers it to the appropriate floor, but this corpse is being taken underground and Carl adds sheepishly, "Oh I forgot to say that some corpses cannot be used again so they are dissected for er..er... other purposes!"

"What other purposes?" I enquire nervously.

"Well, you have to understand that as yet, we are on the verge of building a new planet and food supplies can be a little scarce, so we use cells from er...er... tissue and re-grow it and rebuild it in a printer which creates and makes slabs of meat."

I am shocked and retort:" But you said there is no death!"

"Well technically, there isn't. You see before soldiers come here, details of their DNA and soul have been stored in a special computer so that at any time a clone can be created if necessary and that information can be used to rebuild a person physically and spiritually."

I am astounded at the technology available and lose my interest in seeing inside the massive hospital, so Carl leads me towards rough terrain where his platoon is waiting for him to climb aboard the waiting wagon. "You see our mission here is not just to fight horrendous monsters and honestly you wouldn't believe the size of some of those god-damn spiders out there; but it's to help build a liveable, peaceful outpost for families, because Mars used to be a thriving planet but the population was wiped out by a major catastrophe cataclysm, and of course we don't know how much longer earth is gonna survive as a sustainable planet?" I smile as he climbs into the truck and thank him for his tour. I wave goodbye and my focus becomes fuzzy. Everything around me dissolves in a sea of misty shapes and I am back in my dream state, waking to a new grey day.

The vision of Mars remains deeply planted in my mind and I cannot forget the feeling of the landscape and its other-worldly vibration. It is so different yet the same as earth in many ways. I know what I have seen to be true and now have an understanding of the vastness, greatness and incomprehensible possibilities which lie waiting to be discovered by blinkered humans on this planet. I am lucky to have peeped through a tiny chink in the Universe's crystal ball to imagine the magnitude of great wonders it hides in secret. One day our understanding will deepen and we will know a little more. Until then I am grateful for what little knowledge has been shared and happy to have the opportunity to share it with you. Yes I am lucky, for I am Lucky.

⟡

# MOVING ON-ALL IS ONE

Now, the grey days, the grey ways of a steel- dull, winter season in oppressive dimness from the grey- lidded sky is strange, as it never varies. Overbearing gloom seeps into the forest and pigeons with their grey feathered cloaks blend into the dreary atmosphere with ease. Grey- a colour mixture of white and black, densely pallid, merging into a murky, pasty shadowland washes the trees in a watery winter glaze. Mid-morning and the greyness silently refuses to lift. Where is the sunshine? What is hiding behind the grey dome? What don't they want us to see? They deny us sunshine but keep pouring rain after rainstorm to dumb-down the radiation leaking into our streets from the 5G meters stealthily installed, while we sleep through the grey haze. Smart meters are smart in their greyness and smart in their deception!

Grey, grey, grey, all the day, fizzing with fine drizzle, almost invisible from inside, until you walk outside. Greyness imprisons souls. Greyness sucks out the life-force of liveliness, leaving only a desire to sleep. Sleep is a relief. Let me stay asleep and be warm and cosy. Let me see the world through a screen. Let me be entertained by virtual games in a virtual reality escaping from the tedious greyness lurking outside my window. Grey clings and cloys the air as I walk my dog through forest parkland cloaked in mist. I can't breathe in the unhealthy smoggy blanket. The damp suffocates. My chest tightens. The silver birch trees are grey and merge into the blanket backdrop.

The lake has a dull, opaque sheen shrouding the water where fish hide. Grey stones sleep in the steel tones of lacklustre decaying ferns, dying into the earth in the winter turn of seasons. When did the seasons become confused? Weather modification rules the seasons for reasons we are not allowed to know. I am in a grey depression and I must force my way into the sunshine. My time here in my quaint cottage is coming to an end. Time to move on and forge a new life, a fresh start elsewhere. Time to create a different environment and surround myself in a brand new mantle of existence. The dance project was a great success and I am lucky to have had the opportunity to use my choreographic skills for a wonderful venture. I have sold my property and have arranged to rent an ancient farmhouse, lacking modern facilities, where you have to trek through the old cow shed to take out the ashes from the fire-grate and the kitchen has no other cooking facilities other than an old Aga which was installed when the farmhouse was first built! New challenges await!

My beautiful Chinese carp died under frozen ice in the cruel winter and so I do not have to worry about leaving them. Rory hardly returns home now and my heart goes out to him, because all that he forewarned about the 'monsters underground' is true! No one believes him and so he is imprisoned in a dark mental tunnel, unable to communicate with anyone. I know what he says is true because I have also been a victim and I believe Daisy too, has suffered because of what has happened to us together in the dead of night. Were we guinea-pigs in some kind of experiment and investigation? Daisy continued to have fruitless piano lessons where she just sat and looked at me for half an hour at a time. The cancer treatment she needed lasted a year but she is now fully recovered. We both shared the same rashes, marks and bruises on our bodies in exactly the same places. When I told her I was leaving she was sad but we both knew that her piano lessons would not be missed.

I discovered the tunnels from the old mansion house, turned hotel, ran under our cottages which were once stables, and lead to underground facilities beneath the factory. Rory was right-the monsters were underground and they came at night! I believe all the horrendous Alien experiences were part of ongoing experiments undertaken by the American military, using Alien type robotic beings wearing typical Grey-Alien suits. The small Greys usually are used as mechanised, unfeeling, automatic servants who do the ground work in preparation for further invasive examinations on humans performed by other beings. I have been told that across Britain there are many underground bases run by the Americans who abduct people for scientific research. I believe that the factory opposite was one such base.

Now, I am sitting drinking coffee pondering what is really happening, and why? I have vague ideas or memories of being taken somewhere underground and lying on a table in the dark with beings and a human doctor wandering around in a darkened room with other bodies lying on tables. I have a hazy recollection of speaking with American scientists and Army people whilst being in a trance. I vaguely recall being in an American Army office speaking to a commanding officer about working for them, but I remember through a hazy dream that I declined their offer. Someone who looked like George Bush Senior spoke to me from behind a large black desk and said he was my Father and that I should use my psionic gifts to work for them, but I didn't believe him and the scene evaporated through a smoky veil. Somehow the hypnotic sequences and the Alien happenings lead me to believe that the ones who abducted me were not real but some form of mechanised computer robot made by the Americans. I believe that many people are abducted while they sleep and the happenings are created in a dream-like fantasy mode so that people think they have been dreaming and are embarrassed and afraid to talk about the experience. I believe that many experiments are performed on people to extract physical, mental and emotional data to be used by the aliens to create hybrids for future habitation on earth.

Now it is bonfire night and I am playing smooth, classical music to drown out the noise of the fireworks for my cats, but they don't seem unduly concerned and are sleeping. A storm is brewing and people have been cautioned to have their bonfire parties early, as the thunderstorm later this evening will spoil their festivities. From my bedroom window I look towards the factory, which has been closed for a month and the sheds flattened and destroyed in preparation for building a new housing estate. There are no runway lights glowing in the dark and the empty compound lies derelict and littered with old factory machinery. A strange anger rises as I search for signs of secret base entrances to the laboratories, which I think exist below ground, but in the dark it is difficult to find clues. Across the way gentle, golden, sparkling stars light the dark night with rainbow flashes of silver rain drops and purple flowers appear and disappear in a myriad of firework displays across the fields. The little girl, Daisy, with her parents are eating sausages around a small bonfire next door and I feel a sad warm glow for her. Soon I will move on and maybe never see her again.

Suddenly the black sky lights up with a searing gnarled finger of lightening pointing downwards through the blasting rockets, bursting Catherine wheels and exploding firework bombs. The storm has begun and the thunder rumbles and threatens from beyond the trees to burst overhead releasing a torrent of rain to wash out the colourful array of firework magic. There is a shattering blast that fills the air with ricochet bullets of vibration which shakes the cottage. The blast seems to be coming from underground and the shock waves are travelling up from the earth. Another thunderous roll echoes across the sky and simultaneously from beneath the earth a bomb explodes. It appears that underground explosions are timed to blast in unison with the thunder and lightning crashes. A thought occurs, as I peer across the garden fence to the factory base, that the laboratories below ground are being destroyed by explosives detonated and timed to occur with the firework blasts and the thunder storm. The operation is being cleverly disguised and orchestrated at a time when the noise is concealed by natural elements and when people are engaged in noisy festive fun. I stare hard at the desolate site to see if I can detect any sign of the underground explosions, but it is too dark and the rain is pelting the earth and trees, thrashing everything in sight with an angry force. The sky is now dark. Gone are the rainbow flashes of instant splashes of fireworks blazing fountains of colour across the starless night. The quiet after the storm is heavy, only the rain battering against the window panes echoes across my empty hallway. Time for sleep. The destruction of the factory has given me some peace. The hypnotic drone and the light circles no longer disrupt my sanity. There have been no night visits or abductions since they left. I am so relieved to be left alone and yet there is a strange sense of abandonment with an 'all-round' awareness of everyone leaving. I am abandoning my curious cottage to forge a new pathway in an ancient farmhouse, but I am not sure why I want to live without modern comforts. Renting the large property, I will not be able to afford to heat the house with the gas central heating the owners have installed, but I plan to make fires and enjoy the cosy solace of a living, breathing blaze from seasoned logs. I plan to make the ancient, dark, abandoned kitchen into a bright, happy eating, drinking and meeting place for family and friends and enjoy cooking on the old aga. I promise myself joyful times ahead, albeit there will be challenges to overcome.

The morning dawns on a bright, wet scene of bonfire aftermath and I stare across at the abandoned site of the factory base. Sure enough there are signs of underground activity. Raised in definite rivulets of disturbed earth are the clear outlines of rooms marked out in sharp contours where you can see the exact location of the chambers. In some places the earth has been lifted and elevated in mounds as though an explosion underneath has thrust the earth above ground. I know now that the proof of underground quarters is staring me in the face, but I cannot prove their use, or even their existence as the bulldozers are entering the arena and obviously have been scheduled to tidy up the mess as quickly as possible to hide any sign of the explosions and the underground laboratories. At least I have the satisfaction of knowing my gut feelings about the factory are correct.

I watch the flotilla of heavy machinery scrape and scratch the concrete rubble and pile it into mounds for the workforce to take away in their lorries. The scheme and clever plan to leave no trace of the secret base is working. No one will ever believe me or Rory or even little Daisy, if ever she remembers what happened to her. This is the end of a period of my life which I cannot forget. The quaint little cottage has been a nightmare ride of horror happenings including the roof infestation of rats which terrified me with their nocturnal scampering and the pungent smell of rat piss and excrement. They destroyed life-long expensive costumes which I stored in the loft. I will never forget the disgust and revulsion at opening one of the large, plastic costume bags to find it soaking wet with rat pee and a dead rat amongst the pretty pink taffeta skirts. I was sick on the spot. All my beautiful outfits had to be burnt and I can never replace them.

So it's goodbye cottage with no backward glance at the past. The present waits with new challenges ahead and I want to escape, to forget the past few years of untold terror. Can I forget? Can I escape the trauma? Can I rebuild a fresh, new beginning? Yes I can and I will! The sun is shining and my lorry load of goods and chattels arrive at the ancient farmhouse. I can't wait to get everything unloaded and begin my planned transformation. The owners have given me permission to do whatever I like with the decor and I am itching to dig into the paint pots and bring the house back to life.

Where is the now? Months later after my move, my daughter tells me I have become a recluse. I entertain family and friends at the farm and teach in my school but never go out. I live on the whole, a solitary existence. I have transformed the kitchen into a bright yellow oasis and have learnt to cook wonderful meals on the aga. Yes, the house is damp and cold at times, but the log fire blazes and the whiskey and ginger at night help to keep me warm. I need time to recover from the unbelievable ordeal and I have to assimilate and assess the emotional impact of the torturous events. I have made a wonderful meditation nest in the trees surrounding the farm and I derive comfort and consolation from sitting under the branches and watching the nesting birds from my secret hideout. I am learning new ways of looking at life and am given wonderful spiritual teaching from my whisperers. Perhaps one day I will be able to write about everything to share my experiences. I know I am truly lucky, for I am Lucky and whisperers whisper through the trees: *"All is one . All is everything. Being alone is as joyful and harmonious as companionship. We are as one in this human condition and as one beyond. We are never truly alone because we are saturated with 'oneness'. We are the 'One'. Together we live on and on."*

And I am lucky to know this. I am lucky for all that life has taught me. I am eternally grateful for all that is and lucky to be Lucky.

# WATCH OUT! WATCH OUT! THE FUTURE IS ABOUT!

My dear Rosie,

now you have reached the last chapter in 'Lucky 3- Knowledge is the Key' and the information I reveal will be hard to grasp, but it is my duty to pass on what I have been told, except that by the time the readers have this knowledge, much of the data will be available to research and be proven. Many whistle-blowers will have spoken about their experiences and no longer the question of 'are we alone in the universe?' will be asked, as it will be common knowledge that there are many types of Aliens living amongst us and always have been before the birth of time.

Also, when you read this, you will be closer to becoming further away from the human-being you were and nearer to the trans-human, mechanised, computerised super-human the future promises, where consciousness assisted technology is in everyday use and where mind meets matter purely through a thought activated process. The world of today will not recognise or understand how humanity can eradicate itself in search of the ultimate goal of the 'singularity' accepting a dehumanised society as being the supreme nirvana for all.

So Rosie, living in the farmhouse was fine for a while, until I found my ultimate dwelling paradise in forest parkland. Surrounded by trees and living a very frugal life, alone with my two cats and little dog, I was able to communicate with beings from beyond and learn about many things beyond the norm. I will tell of what I know and that which has been shown to me in the hope that to be 'fore-warned is to be fore-armed'.

It was a cold, wet Wednesday afternoon in the forest parkland and from my lodge, set amongst the trees, the bleak grey, watery sky was cloudless; only the grey-lidded dome sealed in the day, as in the previous day and the day before that. Watery dimness from so much rain in June was depressing and I felt cheated of a bright summer, not being able to sit out on my decking and enjoy a time of sunshine before the inky blackness of winter dolefully crept in. I remember thinking that it was only ten days before the longest day of the year and soon the days would get shorter and the nights longer. My little dog Freddie was turning circles asking for his second daily walk and I couldn't refuse as the last sudden shower had ceased, leaving only the gentle drip, drip of random raindrops dribbling from the trees. The air was fresh and smelt of new-mown, damp grass. The thick rhododendron bushes with purple and lilac blooms were fading and sodden after so much rain and the trees in their fullness were lush and vibrant. Freddie was keen to track the young fawns newly born from the herd of forty which roamed the forest and the young often strayed or got lost near my lodge. I let Freddie run ahead on a long lead and watched him joyously race through the long wet grass. From afar something moved and caught my eye and on closer inspection I saw a young man sitting on a commemorative bench situated under an ancient oak tree. The bench had been donated by the family of the lady who had previously owned my lodge and who had died there. Freddie naturally lead me towards the figure as he loved meeting new friendly people. The young man smiled. His face looked familiar. I was reminded of an old sepia photograph of my Great Grandmother's youngest son, Jim. He was her fifteenth child and had been killed at the age of fourteen when the railway first came to our village. Jim was playing on the tracks and his foot got caught in between two lines and the train was not able to stop in time to save him. As a small child I often looked at his picture and wondered about him. He was a handsome boy with blonde hair and a winning smile.

The young man seated on the bench looked as though he had just stepped out of Jim's era, wearing a peaked cap over his fair hair, an open-neck striped shirt with tiny rubber buttons, a black waistcoat and rough trousers. He could have been a farm-hand. Freddie galloped up to him and the young man bent down to stroke him, laughing at Freddie's friendliness. I watched as the two got acquainted.

Then the young man looked up and grinned. I felt an immediate connection and smiled asking, "I haven't seen you around here before? Are you visiting relatives?" The young man laughed and said he had just popped by and was enjoying the forest. I wanted to know more but was a little embarrassed to pry. " Do you mind if I sit down?" I asked, my feet were weary and Freddie was happy enjoying the stranger's attention. The young man kindly wiped the seat with a red-spotted handkerchief which he drew out of his pocket and I thought it was a lovely thing to do and that not many young men would own such a hanky, or perform such a gallant task. He then tied it around his neck completing his country look. I introduced myself and he told me his name was Irwin and spoke of his love of the countryside and how he feared things would change. His accent was an odd mixture of an American Southern drawl, Scottish lilting laughter and stubborn Yorkshire dialect. He seemed very young but he could have been early thirties and the way he spoke of 'things to come' was very mature. "Do you think humans agree or have agreed unknowingly to their own extinction?" He asked out of the blue. I was momentarily shocked by his statement and needed time to ponder the meaning of his words.

"Er...er, I don't know!" I replied, as I watched him sit on the back of the bench resting his feet on the seat, placing his elbows on his knees and his head in his hands. He reached for a branch above his head and broke off a small twig, placing it in his mouth sucking on the sap. When I had recovered from his statement, I told him I was researching information about the future and found his question extremely interesting. "Do you believe in time travel?" he enquired nonchalantly. I looked at him with a sincere gaze and replied, "Yes, yes I do for I have time-travelled myself!"" I know!" he added. His words stumped me and I was shocked "How do you know?" I enquired, but he didn't reply and jumped off the bench, staring intently into my eyes. Somehow I loved him. Not in a sexual way, nor

Motherly way but an empathetic way. "Well, you will believe me then if I say I am a time traveller and have dropped into this time zone." I nodded. "Ok hold my hand I want to show you something." He stated seriously. I obeyed and through a gap in the bushes we walked into a classroom.

Strangely the classroom turned into a plush, intimate, Victorian theatre decorated in red and gold.

We stood at the front of a balcony and looked down on a panel of people and beings seated just below the stage. On the cyclorama at the back of the empty stage a large screen relayed roving pictures of the earth sent from a satellite in space. A man in a black suit, seated in the centre of the team held the controls which co-ordinated the part of the world they wished to inspect or what section of the sea they wished to investigate. The instrument had the technology to zoom into the minutest detail required by the panel. A man seated at the end of the table read from a printed sheet;" destabilise and demoralise, the population. Destroy the nuclear family. Eradicate humanity as we know it and make ready for a dehumanised society."

The company assembled cheered and a smart woman in a black dress continued-"so these are some of the suggested 'GOALS FOR THE FUTURE' programme, some of these projects are well underway and we're getting some great results. I must say humans are so stupid!" As she turned her head sideways her Alien, distorted face grimaced. "Psychological conditioning is so easy to implement into the human psyche, especially when they surrender their minds to tv screens night after night, day after day and eagerly soak up all the poisoned propaganda we feed them. Plus biological tampering with all the chemicals they consume in their genetically modified food, dulls their senses and calcifies the pineal gland, so that they are not tempted to reach higher consciousness states. Of course there are exceptions – those humans who make a stand against our conditioning."

"Of course, toxic air, water, food and medication, vaccination, not to mention blocking out the sun with strontium, barium, aluminium and other various metals, is all part of the depopulation programme," stated an elderly woman in a black robe and everyone applauded her.

I looked at Irwin and he shrugged his shoulders in dismay, "you see we have to warn everyone! We have to make them listen and understand that their world is being taken away under their noses," he whispered urgently, just as a creature with a lizard face and man's body read from a report with the facts and figures outlined on the large screen. He pointed out gleefully that the pandemic plot and the vaccination scheme was now yielding results, as people across the globe were dying from heart failure and various other side effects and it was especially effective with young athletes and football players who were affected by the vaccine and were dying across the globe. Again the group heartily applauded the statement. The controller in the middle of the table stood up and congratulated the various characters for the success in their ongoing projects. Then the large screen honed in on pictures of mass destruction of forests, jungle land and nature reserves across the globe with heaps of dead birds and shoals of fish washed up on countless shores and beaches. Another Alien creature stood up, whose misshapen silver ridged head looked too heavy for its body and said in a gruff voice: "Ah, nuclear radiation my friends-what a weapon hey? What an effective silent killer? What has begun, cannot be undone and the effects are sweeping across the world. Thank goodness we have at the ready our underground cities, fast efficient underground rail access to almost everywhere and we have the antidote for radiation sickness and many other new world diseases." Again there was a great outburst of applause from the team.

Next a voice enquired-"What is developing in the cultural scene?" asked the director. A heading in large black letters appeared on the screen-'Cultural Grooming-Educational Prepping-Social Media to replace human interaction.' "Ah," he intoned, " who is taking the lead on this?" A creature with a curvy woman's body but with a reptilian face stood up holding a small, thin glass computer and began to transmit her findings onto the large screen. A graph appeared showing the increase in the number of children with Autism aligned with the increased vaccinations that babies and young children were given. "Autism is the key to the new genius young mind. We are developing what humans term as 'Autism' because the new mind set does not comply with the out-dated mind set.

For the future we need single focussed minds that can manipulate A.I. and understand higher mathematical data. Creating minds seeped in computer technology is our goal leading the new youth away from human interaction and social support to independent thinkers of the New Age Intellitech." The assembled team clapped heartily to show their approval and another alien stood up to recount a different project.


The gun-metal grey creature had large bulbous eyes and what appeared to be ram's horns on both sides of its head. It wore a black suit over its human-like body. It's voice was deep and shakily vibrational as he opened his speech-"as you are all aware that creating fear is our greatest weapon in manipulating humans and it's our job to maintain them existing in the lowest vibrational field where fear and dark forces thrive and where low moral judgement is the key to confusion.

Sexual energy when used in its lowest form has great power to entrap the human psyche. The use and abuse of young children has increased through sexual images of young ones throughout the mass media. Provocative clothing is being produced to encourage paedophilia to flourish and gender confusion is rampant in order to prepare the populace for the arrival of different species to inhabit the earth and co-habit with humans, thus creating new types of hybrids. We are of course, underlying all of this with our religious wars and mass destruction weapons".


I felt sick and disgusted and almost collapsed into Irwin's arms. He realized I couldn't stomach anymore so he held my hand and transported us back to the bench in the forest where Freddie waited patiently, as in his time line we had only disappeared for a few seconds. "No, no, no!" I sobbed, it can't be so? It can't be happening?"

Irwin didn't say anything but hung his head on his chest and we sat for a few moments in silence becoming aware of the sound of nature around us. Then Irwin spoke softly:

" You see, having a broader consciousness in order to survive takes courage. Don't be left in ignorance. Many people are suffering from 'information fatigue' and they switch off to the real truth. Over stimulus and continual bombardment from the media creates vibrations which interrupt thoughts. Menticide is mind confusion technology, which is a form of gas lighting whereby it becomes difficult to believe in yourself and the basis of your reality becomes muddled. You must stand by your internal truth. The art of 'just being your true self is the key to everything'. Knowledge is the key to all understanding but if you do not know or fully understand yourself, you have nothing.

In your life you must strive to know three things-where you came from- who you are- and where you are going."

His words resounded in a truthful, melodic harmony blending in with the bird song and the rustling trees. I looked into his eyes and he smiled. Without speaking he told me he would be back some day to take me beyond the beyond and I watched as his image, like a glowing mirage in the desert, shimmered into nothingness.

Now, in the now of everything, a question arises in my mind -how much does a lie cost? Can our hearts and souls be abducted by greed and blinded to the real reality to allow such deceit to flourish under our noses? Are we so blind not to see our freedom slipping away inch by inch? I am uncomfortable with the inside knowledge revealed in the woods with Irwin and feel helpless under the weight of the burden of the truth revealed. Suddenly a voice from behind interrupts my train of thought. It's a voice I have come to know so well and respect as he addresses me with –"well soldier, we meet again!" states Colonel J.R. Gerald, smiling cordially. He stands beside me and pats me on the shoulder adding:" you know all you can do is present knowledge to the people and leave them to do the rest themselves. Knowledge is the key to everything and if they want to use it to unlock the truth, then so be it! You can do nothing more, Soldier! If you have done your best then you have achieved your quest!"

I stare into his sincere eyes accepting his authority, knowing he is right. He pauses in the stillness of the moment and then continues- "I expect you're wondering why I'm here?" I nod questioning his presence. " We have another mission for you!" he states boldly.

"We?" I question, as a familiar face appears bearing a chimpanzee grin.

"You remember Mr. Alexander from your previous mission of returning little Marta from the future to take her place as the first black woman President?

" I do indeed!" I reply laughing. How could I forget his monkey-hybrid antics of dangling me out into the open air from a high-rise window in order to teach me a valuable lesson? I am pleased to see Mr. Alexander again with his short monkey body and long dangling limbs and his bright brown eyes revealing a hidden depth of knowledge, high intelligence and genius mind. He shakes my hand enthusiastically and we both laugh remembering our first meeting.

"The art of just being yourself in truth, in love, in goodness is the key to everything!" Mr. Alexander adds as though reading my mind from a few moments ago. I nod bowing to his infinite understanding.

"Well, that's that then!" commands the Colonel. "Time to get down to the nitty-gritty. As usual Soldier, you can of course refuse the mission, but something tells me you will be game for the new adventure. This time you will have myself and Mr. Alexander to help you."

"But what is it?" I interrupt abruptly.

"Portal doors my dear, portal doors!" exclaims Mr. Alexander in a hushed secret tone.

"Let's not get too technical right now Auguste!" affirms the Colonel, addressing Mr. Alexander informally.

And that my dear Rosie, is how I got drawn into the next mission. The file for Lucky 4-Portal Door is in the bottom of the drinks cabinet and I am sure you will be fascinated by all that is revealed.

Just as Rosie is bending down to investigate the said drawer Estrella walks in and jokingly adds, "Don't you think it's a little too early for a gin before lunch Rosie?"

Rosie laughs and explains that she is looking for the manuscript for Lucky's next mission. Estrella smiles saying," it's just like her to place it next to the booze!"

"Well she was always one to enjoy a little tipple and it seems that another amazing journey is about to be unravelled?"

"Oh Rosie, I am so glad you are here to manage everything!" sighs Estrella.

"But of course, I am the only one she entrusted to do this work and believe me I am lucky to have experienced beyond the veil with her. Lucky to have known her the way I did, for she was and always will be our Lucky.